NATASHA KARIS

The Four Loves Of Alex Hayes

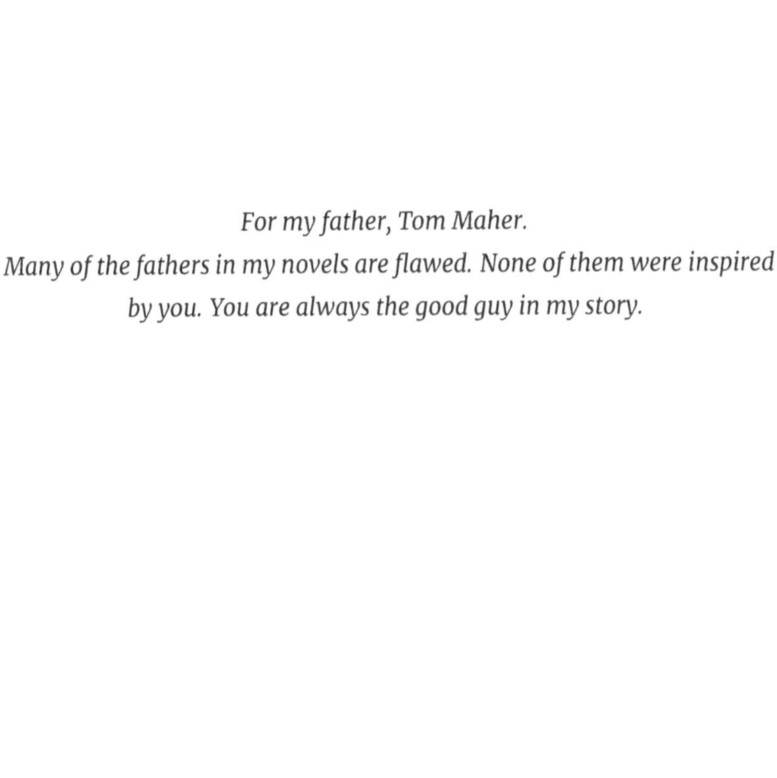

For my father, Tom Maher.

Many of the fathers in my novels are flawed. None of them were inspired by you. You are always the good guy in my story.

Contents

Playlist

All I want by Kodaline
Crows by Talos
All Too Well by Taylor Swift
Let It Be Me by Ray LaMontagne
Love Will Tear Us Apart by Nerina Pallot
I'll Never Love Again by Lady Gaga
Only Love Can Hurt Like This by Paloma Faith
Waking Up Slow by Gabrielle Aplin
Cardigan by Taylor Swift
Lost Without You by Freya Ridings
Always Remember Us This Way by Lady Gaga
It Was Always You by Daisy Jones And The Six
Margaret by Lana Del Ray
I'm Kissing You by Des'ree
Dog Days Are Over by Florence and The Machine. (Lyrics version)
Get here:
https://youtube.com/playlist?
list=PLXUprm9AeVXckeiFVWbbmURrvrMKMsloW&
si=UkQ0Uj9IqK4rWHSB

Chapter 1

Sergeant Vicky Fitzgerald forwarded the CCTV recording until it hit the 10.47am mark, then pressed play. Seeing the black SUV, she stopped the tape and tried for at least the third time to decipher the licence plate. She zoomed in until it became a pixelated mess. Nothing. Vicky scribbled in her notebook:

What did he use to cover the plate?

The SUV sped up as if trying to pass the traffic light before it turned red. For some reason, at the last second, the driver changed his mind, coming to an abrupt stop. As he braked, the car behind didn't. It bumped the SUV. Not hard enough to do any damage, but enough to draw attention. A second later, the guy in the SUV stepped out. Vicky noted the body language.

Fast walking. Hands on hips. Chest puffed out.

She pressed pause again. The man wore a cap, of plain black fabric with no image or label. Dressed in a black hoodie and dark jeans. Zooming in, his face pixelated, but she could definitely see lighter hair, more blond than light-brown.

She wrote: *Find someone to clear the image.*

The man in the black cap opened the driver's door of the car that bumped him and grabbed the person by the collar, dragging him out on to the street. Witnesses and family identified that person as Alex Hayes. The man from the SUV shoved Alex against the car's back door. Alex held his hands up as if in surrender. An exchange carried on between them. Vicky timed it, over ten seconds. At no other point could she see the other man's face, as the camera position only showed the back of Alex's head and his side profile. Blocked from sight, their hidden mouths prevented lip reading.

Body language suggested Alex was trying to calm the situation down. His hands were up, as if trying to pacify by showing he wasn't a threat or offering peace. The man gesticulated with wild gestures, pointing at the ground, at the sky and then at Alex. That's when Alex dropped his hands. The man shoved Alex and stepped up into his face. At this stage, the driver behind heard the man in the black cap shout at Alex that he would kill him and blocked Alex from entering his own car. Alex tilted his head nearer to the man, possibly saying something, his hands back in the air again as if trying to calm the situation. The man backed up towards his car and looked like he would leave. Alex turned, appearing to fumble with his door. Before he could open it, the man returned from the SUV holding an object, confirmed later from witnesses that it was a knife. He charged. Alex ran, sprinting across the road and disappearing into a derelict building. The driver behind Alex Hayes's car, Carmel Rowan, rang the guards as soon as she saw the knife. Too afraid to approach, which, from the way it turned out, was probably for the best. For her, anyway.

Less than five minutes after entering, the man in the black cap ran back out. He returned to his car and sped off.

The ambulance got there in nineteen minutes. Sergeant Barratt from the Ballinroe Station arrived three minutes later.

'Only few days I take off every year and it turns out to be *those*,' Vicky muttered.

When the paramedic arrived, he found a man lying on the floor covered in blood. He tried to stem the blood flow, but the wound continued to seep.

The journey to the hospital took another fifteen.

Alex Hayes died before they entered the hospital. The emergency services still tried to resuscitate him for twenty minutes but declared him dead at 11.58am, just over an hour from the altercation.

Chapter 2

'Sergeant Fitzgerald?'

'That's me.'

'This is Shannon Reeny, the pathologist who examined Alex Hayes. I already spoke to Garda Barratt; I think that was his name?'

Vicky couldn't help clucking her tongue. 'That would be him.'

'The line is muffled, I can barely hear you.'

'Sorry, I'm driving. I was on holiday for a few days; I just cut short my break to get back.'

'That's dedication. Barratt left me a message informing me that since Knockfarraig is your area and he was just covering, you needed to know, too. Not sure why he couldn't call you himself, but out of courtesy, I'm ringing to confirm I completed the autopsy and released the body of Alex Hayes for the family to arrange funeral arrangements.'

'No need for an inquest, then?'

'I don't think anyone will deny the man died from a knife wound, so no, no need for an inquest.'

'That's one positive. No point letting the family suffer any more than they have to. Anything you can tell me? Anything of note?'

'There is significant contusion to the facial region, consistent with blunt force trauma, likely from a fist. Posterior cranial bruising suggests impact with a flat surface, most plausibly resulting from a backward fall. The primary cause of death is a single penetrating wound to the thoracic cavity, which resulted in traumatic cardiac arrest. The wound track is clean and lacks evidence of serration, indicating a smooth-edged blade, most consistent with a kitchen or butcher-style knife.'

'Can I see him?'

'Already in the undertakers. According to Barratt, the wife positively identified Alex Hayes at the morgue in the hospital with him present. All the details will be in the report, I promise.'

'How long do you think it will take for a detailed report?'

'Obviously, I'll have to wait for the bloods and toxicology to come back to write it up, and there being only two pathologists in the whole of Ireland, between you and me, I'm pretty swamped with bodies before I can sit down and write the paperwork. But honestly, Sergeant, here and now, the man died from that stab wound.'

Chapter 3

Saoirse

Three times I fell in love with the same man. Once when I was a little girl and discovered how it felt to have a friend. Then, as a teenager, I found my first love. And again, when our paths crossed once more.

Three times the same person broke my heart.

The thing about pleasure is, it doesn't last. Only pain remains.

It was still worth it, though.

One second of pleasure with Alex was worth thirty years of grief.

Chapter 4

The floor is cold against my cheek. Porcelain. White. A terrible choice for a kitchen. Too slippy. Shows up every morsal of dirt even when you've just scrubbed, mopped, then scrubbed it again. It is full of specks now, specks of my blood. And cold, always cold.

I cannot move.

As I lie on the floor, all the bad choices I've made run havoc in my head; I wish the flooring was the worst of them.

Not by a long shot.

Chapter 5

'The day we cremated Alex; it was bright outside. Surprisingly warm for March. One of those days you would usually look up at the sky and feel blessed that the winter was finally leaving. It felt wrong. If the weather was an accurate reflection of my feelings, the sun wouldn't dare to shine. I wanted gale force winds, pelting rain, I wanted hailstones the size of golf balls to smash into us all. Instead, the sky didn't have a cloud and the brightness of the sun made me squint enough to wear sunglasses, which I really hated. All the onlookers were probably whispering to each other, having a grand old bitch saying, "who does she think she is, Jackie Kennedy?"'

Melinda's posture deflated with the last puff of the sentence. 'What am I talking about the weather for? You were there, you saw what the day was like.'

Sergeant Vicky Fitzgerald scribbled in her notebook. 'No, it's good to hear. Gives me your perspective. Carry on.'

'I'm not making much sense at the moment. All I'm doing since I heard is rambling; I'm a mess.'

'It all helps, Melinda. Just talk. I'll point you another way if I need to.'

Melinda stroked the wooden side locker.

'The coffin was brown and ugly. *My* first choice was the casket. Smooth, black, the most expensive. But a voice in my head kept saying,

Alex wouldn't like it.'

She folded her arms and sat back in the chair, making eye contact. Initially stern, she then softened, slumping her shoulders as if giving in to the thought. It seemed to be a pattern with the woman, rotating from clipped hostile gestures to almost flopping in surrender. Starting with straight-backed angular postures that took too much energy to preserve. *Pain does that*, Vicky thought.

Except for tear-matted cheeks, her appearance was the same. Long, blonde hair hung in waves past her shoulders, her fringe cut across in a hard line, like a golden-haired version of Cleopatra, which only highlighted the softness in her eyes. A striking contradiction.

'He wouldn't have liked the black one, I knew that. If he had the choice, he would go understated. No fuss, plain wood, because that was Alex. See, if I'd been spiteful, I would have chosen the casket. And I would have been well within my rights because it wasn't his choice anymore, only my decisions left now.'

She blinked rapidly, as if the flutter of her eyelids would stop the brimming. It worked.

'I couldn't do it to him, couldn't have Alex lie in a box he would hate. So, there I was at his funeral, staring at the ugly brown instead.'

Melinda reached for a piece of lint on her trousers, grounding it into her soggy tissue, then threw it into the unlit fireplace. She took another tissue from the box on the side table and balled it into a fist. Started again.

'At the funeral, I discovered he had been unfaithful.'

'How?'

She shrugged. 'At first it was just a feeling, an intuition. The first inkling came before the service, in the church, when I looked behind and got a shock from the number of women there. They were everywhere; every pew had at least five women dabbing at tissues. There were men there too, don't get me wrong, but the ratio was way off. Grief is a complex emotion. Everything is a blur since I found out Alex was murdered, but this I remember clearly, I remember the *amount* of women I didn't know there. That hurt, I won't lie. Because straight away, before we even cremated him, still reeling from how he died, I questioned our relationship, wondered whether I knew him at all. His death put everything in doubt.

She gave an apologetic smile, then stared for a few seconds at the fire, unmoving. The knuckles gave away her inner thoughts, though, turning white from clenching the tissue. When she looked away, her eyes were filmy.

'Of course, one woman he had definite history with sat across from me, as if she had as much right to be there, even though she put that man through hell. His so-called family just because she gave birth for him. When all she did was make Alex miserable, while all I ever wanted was to make him happy.'

She blotted her face with the tissue. Mopped up the damage and threw the sodden tissue, now disintegrated strings, onto the growing pile on the fire.

'And look how he repaid me.'

She flicked her eyes at Vicky, looking rueful.

'It wasn't an obvious discretion. There were no whispers in the church. No one professed undying love or claimed to be having an affair with him. It was just these strange women dotted around were as upset as I should be. They were crying. Not with I'm-sorry-for-your-loss tears, but sorry for *their* loss weeps. Their tears highlighted my lack of them. Shining a spotlight on my ungrieving. Their occasional bursts of sobs echoed along the pews, the sound strong enough to slap me across the face. Their wet cheeks put me to shame. No matter how bad it looked to other people, I couldn't cry for him. Not yet. No, I was livid.'

The Sergeant's pen scratched the pad as she wrote, causing Melinda to wince.

'Livid? Why?'

Melinda straightened at the question, mulling it over as if surprised at the need, as if her answer was obvious. When she did talk, she spoke clearly, as if needing to get her point across to someone having trouble understanding.

'Because he left me, and he wasn't allowed to leave.'

Chapter 6

The Sergeant didn't question Melinda's answer, happy to sit in silence until Melinda added to her last statement. Melinda hated awkward silences.

'Look, I'm probably coming off harsh; I have a tendency to do that. Alex softened my hard corners. Of course he could leave. Anyone is free to leave any relationship; it wasn't like I chained him up or anything. Him leaving was always my worst fear; Alex knew that.'

'Was Alex leaving you?'

Melinda narrowed her eyes.

'Be careful, Sergeant, you're twisting my words. Dying is a pretty hard place to come back from, isn't it? All men leave in the end, whether physically or emotionally, I told Alex that when we first met. He promised he would spend his life proving he wouldn't. Turned out Alex was a liar.'

Satisfied, Melinda went back to staring at the fire. Smoothed her hair, checking no wayward pieces had escaped. The blow dry had held up since the funeral. *The only thing of hers that had*, she thought.

'Who did you attend the funeral with?'

The question snapped her back.

'You saw me there.'

'For the record,' the Sergeant prompted.

Melinda's eyes narrowed further, resting in slits. The question was a low blow.

'In the church, I sat on my own. Had the entire front pew on the left-hand side. No family left of mine; no parents for Alex. Well, his mother Cassandra is alive, but as you know, she couldn't be there. His mother would have sat beside me; we would have supported each other.'

'You get on?'

'With Cassandra? As much as you can with a mother-in-law, I guess. Tolerate might be a better word. Alex and his mother were as close as can be. My relationship with her was more complicated. She loved him, no doubt about that, and she would have been there if she hadn't collapsed the day before. From the shock of it, no wonder. No parent believes they will outlive a child. I wanted to postpone the funeral, I said so to her at the hospital but she insisted I go through with it. She said she'd never handle it even if we delayed it for a year. If she had been able, she would have sat with me, not with *her*. I want that included in your records.'

Vicky nodded, her mouth straight and solemn as if to affirm the last sentence.

'Alex was an only child, same as me, another thing that drew us together. You know already we had no kids together, met too late for that. Too late for Alex, anyway.'

Vicky tilted her head.

'Vasectomy.' She tapped the air. 'Just to be clear, his relatives and their partners never had an issue with me. On the day they probably would have sat beside me if I'd asked them to, but I wasn't thinking straight.'

She shifted in the chair, folded her arms across her chest. 'When they saw me sitting at the edge of the pew, they must have assumed I was blocking the entrance, putting an impassible wall up. Sometimes people think I'm standoffish.'

She ignored the smirk from the Sergeant.

'Anyway, whatever their reasoning, instead of sitting beside me, they offered their condolences, then sat on the pew directly behind.'

Melinda leant forward, pulled out another tissue from the emptying box and folded it on her lap, then looked up, her eyes doe-like, genuine.

'I wasn't, by the way. Blocking the entrance, I mean. It was just the nearest spot to where the coffin would be and, for the time left, I wanted to be as near to Alex as I could. It felt lonely up there, being the only one on that long bench. Especially when *she* sat on the opposite pew. With her stupid spectacle of a hat balanced on her head. It was a statement, a piece of fashion that screamed: "Look at me, I'm the true Mrs Hayes."'

Melinda shredded the tissue. 'There Bernice was, full on glamour, while I barely had the energy to throw lipstick on. If I hadn't gone to the hairdressers, I don't think I could have even brushed my hair. I wore the first black thing I found, whereas she looked like she'd just stepped out of a fashion show. That was Bernice all right, always putting her priorities first. Her two children fidgeted all service in their uncomfortable clothes. Alex's children. Have you met his kids yet?'

'Over the years, I've seen them around Knockfarraig, but I haven't spoken to them, no.'

'The girl, Lily, is the image of him,' Melinda smiled. 'She's lovely. Acts younger than eight, comes across as so innocent. Even when she's cross, she has a tantrum in the cutest way; you honestly have to fight yourself not to laugh. At the funeral, it must have taken all her concentration not to smile. Completely unnatural for the girl, I could see the effort it took not to wave at relatives she loved. Almost white hair, identical to her dad when he was a kid. Dark-blue eyes, the colour of the Atlantic Sea. The son, Kenneth, is more like *her*. Dark. Mousy. Shrewd.'

She pulled one shred of tissue free, balled it between her thumb and finger, then rolled it back and forth.

'Sorry, take that last statement back. Kenneth is a good kid, great with his sister. If she gets upset, he'll pick up one of her toys and do accents to distract her and if she demands to play, he never refuses. Most boys his age, being nearly at teenager, won't do that, from what I've been told. Sorry, I'm rambling again, but it's important to know that throwaway statement isn't how I really see him. It's just the anger coming out. The grief. Because I want someone to blame or need someone to rage at, I think, when it's all so sudden, so disgustingly unfair. I'm not myself at all. Everything feels upside down, like I'm looking out from inside a jam jar, distorting my view.'

'I get it,' Vicky said.

'There should have been more time. We should have had more years together. And now there's nothing and I'm alone again. A murderer ripped away the love I waited for, spent my whole life waiting for.'

'Grief is understandable. You said you found out he'd been unfaithful. Was that what made you angry on the day of the funeral specifically?'

Melinda didn't like the way the pen hovered at an angle towards her. As if pointing.

'Hadn't I good reason to be? One minute I'm choosing where we'll holiday next, and a week later, I'm planning my husband's funeral. Whoever did this took my future, took any future away from Alex. Isn't that why I'm here? To discover what happened. And what do you have? Nothing. No clue who killed him and instead of being out there searching for the culprit, you sit here making me run through the funeral. Which happened *after* he died. Why are we wasting our time on this? You should be out there, searching, going through the CCTV, figuring out who the person is, not wasting time on where I sat in the church. Why are you asking me all this?'

Sergeant Fitzgerald pinched her nose. 'Because, Melinda, we believe the murderer was at the funeral.'

Chapter 7

Melinda shifted in her seat.

'Who was it?'

'I cannot say.'

'Why? Are you insinuating it was me?'

Sergeant Fitzgerald stayed silent.

'Just because I was angry?' Melinda stood, held out her hands, wrists together facing the sky, to the Sergeant. 'Well, if anger indicates guilt, lock me up.'

'Please sit, Melinda.'

She stayed where she was. 'Do you know what I wanted to do most of all at the funeral? I wanted to scream. I wanted to stand up on the pew and scream until there was no more voice left in my throat. Not sit and listen to the priest, or look around at all those sad women, or be the dutiful current wife letting the ex-wife take over. Do you know what I also wanted to do?'

Melinda didn't wait for a response. She stepped towards the Sergeant.

'What I wanted more than anything was to run up to that coffin and shove those wreaths on the floor and stomp on them until the petals turned to sludge, because they had no right to lie on top of my husband. They had no right to exist. And I still feel this way, days later because I'm angry all the time; I want to hurt someone; I want to beat my fists against something until they burst bone. Alex should still exist. He should not have been in that stupid box. In that stupid suit. That stupid suit that when I saw how handsome he looked in it at our wedding, I thought I would pass out.'

Her voice lowered, as if only talking to herself. 'I couldn't sleep with the thought of the darkness in the closed coffin. Alex never liked the black of night, always slept with some form of light peaking from another room. The thought of him in eternal darkness was too much. In the end I had to take a sleeping tablet, I had to erase the thought. Maybe if the coffin was open, there would have been more closure. Maybe then it would have felt real.'

She lifted her hands in the air. 'Sorry, getting away from the funeral again.'

Sergeant Fitzgerald waved her hand. 'No, this is good. It gives me an insight into who Alex was.'

She tapped at her notebook. Opened her mouth to speak, hesitated, then spoke anyway. 'Distracting yourself works.'

'Works for what?'

'You said you are angry all the time. If you don't want it to consume you, if you need a break from it, the best way to do that is to distract yourself.'

'How?'

Vicky shrugged. 'Doing something pleasurable works.'

Melinda arched her eyebrow.

Vicky rolled her eyes. 'Work. A hobby. Go for a walk where there's plenty to look at. Read a good book. Anything that might help you forget.'

'You know what would cure my anger instantly? Finding out who killed my husband.'

'Working on it.' Vicky leant in. Then spoke in a softer tone than before. 'You only think that's the answer. Knowing who did it will create more anger than you can understand.'

'If you know who killed my husband, please tell me.'

'Everyone is a suspect at the moment.'

'If that's the case, why do you think the murderer was there at the funeral?'

'As soon as I know more, I will tell you. Carry on if you can.'

Melinda nodded. 'Mostly, what I thought about as I looked at the coffin, was that I missed him already,' she sniffed. 'He was good in those scenarios, at funerals and weddings; Alex always knew the right thing to say. He would remember the little things, the intricate details that made up the cobwebs of someone's life. Alex would ask someone a question and they would look shocked for a second, either surprised they had confided in him or forgotten the conversation even happened. That was Alex. I usually clung to him at social events. Hid behind him, if I'm honest. It's not that I was a total introvert, I've just always preferred to be a bit of a recluse. The quiet one. Dependable. Genuine, I like to think. Strange for an artist, people think of creative people as flamboyant and loud, but I love nothing more than to hide away in my studio with just my canvas.'

'Is that a London accent?'

'It is. I moved here to be with Alex. Our meeting had been complete fate; a blink and you'd miss it exchange. Alex was only visiting for a nurses' conference. One extra minute and we wouldn't have sat next to each other on the tube. Or if something hadn't disrupted the line, we wouldn't have talked for over thirty minutes before realising every other passenger had cut their losses and left to jump on buses instead. He hadn't known London, so asked me the best way. Going in the same direction and liking what I saw, I offered to walk with him to the next station. In the space of five minutes, I saw and heard enough to suspect Alex was different. When his credit card didn't work on the turnstile, I paid for his ticket. He offered to buy me dinner as thanks. And that had been it. Before we even finished our starter, I knew I would sell my soul for a second date with Alex Hayes.

'We tried long distance until it became agony to say goodbye, but it was a big step to leave my whole life behind for a man. From the first date, Alex had been clear that leaving his children wasn't an option. As an artist, I was free to follow him.'

She flashed a "blink and you miss it" smile. Then her expression turned distant, lost in a memory.

'Sometimes, I used to watch him at those parties, when I could get away with tucking into a corner. There, the chatter would blend away and I'd just watch him weave through the room. He was always my favourite person there.'

She shook her head. 'Alex was one of those rare people who could turn any uncomfortable situation around and do it in a way that the people involved would think it was all their making, even pat themselves on the back for it. I think that's why he made such an excellent nurse. He cared. Didn't have the ego needed to be a doctor. All he wanted was to help. That's what makes this whole thing with the man in the car even stranger.'

'What? That Alex would approach him?'

'No, all day long, Alex would try to defuse the situation. What's confusing is that Alex might fail.'

That scratchy pen again. 'You think Alex was trying to defuse the situation?'

She screwed her eyes. 'Don't you?'

Vicky didn't answer. Her silence made the hairs on the back of Melinda's neck rise.

'Why do *you* think it happened? Who would want to hurt him?'

'We are still investigating all avenues of inquiry.'

'You have more avenues than interviewing me?' Melinda raised an eyebrow.

'Mrs Hayes, this is an informal chat. If I believed you were the only avenue worth investigating, this conversation would take place at the station. Can we go back to the funeral? What did you notice?'

'Not before you record what I just told you. You might think I'm rambling, but it's important you know what type of person my husband was. Alex was *never* violent.'

Vicky wrote something in her notebook. 'Noted.'

Melinda straightened, smoothed her clothes. 'If you are saying the murderer was there, was someone at the funeral, if you are saying you have reason to believe someone there hurt him, then I can tell you exactly who it was.'

Chapter 8

They both jumped when Vicky's phone beeped.

'Sorry about this. I've warned Phyllis not to interrupt unless it's something important. I'll just go outside for a bit, yeah?'

She ripped out a piece of paper from her notebook.

'While I'm gone, can I ask you to jot something?'

Melinda took the offered pen and paper. 'Okay?'

'My name is Melinda Hayes.'

'Okay,' she chuckled. 'Is that all?'

'That's all for now, thanks.'

Noting the woman's confusion, Vicky stepped out of the room, opened the front door and walked to her car. She kept her voice low. 'Phyllis, this better be important.'

'Phone call from the big man. He didn't want to be put off again. Said you keep ignoring him.'

'Right. I'll ring him there.'

Stepping into her car, she dialled the superintendent.

'Afternoon, Mara.'

'Do you ever have your phone on?'

'Not when I'm interviewing the wife of a murder victim.'

'You're at Melinda Hayes' house?'

'Sure am.'

'You don't think it's too soon? The funeral was only two days ago.'

'You said yourself we need to get moving with this case.'

'I did. I also told you to work with Garda Barratt but he's just informed me you dismissed him, saying there was no need for him to be involved.'

'Come on, Mara, he'll only get in my way. He briefed me over the phone. Anyway, he seemed happy for me to take over.'

'Happy not to get an earful, more like.'

'Knockfarraig is my area. It wasn't my fault I took a few days off.'

'You know procedure, Fitzgerald. Barratt was first on the scene. He was also the attending garda at the identification at the morgue. If anyone should back off, it's you.'

'Do you want me to back off?'

The line stayed silent.

'We both know I have a better track record than Barratt. Have you had a conversation with the guy? Honestly, if I have to work with him, you'll be investigating two murders.'

'I'll cross that bridge. Next time I talk to you, I want confirmation you've worked together. Expect him later today. Got it?'

Vicky bit the inside of her lip until she could taste blood.

'Got it, Fitzgerald?'

'Got it, Mara.'

'Good. Now, spill.'

Pulling the car mirror down, she checked her reflection and then wished she hadn't. She hadn't slept properly in days.

'Here's what I know about Alex Hayes so far: the man acted like a saint. From the sounds of it, his wife Melinda was jealous of every woman who came near him within a five-mile vicinity.'

'Warranted?'

'Haven't established yet. Everyone I've spoken to so far won't hear a negative word spoken about him. Also, the obvious fact is a stranger killed him in a road-rage incident.'

'You're going with road rage?'

She waved her pen.

'Well, that's all I've got to go on. Cannot make a connection between the two men at all. Did you get the CCTV footage I sent over?'

'Yep, is there a way to improve the image of the suspect?'

'Looking at companies now. Rarely have a need for one in Knockfarraig.'

'I'll get you a name.'

'That would be great, sir.'

'How long did the ambulance take to get there?'

'Nineteen minutes from the Garda call. Not unusual for our neck of the woods. I assume there were no local ambulances on duty and they had to deploy from Wilton.'

'What have I told you about assumptions, Fitzgerald?'

'Noted, Superintendent.'

She wrote: *Check what delayed ambulance.*

'Other leads?'

'Plenty. The ex-wife wasn't on good terms with Alex, according to Melinda. From court records, Bernice seemed to prefer if her previous husband would leave the kids alone. Melinda has definite trust issues. My hunch is she wouldn't have it in her, but hey, no assumptions, like you say. She was just about to tell me who she thought killed her husband when I was told to give you a ring, so I'd better get back. I'm not holding my breath.'

'Why's that?'

'If the woman had any concrete information, she would have been straight out with it.'

'Assumptions, Vicky.'

'Right, Superintendent, I'll keep you informed if she sheds any light. As soon as your guy clears the image, we'll run it through the system and if nothing shows up, release it to the press, if we have your permission, of course.'

'Sergeant, if that's what we need to do, we do it. As soon as, understood?'

'Understood.'

'What about the murder weapon?'

'No sign of it so far. Barratt already did an intensive search but I'll return to the scene after I finish with Melinda and make sure he didn't miss anything.'

'No sign of the car either?'

'No sign of the man or car, no.'

The superintendent breathed heavily. 'What about the writer of the note?'

'I've just asked Melinda to give me a sample of her handwriting. I'll do the same with every person I interview. We'll get there.'

'Don't go running in a different direction like you often do. Road rage seems the most likely.'

'There's more to this story, Mara; I can feel it.'

'Do you know how many times I've heard this from you?'

'Do you know how many times I've been right?'

'No garda makes note of what you do right, only your wrongdoings. I don't want time wasting here. This hitman theory, it's pretty out there even for you. And wanting to interview all the women in his life, why?'

'Because one of these women holds the key, I can—'

'Feel it, yeah, I know. You're like a record on repeat. Do you know how many newspapers are ringing up this office to ask if there is any new information? The public is reeling from this, and the only way to calm them is to offer justice. They can't understand how something like this can happen to a good person right out in the middle of the street in a town like Knockfarraig. We have to restore their faith. And we have to do it quickly.'

'Understood. I'm on it.'

'Well, hurry up, would you?'

'Don't rush a genius, boss.'

'Is that what you're calling yourself these days?'

'Better than what you probably want to call me.'

'Get back to work.'

Chapter 9

Vicky smiled at the steaming teapot on the table. 'It's like you read my mind.'

The piece of paper with Melinda's handwriting was next to the empty cup. Vicky examined the handwriting then pocketed it.

Melinda poured. 'Did I pass?'

Vicky hesitated.

'Melinda, I'm going to tell you something that I probably shouldn't, but it might help jog your memory. Someone left a note at the crematorium. Just before they had closed the privacy doors I caught sight of something, a little triangle, a glimpse of white peeking out from the back end. I approached the undertaker and asked him if they burned the coffin right then. He had sneered his lip in disapproval at the term, then explained that they didn't actually cremate the body until after the services, which on a busy day, could be hours after. Once everyone left, he allowed me to be present as they lifted it. There, badly wedged into the back of the seal in the coffin, was a handwritten note.'

'Saying what?' Melinda looked genuinely shocked.

'Please forgive me, I didn't want to kill you.'

'What? Like it was an accident?'

'Maybe, I won't jump to any conclusions.'

'So, someone in that crematorium knew what happened to my husband?'

'Well, the writer knows something, at least, which is why it's important to find out who they are. Anything at the funeral that struck you as strange could help.'

'Everything at a funeral is strange.'

'You know what I mean. Before I left the room, you said you knew who killed your husband?'

'I don't know for sure that she killed him, just that she would have reason to.'

A pen tapped the notebook. 'You know the murderer was a man, right?'

Melinda shrugged. 'Women hire hitmen.'

Sergeant Fitzgerald's pen stopped tapping. 'I'm listening.'

Melinda laid a hand on her chest. 'As his next of kin, as the legally recognised wife, I could have pulled rank, could have made life difficult. Even though I didn't have to, I allowed *her* to play a part. I chose the first reading, a dig I admit. "*His soul being pleasing to the Lord, he has taken them quickly from the wickedness around him. Yet people look on, uncomprehending; it does not enter their heads that grace and mercy await the chosen of the Lord.*"'

Melinda chuckled. Then furrowed her brows.

'She chose the second, a dig at me. "*Love does not come to an end. In short, there are three things that last: faith, hope and love; and the greatest of these is love.*" Bitch. Like it was loving of her to sleep with his friend. That's right, scribble that down in your book.'

'Which friend?'

'Eamonn O Sullivan. His friend from college.'

'Did Alex confront him or her about it?'

'Alex found out after they broke up. Eamonn admitted it to him after a few drinks.'

'Did they keep in contact?'

'As far as I know Eamonn lives somewhere hot. Dubai, I think.'

She leant forward in the chair, enjoying the revelation. 'I saw how she used the children as pawns while she negotiated more money. Even when he gave her the house, when he left himself homeless and had to move in with his mother, she would change the visiting arrangements at a moment's notice. She didn't care. It was like she wanted him to just disappear. Three years ago, when we thought he wouldn't make it, I called for the children, asked her if they could come to the hospital. She refused, wouldn't even let them say goodbye.'

'Three years ago?'

Melinda nodded. 'Liver failure, due to Bacillus cereus. He nearly died. They told us to contact his loved ones. He called out for them, cried out for his kids, so I made the phone call. Told her of his wish to see them. She said it would be too traumatic, that it would be better they keep the memories they had rather than remember him dying. She said to me, tell him we love him. Tell him we said goodbye. I'll never forgive her for that. Letting a dying man go without seeing his children one more time. Denying him a chance to tell them the things he needed to say. But that was Bernice. Controlling every situation, even if it was her ex's death. Only she didn't get her way, because that time he didn't die. That time, he pulled through, a doctor figured out what caused it and treated it quickly. After he recovered, Alex made sure his children had a way of contacting him without going through their mother. If there was ever any other emergency, he wanted to ensure I or him could contact them. *If.*'

'How did he ensure that?'

'Gave them secret phones.'

Vicky made a note.

'Alex changed after that scare. Became braver. Tried more. Lived more.'

The pen tapped the page.

'It doesn't matter now. She still won.'

'Why?'

'A man can't have custody when he's dead.'

'Are you suggesting Bernice had something to do with Alex's death?'

'I'd check her out if I were you.'

Melinda sighed. 'God, I miss those kids. It's ridiculous. Do you know how many weekends when I first moved over that I secretly wished for some time alone with my husband? How many times I resented them robbing our time?'

'Did you bring this up with Alex?'

Melinda guffawed. 'Never. That wouldn't have gone down well. Not that Alex would have argued or anything. Only once did I ever see Alex lose his temper the whole time I knew him. Anger I've dealt with before, anger I can understand from a partner, but with Alex, if I pushed his buttons, he turned quiet until he could process his hurt. Voicing my annoyance over the kids would have hurt Alex deeply; he would have been offended I even considered such a thought. All the resentment means nothing now. As much as I missed having some alone time with my husband on the weekends, I see now I didn't just lose Alex when he died, I lost those kids too. My weekends are back to being free. Back to nothingness. What I would give to fill that empty house with laughter again.'

'Maybe Bernice will allow them to visit?'

Melinda scoffed. 'Please, have you met her? She wouldn't even let Alex see them if it didn't suit.'

Vicky tapped the pen again. Melinda had a sneaking suspicion the Sergeant was doing it to keep her from running off tangent too much.

'You mentioned Alex lost his temper once? Can you tell me about that?'

'Oh.' Melinda pulled on her earlobe, then shook her head. 'Honestly, I can't remember.'

'Really? If my husband only lost his temper once, I'd never forget.'

Melinda flicked her hand. 'He was sick, and he wasn't himself. Delusional even. Started accusing me of all sorts. It was the medication. As soon as he was better, there was never another word.'

She ran her fingers along her bottom lip, watching as Sergeant Fitzgerald wrote. The scribbles went on for a long time.

Chapter 10

'Can you tell me about the rest of the funeral? Did you notice anything unusual?'

'Most of it passed in a blur. My only focus was on Alex in the coffin. Alone in that box. I knew it was nearing the end, the saying goodbye and I wasn't ready. There was no way I could say a few words or write a eulogy, I couldn't stand up and say a reading, my legs wouldn't have been strong enough for that walk. I would have collapsed. Or if I did somehow make it, I would have broken down up there for all to see. I barely kept it together as it was.'

'Do you need a break now?'

She shook her head.

'Then it was over. The priest gave the men a nod, and they took their places. They shouldered the coffin and as they hoisted him, it dipped forward and for a terrible moment, I pictured the coffin sprawled out on the floor. Imagine the sheer horror of seeing Alex that way.' She waved her hand as if brushing the thought away. 'Course, it was just my overactive imagination and they were fine. Powerful men, well able. Sure, Gerry and John at the back, played rugby with Alex back in the day, and they never lost their muscle. Ernest at the front always kept fit. His cousin Rory played to nearly professional level soccer. Carrying my dead husband should have been a walk in the park. Then it was my turn to move, to follow. I stood, clung to the pew as I edged out to keep myself upright. In the aisle, I froze. It is tradition to let the first row lead with each row following, so in order to get things moving, I gestured to the children to take the space, letting them know they had as much right as me to walk directly behind too. Kenneth and Lily saw my gesture, came out all coy. It didn't surprise me when Bernice walked ahead. Kenneth followed her, but Lily held back; she walked beside me instead.

As I left the church, I caught a sight of the sea, between a gap in the street across. I breathed a long breath. I didn't know if I could get through the rest of it.'

'Did you notice anyone that shouldn't have been there? Anyone stand out?'

'Then? No. I didn't look at anyone. All my effort went on what would happen next.'

She gave a disapproving look, as if Sergeant Fitzgerald annoyed her for even suggesting she look around.

'So, that leaves the walk from the car to the crematorium. Can you list those people for me?'

'Alex's last walk.' She dabbed at her eyes and flapped her hands. 'Sorry. You'd think I would be all cried out by now.'

'That's understandable, Melinda.'

'No, I have to stop. I have sores on my eyelids from tears.'

She waved her hand in front of her eyes and once satisfied the eyeballs were dry again, continued.

'For the last walk, it could only be his friends. Ernest sorted it.'

'Ernest? They were still that close?'

She scribbled some notes.

'The best of friends. Known each other since they were in nappies. More than once I said to Alex his life would have been much simpler if they had married each other.'

'They were like that growing up too.'

'You knew Alex when he was younger?'

'Hard not to know everyone in a small town like Knockfarraig. Who else carried the coffin, carried Alex, I mean?'

'You know most of them I would think. Alex's friends. Ronan and Con, both known him since primary. Ernest again, best man at his wedding, both his weddings. Simon and Greg studied together in college and Eddie, from his team.'

'Ronan, Con, Ernest and Eddie all hail from Knockfarraig. Tell me more about Simon and Greg.'

'What do you want to know?'

'Surnames mostly. Were they nurses too?'

Melinda sucked in a breath. 'Simon Bracken and Greg O'Farrell. Neither were nurses and they loved to rib Alex about that, weren't even medical. They shared digs together and all went their separate paths in UCC then hung out together in the evenings. Being a straight man, Alex found it hard to socialise with the other female nurses. Back when he was studying it was rare to see a male nurse. Nights out with the girls would often turn into one of them trying to make a move and, according to Alex, he didn't think it was right to mix work with relationships.'

'According to Alex?' Vicky asked with an eyebrow raised.

'Well, how much truth is there in what a man really tells his girlfriend about his past dating history? Anyway, a year later he was married to Bernice.'

'They stayed close throughout: Alex, Simon and Greg?'

'As close as men can who live a distance away and all have kids. They tried to meet up at least once a month for a pint but over the years it could often go every couple of months.'

'No arguments?'

'They were friends, Sergeant Fitzgerald. They could get heated about who they believed won the World Cup in 2002 – but, as I said, Alex was gentle. Alex never fought with anyone.'

'Who would you say Alex was closest to?'

'Me.' Melinda straightened, looked Vicky straight in the eye, with more than a hint of defiance. 'Friends come and go. They were acquaintances, mates he sat and drank a pint with, shot the breeze for a couple of hours at the most. If you are asking who in the world Alex was closest to, the answer is me.'

Vicky scribbled in her pad. 'Was there a reason they didn't come to the wedding do you know?'

'Who?'

'The relatives?'

Melinda tilted her head. Vicky waggled her pen. 'Any animosity between the family? It all helps piece together the jigsaw.'

'Not as far as I know. They all gave what seemed like valid excuses. We married mid-week so getting time off for most people wasn't feasible and honestly, we didn't want a big do, it was Alex's second time remember?'

Vicky's pen stayed in the air. 'You didn't mind?'

'What do you mean?'

'Alex had walked the aisle before but you were still a first-time bride. You didn't want a fuss?'

'I wanted to marry Alex the day I met him. I would have walked into a tornado to do it. Marrying mid-week was hardly a sacrifice. As my family and friends were flying over for the wedding, most of them were making a week of it anyway so it didn't matter what day it was. Sorry, but why are we going off tangent here?'

'You'd be surprised what adds up. I prefer to have too many facts than too little. Anything else to add?'

'Only that as far as I know there were no problems between Alex and his mother's family from Galway. There was, I think, at one stage, when his mother left Galway. Alex's dad was, for loss of a better word, an absolute ogre. They hated him, didn't want her to go out with him let alone have a child with the guy. Thinking it was all romantic, she ran down to Cork with him. Left her whole family. Left her all alone.'

'Like you?'

Melinda crossed her arms. 'Don't compare my relationship with Alex to the train wreck of his parents.'

'Why do you say that?'

'Alex's father was a drunk. Died at the foot of the stairs after falling over an empty bottle of whiskey and, from the sounds of it, all it brought was relief. That man gave Alex, gave his mother, a desperate time. He abandoned Cassandra in Cork before she gave birth. She told me she was too ashamed to go home and admit they had been right about him. After John's death, Cassandra's brothers reached out. There was no feud. They loved their sister, always had. When she realised they had been right all along about her husband, when he showed her the man he really was, she felt it was too late. Have you met Cassandra yet? Proud would be one way to call her.'

'I would know of Cassandra. Spoke to her around Knockfarraig. What was her maiden name?'

'Dalton. It should be her telling you about this, not me.'

'Like I said, I like to gain each person's perspective.' She wrote something down. Melinda huffed; the woman's scribbling was getting annoying.

'In the crematorium I thought about jumping in with him, about the practice of Sati.'

Melinda frowned at the Sergeant's blank expression.

'In ancient Hinduism, the wife either threw herself or was thrown onto the pyre when her husband died. The belief was that the woman was a part of the husband, an appendage that had no right of its own to survive. Before, the tradition maddened me, but that day I understood it completely. I imagined all the people who died from a broken heart.

Imagined Cassandra in her hospital bed, her heart nearly bursting with the shock. Did she make a conscious choice; did she force her heart to give up? Did her brain command it to stop, or was it more subconscious? Did the people who succeeded just crack open from grief and let go of life without even thinking of it? Would I die from the pain? Should I? Did living on mean I loved him less?'

She stopped. Put a hand to her breast.

'The pain in my chest could have been an indication of death. I've never felt a sensation like it. It was like how I imagined drowning must feel. Breath wouldn't come. The closing in, the tightness pressing down. Perspiration beaded on the bow of my lip. Fainting was a real possibility. And then a hand slipped into mine. The girl. His Lily. Her eyes were like saucers in her tiny face. For a second, she broke the sorrow and made me smile. I looked around then, more for a distraction than anything else, and there she was, Bernice, staring back. She nodded at me, just once. Most things I will ever say about that woman will be uncomplimentary, but she recognised I needed Lily, and she didn't call her away. Maybe it was guilt. Maybe it will come out that all of this is her fault; I truly wouldn't put it past her. There was no love lost between us, but I'd always been civil, always calmed Alex down when she did something unfair.'

'Unfair?'

Melinda shrugged. 'You know, typical acrimonious end of marriage, ex-wife behaviour.'

'Like?'

'Like, she would change the kids' availability at the last moment. Or not pass on messages about school concerts or play dates or matches until Alex insisted they add him to the notifications list. One time, she announced the children couldn't go with us the night before we were flying out to Tenerife. We had scheduled it a year in advance, court approved and everything. We bought the kids their own luggage and let them choose what they wanted to fill inside because we wouldn't chance her pretending to have forgotten their gear. She didn't even give us a proper excuse, just left Alex a message saying the kids wouldn't be able to fly. I'm sure she thought we would just get on the plane, the two of us. She didn't bank on Alex already being a step ahead, sending a pre-prepared solicitor's letter back stating she would have to compensate every penny of the cancelled trip and arrange another holiday for a particular week she booked to take them away. Funny, after that the kids made it onto the flight.'

She smiled. 'It was a great holiday.'

Then, her face dropped. 'Our last.'

'Is that why you think Bernice is capable of murder?'

'You must look at me and think, of course the second wife is going to have a problem with the first, but honestly, if Bernice hadn't given reason to dislike her, for the kids' sake, and Alex, I would have tried. On the morning of the cremation, after she let Lily stay by my side, when we looked at each other, there was something new between us, something different than what we had throughout the years, like a sharing of pain. An acknowledgment of grief. Never before, or after for that matter, have I felt the same and it was gone by the time we walked out to the car park, but in that one tiny moment I felt her regret. Before, I wondered if she was even human. Even if her grief was genuine, she can't erase the pain caused through the years.'

'In what ways?'

'It is unforgivable that he had to fight her to see his children. I understand women who have to do what it takes to protect their kids from abusive partners, where they would rather risk jail than hand over their kids to a dangerous man especially without supervision, and I can sort of get the logic with women who stop visitation when the husband doesn't pay maintenance, although I don't agree with this form of emotional blackmail, at least they have a reason. There was none of that with Alex. He adored those kids. He was a good father, you know? Not just with paying maintenance or turning up for the obligatory Christmas show, either. Alex was the kind of dad that ran up the stairs to tuck his kids into their bed just so he could spend extra time with them.'

She rolled her eyes, then smiled. 'I often had to go up when the laughter was still travelling down two hours later. Or I'd find him asleep in one of their beds, cuddled into them like he couldn't bear to let go. Mondays were the worst. When he'd wake up and see an empty kitchen instead of them sitting there eating breakfast. The house was too quiet for Alex, too empty when they left.' She pinched the bridge of her nose, took a deep inhale of breath, then looked up.

'All that disappeared the day Alex died. No more problems with Bernice. No more custody visits.'

'How often did Alex see them?'

'It was the strangest thing. Bernice went from messing him about to one day offering him the majority of custody, us getting four days while she got three. I never knew exactly why she changed her tune there. Whatever happened between Alex and her, he would never allow a word said about her as a mother. And I have to say, looking at those children, she must have done something right.

'At the cremation, Lily didn't have to stay with me, but she did. And, I was thankful for her hand in mine. When they closed the doors of that little compartment where the coffin was, it hit me that there were no more chances, there was no more hope, Alex was never coming back. I lost my breath. No, lost is the wrong word; I gave up my breath, I clamped my mouth shut and decided that was it, no more would I go on. My chest started juddering, struggling to get air, but I didn't care. And then her little hand squeezed mine and for a minute I didn't feel alone. When I heard her crying, I couldn't bear it, because I knew as long as a child of Alex's was alive, I had a responsibility to him. I took her into my arms and hugged her and didn't care what her mother thought. As I held her, I wished we could stay like that, imagining Alex was still alive, still with us. I remember wondering how long could I hold her without it looking strange.'

'At the start of the conversation, you mentioned your husband had been unfaithful. Did you gather that only from all the women crying?'

Melinda folded her hands in her lap, unhappy with the intrusive question. Then her shoulders slumped, giving in to the memory.

'Did you ever think you knew someone in their entirety? That was the way we were, me and Alex. He was kind, and loyal, and he taught me it was okay to trust men. That one sentence doesn't do him justice, but it is the truth. Many men hurt me. When I met Alex, I had given up on love, was not looking for a partner, fought against it actually. My husband was the first man to show me love could be different to what I knew. If you'd asked me who my husband was before his death, I would have listed those words without hesitation.'

She held her hands out in admittance. 'Yes, there were times I doubted Alex but once reassured, once I spoke to him about it, I knew it was just because of my past. Because of what had happened before Alex. It must seem completely irrational to talk about the women in the church. Even at the time, I knew I was delirious, but my gut told me to be suspicious. In the crematorium, that changed. There was a side to Alex I didn't know, mustn't have known. Because the Alex I knew was selfless. If he *was* unfaithful, that changes the person I knew completely. It changes who he was. No, I didn't conclude Alex had been unfaithful just from the amount of women crying. It got my back up but didn't convince me. It rattled me was what it did. My conviction came when I met *her*. Inside that crematorium I still didn't know the woman existed. As soon as I saw her, though, I knew she had been with my husband. And without you telling me anything, without knowing one thing about the woman, I also knew she had something to do with my husband's death.'

'Can you be specific? What was it that made you think that?'

'It was her guilt. Every step she made, every time she looked up, it covered her, wrapped her up in it like a blanket. She acted like she was terrified, like she felt she shouldn't be there but couldn't stay away. Like she wanted to hide yet wanted to jump into the coffin, too.

'I'd never seen her before, yet I recognised something in her. At first, it wouldn't connect. Until later, when they were lifting the coffin, and she looked as if she might break. Then I understood; it was her grief. She was not just crying like the others. Not just sad at the unfairness of Alex dying so young, or shocked at his violent end. She was as broken as I was. That's the exact moment I knew. You think I'm crazy, don't you?'

'Did you approach the coffin in the crematorium?'

'Yes. I kissed it and said goodbye.'

'Did you see anyone else approach it?'

'No. Bernice and the kids maybe. Do you know who she is?'

'Who?'

'Oh, let's see.' She tapped at her cheek, then scowled. 'You know who I'm talking about.'

'I don't. Who are you talking about?'

'I can't say her name.'

She stared at Vicky's pen, as it hovered, waiting for her to speak.

'I can't say her name because I don't know it.'

Chapter 11

Ivy Harrington wiped at her eyes roughly, then, smoothing her unruly black hair back and securing it in a ponytail, threw her arms out wide. 'I'm sorry, I don't know why I'm still crying. Ever since I heard, I can't stop.'

She blew into a tissue.

'I've no right to be this upset; I didn't even know the man that well. It's just so unfair. There's plenty of arseholes in the world, why couldn't it have happened to them instead? Why do bad things happen to good people?'

She pointed the tissue at Sergeant Fitzgerald, waiting for an answer.

Vicky cleared her throat. 'It is unhealthy how many times I have asked the same question. You considered Alex Hayes a good man, then?'

Ivy leant back in the chair, the tears all dried up now it was time to talk. 'The best. He helped me, helped my family. Behind closed doors can be another story, of course.'

She wagged her finger. 'I found that out the hard way and met many a scumbag. From what I knew of Alex, he was a kind man, a good man. When you've met the amount of losers I have, it becomes easy to spot a great one.'

'How did you know him?'

'From the hospital. When I say Alex Hayes saved my son's life, I mean Alex Hayes *saved* his life. Saying I owe him everything, it isn't an understatement.

'I'd already put down a bad night with Eric, that's my son, which was after two days of him lying in the bed at home. At first, I thought he was just being a typical teenager, lazing in the bed, but then he turned lifeless. Couldn't move his neck. Now, most people on the street know what to look for, but back then, I hadn't a clue. The doctor told us it was a virus, like the flu, but I never saw any flu like that. He put Eric on an IV drip and said they would keep a close eye. In the night, Mr Hayes must've only started his shift because it was my first time meeting him when he came in the room to check on Eric. Back then I thought it was strange him being a nurse; I'd never met a male nurse before but he seemed sound, made sure he introduced himself when some wouldn't even look at you. He even asked was it alright to approach Eric, which I thought was like he saw me, like I mattered. When he lifted the sheet, Eric groaned at seeing the light, Alex checked his pulse, and it all changed. He rushed into the corridor and tried to ring someone on the phone. I freaked out then. The way he kept punching the numbers into the handset, I knew it could only mean trouble for Eric. After about five attempts, he slammed the phone down, ran into another room. I paced the hall, went back into Eric. In five minutes, he had deteriorated even more. Every couple of seconds, he moaned and when I tried to shift his head on the pillow, he cried out in pain. Mr Hayes came back and I'll never forget the look on his face. It was enough to make my legs buckle. He said, "Mrs Harrington, I believe I know what is wrong with your son, but if we wait for the test to confirm it, if I wait for the doctor, or the lumber puncture, or a rash, it will be too late. He's in grave danger."

'I don't know if I went into shock or something 'cos he grabbed both my arms and said, "Mrs Harrington, if we hesitate, Eric might not survive." Even in shock, I liked that, how he used my son's name. It was as if my son already meant something to him, like he wasn't just another patient, like Eric's survival was important to him, too. "What do we have to do?" I asked.

'He told me he needed to give him an antibiotic straightaway. When I asked what he thought was wrong, he said he thought Eric had meningitis. I damn near collapsed at that. Horror stories made the news about that illness. You heard of kids dying. Being there one day, gone the next. Losing arms and going into comas.

'Alex told me we needed to treat him with a particular antibiotic that he had to get approval for. Something about that man made me trust him straightaway. With most doctors their eyes are cold; I'm not saying it the right way, but they are all business, you know? Like when they are telling you about your child, they might as well be listing off their weekly shop, but not Alex Hayes. I said to him, "do whatever you need to, you have my full permission." And if he had been wrong, and the worst happened, I would still never have blamed him because right there, it was like I could see what was in his heart, because he was doing what he believed was right. He took Eric off the medication. Against the doctor or consultant's instructions. It worked. My Eric pulled through. It didn't stop Mr Hayes getting into trouble. When the doctor arrived, he called him out of the room with a pure frosty tone, like a headmaster about to cane a student, and I just knew he was gonna take flack. That bigwig pulled the curtains but I could still hear; I'd say everyone in the ward could.'

'The exchange became heated?'

She snorted. 'More like an inferno. I heard the guy say if he ever went over him again, it would be his last day at the hospital. Alex just kept repeating the same words over and over. *It needed to be done.* Afterwards, the test results proved Eric had meningitis. By that stage, I didn't need any confirmation. Seeing Eric on the mend was enough. When I thought of how much worse it could have been, it didn't bear thinking about. Every year, every anniversary, I never forgot about the decision Mr Hayes made, about how much I could have lost. As Eric grew, I never forgot. Mr Hayes must have only been fresh out of nursing college, only in his twenties, younger than what Eric would be now. Every occasion Eric has celebrated since I have thought of that man: every birthday, when he met his partner Fay, when he made me a grandmother last year, the first person I wanted to tell, to thank, was Alex Hayes. Alex saved my family. As far as I know, he never got an apology either. When I asked, he just rolled his eyes, said not to worry, it all worked out in the end. I wasn't the only one either. There were tons of us at the church, hundreds I'd say. Like a little Alex Hayes fan club. All with stories of how he saved our lives or someone close to us. It's people like Alex we should line the streets for, that we should commemorate, not politicians or state leaders. It's men like Alex Hayes that are the real supermen, the proper heroes.'

'Do you have the name of the doctor?'

'I'm not sure if he was a doctor or a consultant but his name was Jefferies, that I wouldn't forget.'

'Could you describe him?'

'Sure. Tall. Dark hair. Beard. Mean looking.'

She waited for the scribbles to stop.

'Alex always brushed away a thank you. Kept saying it was his job. And then, this is the way he died! Such a violent death. Nobody deserves to die that way, but Alex, he definitely didn't. My heart breaks for his family. His son at twelve now is nearly the same age as Eric was when he caught meningitis. Every Christmas I dropped in a hamper for him at the hospital. If I was lucky, he would have a minute to chat. He always made me feel like I wasn't imposing, that it was always the right time. His eyes crinkled and his lips went upward whenever he said his son's name. He couldn't stop smiling when he told me he was about to become a father for the second time. And the next year, when he told me they called the baby Lily because she was as beautiful as a flower, I remember thinking it was nice for a man to talk about his child that way. Rare, even.'

45

Chapter 12

Face in face. Teeth bared, snarling like a cornered animal.

There is no corner.

I have tried to give enough space, but I need more, need to remove myself from danger. I back away, one tiny inch at a time, trying to escape without notice. Not far enough, for spit lands on my skin. Nose nudges my nose. I need to move, to get out of danger. Quicker now, I step back, again and again. I do not notice the edge of the stairs until I tip over. Each step I hit on the way down hurts.

This time, bones break.

Chapter 13

'Barratt,' Vicky said in greeting, but she didn't look up from her desk. Vicky didn't care if it appeared rude, in fact she wanted it to. Looking at Barratt was what got her in trouble before. Never one to mix business with pleasure, she had hooked up with him when she first moved back to Knockfarraig, on the assumption that Ballinroe Station was far enough away not to matter, not realising how much a rural station manned by only her would need to interact with a bigger station twenty miles away. Barratt leant against the back wall, his crossed arms enough evidence that he didn't want to be there either. Vicky softened.

'Look Barratt, I know Mara summoned you. Let's just do what we need to do and keep out of each other's way.'

She pointed to the seat in front of the desk.

Barratt sloped over. 'You actually going to talk to me this time?'

'I'll talk. Just … let's keep it professional.'

'You say that as if I want something different. Believe me, it's better for everyone if we stick to the case.'

'Okay then,' she said, making the mistake of meeting his eyes. Dammit. Dark, dumb and handsome, just the way she liked her men. These days, anyway. Barratt in fairness, had been discreet. He could have turned their night together in his favour with the other lads at Ballinroe, who would have loved nothing better than to rib her. Still, though, working together now was proof why she should never mix business with pleasure. It's harder to rip into someone when you've seen them naked.

'Right then, what have you got for me? Start from the start and tell me everything.'

Chapter 14

Ernest Morley stuck his head around the door and walked in.

Vicky stood. 'Thanks for popping in; it shouldn't take long.'

Ernest smiled. 'Am I in trouble, officer?'

Vicky, hands on her hips, smiled back. 'I don't know, should you be?'

'Knowing you, Vic, if there was any inkling of wrongdoing from someone in this town, you'd have arrested them already.'

'You know me too well, Ernest. No trouble, just hoping you can help me figure out what happened.'

'Fire away with the questions. If I can help Alex, I will.'

'Sit so.'

He pointed to the chair. 'Isn't that where you seat the criminals?'

'Criminals, innocents and anyone in between. In a station this small, you sit where you can. I ate my lunch here this morning.'

'Right so.' He sat. Shifted in his seat, then settled his hands on his lap. 'Ready when you are.'

'Here,' she slid a piece of paper across the table. 'Just write something down for me.'

'Like?'

'Let's see. Please give me lunch. I didn't mean to forget to eat.'

'Strange one but okay.'

'Ah there's always a method to my madness.'

'And I bet you're sworn to secrecy too.'

Vicky tapped her nose. 'How long were you and Alex friends?'

'Since the day I was born. Alex loved to tell people he was five weeks older. Went to the same school, our mothers knew each other from way back, so they raised us together. They were best friends until my mother died twenty years ago. Growing up with four sisters, Alex was the closest I had to a brother, really. We drank our first beers together, then he rubbed my back when I needed to vomit it up. Best man at his wedding. At both of his. It would be an understatement to say we were friends.'

He scratched at his stubble. Vicky wondered if he grew it to hide the hollowed cheeks. His dark hair was unkempt. 'You look pale, Ernest. You taking it hard?'

'As hard as you can imagine. Sorry, I know you can relate.'

Vicky straightened. Sometimes she hated living in a small town where everyone knew your business. This was not the time to talk about her.

'Did you ever fall out with Alex?'

'We had our moments, like anyone with a friendship that long does. Doesn't mean I killed him, though.'

'That's not what I'm asking, but now I'm wondering why you're going on the defensive.'

He smiled. 'Guilt, probably. There's a lot to feel guilty over.'

'Why?'

He stayed silent, but there was a flicker. Doubt or guilt? Whatever it was, Ernest was holding something back.

'Did you notice any change in Alex running up to the murder?'

He scratched at his eye, as if trying to prolong the answer, as if it would help to avoid the question. Vicky waited, raising her eyebrows when he still hadn't spoken. He spread his arms. 'A sudden change might not be accurate. In the last month or so he was happy. Before that, I'm not sure. We hadn't spoken for some time.'

'Why?'

'A conflict of opinion.'

'About?'

'His choice in women.'

'You didn't like any of them?'

'With Bernice, you could definitely say that, yeah. With Melinda, I had nothing against the woman actually, I just didn't think she was the right one for him.'

'What about Saoirse?'

Ernest jerked his head, as if shocked. Then, he laughed. 'Sometimes I forget you grew up here too; you were away for so long in the city. Saoirse and Alex finished fifteen years ago.'

'Yeah, but you can't deny how much they loved each other.'

'Nobody could deny that. Do you know what ends up happening with those relationships? They burn out. If you're lucky, they stay in your memory as a benchmark for what you deserve in your next relationship. Both of them settled for much less.'

'You kept in contact with Saoirse?'

'From time to time. Mostly it was one way traffic with me emailing her every so often. She never told me where she lived or how I could find her.'

'Was Alex aware that you were in contact with Saoirse?'

Ernest looked away. 'He was not. You asked me what I felt guilty about, well that is it. All the time I wasted.'

'Your time?'

Ernest looked at her. 'Theirs.'

'What stopped you and Alex from speaking?'

'We didn't fight or have an argument. Stopped speaking is the right term. We just didn't pick up the phone or call round. Some of his choices frustrated the hell out of me but I still loved the man, and I knew he still loved me. Look, we often went spells where we needed space. Alex is, was, quieter than me, whereas I'm more opinionated, as you well know.'

'Yeah, I've witnessed you losing game night down The Kings.'

'That night is still debatable, Vic. Google proved their questions were dodgy.'

Vicky laughed at how serious he was.

'Look, I'm impulsive and say the first thing on my mind, whether that hurts or not. I'm not one to stay quiet if I see something I disagree with, and I can act first and think later. Alex didn't always agree with that.'

Ernest rubbed at his stubble again.

'Vic, what I'm trying to say is even though sometimes our opinions clashed, the time we went without speaking was only breathing space. We both knew if the other's world came crumbling down, we'd be the first to pick up the pieces.'

'What did you love about him?'

Ernest broke out into a smile. 'Alex was the kind of guy that you could bend his ear with a problem and you wouldn't overhear it doing the rounds the next day. Good man to have a pint with.'

'Why, so?'

'Guaranteed interesting conversation, even better as a listener.'

'What about as a wing man?'

'Nah, Alex wasn't the kind to stand in a nightclub getting locked and looking up girl's skirts, if that's what you mean. He was just straight up. If he liked you, he liked you and if he didn't ...'

He hesitated.

'If he didn't?'

He shrugged. 'Then he left the room.'

'Why did you hide speaking to Saoirse from Alex?'

'She made me promise not to say anything. Swore she'd never talk to me again if I betrayed her. They ended abruptly.'

'What happened between them?'

'From what I gather, they had an argument.'

'You weren't there?'

'There, but not around them. I snuck out of the dance with another student. It was a secret thing, so I didn't tell anyone where I was going. When I came back, I heard Alex was messy drunk and Saoirse had run off somewhere. The next day, Saoirse left town without a word. Neither of them ever spoke about what happened; I got the impression it was off bounds for the two of them.'

'You didn't see them that night?'

'Saoirse, I did. She was a mess. When I went looking for them, I only found her. She wouldn't tell me what happened, but it was clear when I dropped her home that there was no going back.'

Vicky made some notes.

'How did Alex handle her leaving?'

'He was distraught, of course, but his father dying and a funeral to arrange meant he didn't have the time or the energy to cause a fuss. And anyway, what could he do? Unless she rang or emailed, there was nothing. Saoirse planned to go into nursing with Alex. He hoped she would be there when he started, but she wasn't. He had no other leads.'

'You didn't tell him you were in contact, knowing he was trying to find her?'

'Vic, I'm not heartless. Back then, she didn't contact me either. Alex saw she hadn't responded to my emails; he was with me when I sent some of them. I guess he hoped she might answer mine if she didn't want to talk to him. When he got with Bernice, I stopped talking to him for a while. By the time Saoirse did contact, Bernice was pregnant, and they were married.'

'You weren't talking to him, yet you were best man at his wedding?'

'He knew how I felt about Bernice, but I wouldn't let him stand at the altar alone, even if I believed he was making the biggest mistake of his life. He was only twenty, Vic, still studying, with no wage coming in. Just a baby himself. When I heard Bernice miscarried after the wedding, I told Alex he should run. That didn't go down well and cost me his friendship for some time; Alex was loyal to Bernice even if the trait wasn't reciprocated.'

'Do you think Bernice is capable of murder?'

Ernest pursed his lips, screwed his eyes. 'Have you met Bernice?'

'I have.'

'It's safe to say she is not one of my favourite people. If I had to use one word to describe her, I would say sneaky. Manipulative. There, that's two. Capable of murder, though? I think most people could be capable of murder in the wrong circumstances, Vic. Do I think Bernice did something? I'm not sure. There was trouble in that marriage and when Alex called to say he wanted to leave her, I punched the air with joy. When he left, Alex strengthened and Bernice, well, she kind of weakened, like the air quickly leaked out of her the way a balloon deflates. Don't get me wrong, she did his head in with all her chopping and changing of visits and he had to bring her to court, but she was a quieter girl than she had been, that's for sure.'

'So, Alex grew stronger when he left Bernice?'

'Oh no. Alex fell apart after he left Bernice. He left with nothing. But then he grew stronger. Until he met Melinda a year later. At first, I supported them, hence why I was his best man at the second wedding. But then some things filtered through, mainly from other people, and I told him I thought he was repeating the same mistakes. Alex did not like that. Told me if I couldn't keep my opinions to myself, then I was no friend. That killed me; I won't lie.'

'What, that he could get rid of you?'

'Not get rid of me. Rather that he could choose two women who weren't right for him over me.'

'Was it left that way until he died?''

There was a flicker of hesitation from Ernest. 'Until he died, no. We made up with each other beforehand.'

'Hmmm. Never knew you to back down from an opinion, Ernest.'

He grinned. 'And you would know me, right?'

'What changed?'

Ernest shrugged. 'Alex wanted my advice.'

Vicky sensed the truth of that statement. 'What did he need advice for?'

'He wanted to leave Melinda.'

Chapter 15

The first smell that hit as you walked into the hospital room was bleach. The second was from a bunch of flowers threatening to spill from a vase on the side locker. A spacious room with plenty of light and a view of the shopping centre, Vicky whistled as she entered.

'Nice. Your insurance must be top-notch to land a non-sharing.'

'That, or the hospital staff know my son, their colleague, was murdered and thought I might need my privacy.'

Vicky didn't blush or look put out by the comment. 'Is it okay to talk, Mrs Hayes? I don't want to compromise your health.'

'If you did, maybe you'd be doing me a favour,' she smiled wryly. Cassandra Hayes, although pale, despite just having a heart attack, had brushed her hair, her blonde bob neatly tucked behind her ears. Vicky estimated Cassandra was about sixty years old.

'Is there anything you want to tell me about Alex?'

'I want to tell you everything about Alex, but I'm afraid none of it would help his case.'

Vicky sat in the seat next to her. 'If it helps you, tell me everything.'

'The only thing that can help me is bringing my son back.'

'I wish I could, Mrs Hayes.'

'I wish you could too.'

Cassandra tilted her head back until it rested on the pillow.

'Maybe talking about him will help. Stop me if it doesn't.'

Vicky nodded. 'Anything helps. Even if it's just to let me know what he was like.'

A bird landed on a tree branch next to the window. Both women watched as it deposited a worm into the open beak of its chick.

'Since he died, I keep getting flashbacks of Alex as a child. Of all the different stages of his life. Alex's birth gave me my first taste of death. Before that, I didn't know being in that much pain was possible. It was intense enough to convince me death would take me from that hospital bed. From this earth. After, there was no husband to tell me I did a great job. Nobody at my side to tell me what I had given birth to. As I tried to regain my sense of what had just happened, I waited for them to hand me my child. I waited for a cry. None came. The midwives huddled over my baby; their hands patting, scooping, tapping, and rubbing. Time continued, enough space between to alert; I panicked then, tried to sit up, called out. Why had the nurses not shown him to me? Why were they fussing with him?

'Then I heard a little cry and my insides calmed.

'A midwife, the nice one, carried my baby to me, wrapped in a little blue blanket.

'The nasty one, the one who sneered from the moment I came in, who kept on calling me Miss when she addressed me, to highlight the lack of Mrs, who whispered to me when I roared that something was wrong, that I wouldn't be so quick to get pregnant again, now lit up. That's the beauty about after a birth; I forgave her instantly. The early nineties in Catholic Ireland wasn't very forgiving for a single mother.

'Once he was in my arms, everything that came before him became insignificant. Alex gave me my first glimpse of death, but he also gave me my only real experience of love. Within a second of laying eyes on him, I forgot the pain.'

She frowned.

'Not forgot, wrong word, more like pushed aside, shoved away as irrelevant. Because the love I waited all my life for, had finally arrived. This little thing, with it's puffed out features, this weird, distorted looking, living creature, lay in my arms, filling me with love. Whose lungs once shared my oxygen. Whose blood came from my blood. My son looked at me as if he had waited for me too. As ecstatic as I felt, sadness blended, too. Because one day this little, tiny boy would break my heart. One day, he would leave me. Within a second of knowing him, I understood I would never cope with the loss. My Alexander had given me more in that fraction of time than anyone else in my whole twenty-five years before him. But you're not here to listen to this, are you?'

She didn't wait for an answer. Just looked at the IV drip.

'You're probably wondering where I'm going with this. Probably thinking, why is the old bat talking about the way the murder victim came into the world, but it's important you understand how linked we were and what Alexander was like, I mean really like. You will have a lot of conflicting opinions, I'm sure. This is important, though. I've had two close brushes with death. The first, the day Alexander was born, the second the day before he was cremated.'

'How are you recovering, Mrs Hayes?'

'As well as anyone who has just had a heart attack can feel, I suppose.'

'Was there a blockage?'

She clasped her hands, as if in prayer. 'They said so, yes. I'm sure it was, but there was a definite want on my part.' She leaned closer. 'Have you ever wanted your heart to stop?'

Vicky hesitated. 'I've come close.'

'I never had. Until they told me Alex was no more. I remember thinking it, thinking: "I want to die. I want to just collapse right now."'

Her thumb stroked her other thumb.

'The shock of those words, of hearing he was gone, forever; it was the worst feeling I've ever felt. Even this morning, when I opened my eyes, my first thought was of Alex, of him being dead. My second thought was, how do I join him? Wrong of me when he has kids to keep an eye on, but the thought of carrying on without him, it's just too much. I can't believe he's gone. It just feels unreal. Like it's all some unfunny joke. Maybe if I had been present at the funeral it would be easier to accept, might have given me some closure but now, being here, it just doesn't feel real.'

'You were close?'

'As close as a mother can be to her son. Closer even. For years, it was just the two of us. Alex was a good boy.'

'I know you requested for time to recover, but I have to ask, is there anything you want to tell me? Anything you think might help the investigation?'

Cassandra stayed quiet.

'Any enemies? Do you know of anyone who wanted to harm your son?'

She narrowed her eyes as if thinking. 'I don't know of any man who would want to hurt Alex. The people that harmed Alex the most were the women he loved.'

'Melinda?'

'Her, yes. Bernice definitely. And Saoirse.'

'Saoirse harmed Alex?'

'Saoirse Thomas destroyed Alex. She broke my son's heart. He was never the same after she left.'

Vicky scribbled some notes.

'Did he have any recent contact with her?'

'As far as I'm aware, Alex never laid eyes on her for over fifteen years.'

'If I showed you a picture, would you be able to see if it brought any recollection?'

She tipped her head in agreement, took the photo. Cassandra Hayes put the photo close to her face.

'Sorry, I've no glasses here. Is it just me or is it very blurry?'

'It is. We are working with someone who is trying to make it clearer. But that takes time and if you could just check if the man bears any resemblance to anyone Alex might have known?'

Cassandra peered as close to the picture as possible. Then angled the picture to shift towards the light.

'From what I can make out, he doesn't look familiar. Do you think Alex knew him?'

'We are trying to work that out. None of your son's, I mean Alex's, friends or family or work colleagues, seem to know the man.'

'And you couldn't catch him?'

'It's like he disappeared into thin air. We have the images of the car circulating on the news every hour. Something obstructed the licence plate number, as if smeared on purpose. We are following up leads, but none are proving fruitful. When we get a clearer picture, we will release that, too. I promise, Mrs Hayes, I will do everything I can to get justice for Alex.'

She nodded, then handed the photo back. 'I'm sorry I can't be of more help.'

'Giving me an understanding of Alex helps a great deal.'

'Well, that I can do. I can also tell you who I believe did it.'

'I thought you said you didn't know the man?'

'I don't.'

'Maybe you fell ill before anyone explained what we know. We have CCTV footage of both cars stopping at the lights. The man got out. Him and Alex argued, then the man followed your son into the derelict building. If you think it wasn't him involved, it would take a lot of convincing to change our minds.'

Cassandra swiped her hand in the air, as if wanting the words moved away from her.

'That's not what I'm saying at all. The man obviously had something to do with Alex being attacked. That man murdered Alex.' Her voice caught, and she clutched at her chest.

Vicky held her breath. She couldn't be responsible for Cassandra having another heart attack.

'Are you feeling unwell, Mrs Hayes?'

Cassandra shook her head. Took a deep breath.

'I'm not talking about the man who did it. What I mean is I can tell you the name of the person I believe caused his death.'

'And who do you think that is?'

'I believe Melinda, his wife, had something to do with it.'

Chapter 16

'Why do you think Melinda killed your son, Cassandra?'

'I'm not saying she killed him. I just want you to know she is capable of it. Although, you'd want to look into Bernice as well. Whatever you say about my son, he chose women with wicked form.'

'Some might say you just have a problem with your son's wives.'

She shrugged. 'You're entitled to your opinion and I'm entitled to mine. I imagine you're getting numerous versions of what Alex was like. What I am trying to make clear is those other versions, depending on who you speak to, may be distorted.'

Vicky scribbled something down, then dangled the pen.

'You'll think I'm just biased, that no mother sees any wrong in their son, but you'd be mistaken. I searched for it in Alex. The sweetness in him growing up turned into kindness as an adult and he never lost that, even with all the hurt he suffered. Even when I thought he might die after breaking up with Saoirse. I prayed he would meet someone after her. When he met Bernice, well, I didn't like her, didn't think she was right for him. Within a few months they discovered she was pregnant. Faced with that news, given his history of being raised first with a single mother before his dad came back on the scene, Alex was always going to do the right thing, despite my reservations, despite being twenty years of age and a broke nursing student. Believe me, I was right to worry about him. Even though this sounds heartless, it always struck me as convenient that Bernice miscarried on their honeymoon. Afterwards, I begged him to get the marriage annulled, but Alex wouldn't hear of it, said he couldn't leave her when she was grieving. A year later, when I had nearly convinced him to leave, she was pregnant again. As Bernice's bump grew, my son's personality reduced. At twenty-one he should have been having the time of his life, partying and meeting people. Instead, he was married and depressed. He withdrew from our conversations, quietened until there was only silence. Unsaids grow louder if you don't get them out. Bernice didn't hide her dislike for me, either, she even banned me from their home. You may have me down as confrontational; I suppose I was when it came to matters with my son. I didn't start off that way. I learned to fight back. Alex didn't, no matter how much I tried to teach him, so I learnt to fight for him. When the marriage ended, I was nothing short of relieved. And then he met Melinda and fair play, she was there for him. But as the years went on, I saw she was very similar to Bernice, similar enough to worry about history repeating itself. He reassured me she wasn't. Bernice was difficult. Melinda was clever. The truth is, we both never got over his first love. Anyone after that was only getting half of Alex's heart.'

'Saoirse Thomas?'

'That's the one.'

'You said Melinda was clever. What makes you think Melinda had something to do with Alex's death?'

'Look, I have nothing against Melinda. She is a nice enough woman. Standoffish, quiet, doesn't have much to say, if you know what I mean?'

She sniffed.

'You're thinking, here's a possessive mother who couldn't let go of her son. It isn't like that at all. I know how it looks, what with me telling you already the whole reason I had a heart attack was because I couldn't bear to live after my son passed away but you would have it all wrong if you think I had it out for her. I welcomed the girl. It was obvious she loved him, *that* I could see right from the bat and after the way the first one he married treated him, she was a saint but ...'

'But?'

'There are many types of love. Hers was the suffocating kind.'

The pen scribbled in the book.

'What made you come to that conclusion?'

'Do you want a list?'

'Just the details will do.'

Cassandra smoothed down the bed sheet until no creases remained. 'For one thing, she was fierce jealous. If Alex so much as looked in another woman's direction, there would be murder, sorry, pardon the pun. I know she's told anyone who'll listen he'd been unfaithful and she never so much as imagined he could do that, and honestly, I'd say she believes it but that's not the case. She was insecure, bordering on paranoid. Alex forgave many of her actions, pandered to her often, when I questioned why, he said men in the past hurt her. In other words, he let her get away with it. Any time she went off on one, he calmed her down, helped her see the facts instead of her fear, but he's not here now to reason with her so her mind is going into overdrive. Whatever she says regarding other women, I can tell you right now my Alex was never a cheater. I raised him right. He saw first-hand what damage cheating could do to a marriage.'

'His father?'

Cassandra nodded.

'Before you go assuming if his father was like that, cheating was probably in his blood, then you should know Alex was nothing like that man. He made a point of being the complete opposite. The only thing the two shared was a surname.'

'You married him?'

Cassandra nodded. 'When Alex was six. Look Sergeant, Melinda might portray herself as a victim, but she isn't the woman she makes out to be.'

'How so?'

'She comes across as quiet, meek even, but let me tell you, if you cross the girl, she has some temper!'

Vicky bit her lip to prevent a smile. Melinda was nearly forty, yet Cassandra saw her still as a girl.

'You witnessed this?'

Cassandra coiled a strand of hair around a jewelled finger. 'Many times.'

'Give me an example.'

Cassandra pursed her lips in thought, then smoothed the sheet again. 'Here's one. For my last birthday they took me out. Booked a restaurant out there at the end point of Knockfarraig; it's called something like The Edge. Have you been there?'

'I haven't. Heard it's quite the place, though.'

'Quite pricey, you mean,' she chuckled. 'It was. I nearly fainted when I saw what they were charging for soup. I said to Alex, how did they come up with that figure when it's only vegetables and water? He just laughed and said, don't worry, it's on me. He was always generous, Alex. Not pretentious though, he didn't make a habit of going to restaurants like that. It was just a special occasion and I have to say, that soup was the best I've ever had.'

'The jealousy?'

'Ah yes. We were just after finishing our starter, when this woman approached our table. Coat on, ready to walk out the door. Beautiful girl now, one of those women who turns heads, about Alex's get up in age. You know already there was an age difference between him and Melinda?'

Vicky tilted her head, asking in silence *how so?*

'Five years means nothing when the older person is the man. To Alex it didn't matter a jot, at thirty he'd already had children and didn't want any more, but to Melinda, being thirty-five, the age gap mattered. It added to the insecurity. So, when women approached him closer to his age, it set her off. And this woman would have made anyone insecure. The sort of woman so immaculately groomed, even in your best gear, your outfit would look frumpy. Straight away, Melinda's back went up. You should have saw the frown on her. Anyway, the woman leant on the table and said she couldn't leave without coming over. She directed her words to Alex the whole time. Two pink dots formed on Melinda's cheeks. The woman said to him, "You probably don't remember me but I wanted to thank you for what you did for my family. In the hospital."

'You must know by now Alex was a nurse. A brilliant one too. Turns out he had called this woman in when he noticed her mother wasn't right. Her and her brother had only just been sent home by the nurse on charge. Alex's phone call meant they made it on time. Now, as a mother, a proud mother, I don't need to hear these stories about my Alex, but I still love to be told them. Not the case with Melinda, I'm afraid; the girl was livid. By the end of the conversation, her cheeks were like purple bruises. Not once would she look the woman in the eye, giving her the side face the whole time, just staring at Alex, as if furious with him. The woman said goodbye and Alex sat on the verge of tears. He was never one for fishing out compliments or searching for them, but it moved him to hear how he affected a patient. All he said was, that was nice.

'There was complete silence. Until the doors swung and the woman disappeared behind them. With that, Melinda caught her wine glass and threw it across the room, hitting the window. The glass smashed to pieces; guests had to duck. She was lucky she didn't hit anyone. Melinda stood, then I swear she hissed. "Nice? Let's see how nice walking home feels then."

'And with that, she stormed from the room. Alex ran after Melinda, trying to reason with her. He came back alone. She left us there, on a clifftop at the end of Knockfarraig. We had to wait over an hour for a cab. I insisted Alex order dessert, tried to distract him. He was no better after that, though. His mind was gone from the room.'

'Her behaviour worried him?'

'Extremely. Like he was living on his nerves. He was jumpy and his eyes kept jerking, not fixing on one particular thing. It didn't matter how many times I repeated if anyone should apologise it was her, he just kept ringing her phone, worrying that she might crash the car or do something stupid. Like she was likely to do something drastic if he ever upset her. I told Alex I didn't like that one bit, that he couldn't live like that. There's a lot you can hold over someone if they fear you might get hurt.'

'Do you believe she threatened to harm herself?'

'You would have to ask her.'

'I'm asking you.'

'It's not my place. I will say there have been more times that I questioned her mental health.'

'Like?'

'Like when she poisoned my son.'

Chapter 17

Cassandra Hayes didn't seem the type to embellish facts. Still though, Vicky didn't give any reaction to the last woman's comment. 'That's a big statement to make.'

'It is. And one my son, if he was alive, would deny. You won't get any admission from Melinda, either. Whatever she says, she was fuming with him that week. And when I say poisoning, I'm not talking about some little stomach bug that had him on the toilet for a couple of hours. It was bad enough to end up in hospital, for them to think he wouldn't make it. His liver went into failure. Only for one doctor working out what caused it and giving him the right medication, he might have needed a transplant.'

Vicky flicked through her notes.

Bacillus cereus. Melinda forgot to mention she was responsible for him nearly dying.

'Do you know why she poisoned him?'

'No. But I know she was angry with him. Alex told me himself that she was giving him the silent treatment.'

'How did she do it? Did he confront her afterwards?'

'He wouldn't speak of it. No matter how much I tried.'

Vicky made a note to speak to Melinda.

'What was it like being Alex's mother?'

'John, Alex's father, took off when he heard about the pregnancy, so I found myself on my own. Being a single mother, I faced many challenges. Determined to change the way life or the social stigmas would have planned out Alex's life, I knew education was key. So, I was strict. There were rules; he could not go out to play until he had read for at least an hour. We sat together and talked about history, or the news, or the wonders of the world. I felt the extra education would stand to him in life. If he believed he was smarter, he wouldn't feel less at school.

'Alex was a soft-spoken kid. Introverted, yet confident enough to stand up for himself if it was called upon. He didn't have many friends, but he was happy. One good friend was all he needed and Ernest and him were the best of friends. In his first year at school, I attended his parent teacher meeting. Each classroom had a few chairs outside lining the wall. As is usual with these meetings, Alex's teacher ran late, so the excess moved to the hall. It was full of mothers and fathers, waiting for their turn. In a waiting room, when a door opens, it's natural to look up and see who's walking in. This was different. Before that day, I'd noticed most people didn't make eye contact when I dropped and collected Alex from school, but I just brushed it off. Usually, I had Nuala, that's Ernest's mother, who I made a beeline for. The last few months she hadn't been around, after having complications with delivering her last daughter, so I dropped and collected Ernest, too. There was only one seat left in between a couple. They just stared, didn't move, didn't offer the seat. Everyone stopped talking, like I'd walked in uninvited. All the unsaid words I could sense from them.

'*Slut. Whore.*

'I moved to the furthest corner and stood facing the door, wishing for my name to be called. These days you can hide behind your phone in an awkward situation; back then there was nothing like that. I had to stretch my eyes to keep from crying because I would not give in to those disgusting people. Just to occupy my hands, just to give me something to do, I fidgeted with the straps of my bag. My mouth parched; I became desperate for some water. Each minute dragged out until I could feel sweat dripping down my back. It wasn't paranoia either. When one man looked my way and gave me one of those apologetic smiles, his wife actually leaned in and whispered in his ear with a look of horror on her face. God forbid anyone was nice to me.'

'That must have been tough?'

'It was a different time back then. It didn't matter if you suffered in life so long as you did it in private. I was fragile. After both my parents died, they left my brothers and I an even share of their savings and with the proceeds from the sale of their house, it was enough to buy a place of my own in Cork and I can tell you, as a single mother, I wouldn't have survived without it. The same week as the parent teacher meeting, the roof leaked and needed to be repaired and I couldn't afford it. Alex's father, John, was back from being away from who knows where, and he kept turning up, asking for another chance. Acting like he was genuinely sorry for leaving me to fend for myself. Also, Alex was getting older and wanting to be around his friends more, and I was lonely. Meeting the teacher was the last straw. She was a prim woman. Married forever and full of judgement, as soon as I entered the room, her nose turned towards the floor as if she was shielding herself from a disgusting smell. She made an exaggerated point of staring at my ring finger the whole meeting. There was nothing bad to say about Alex, so she couldn't hurt me there, but she certainly wasn't offering any compliments, either. What she zoned in on was Alex's introspective nature, about how quiet he could be in class. Asked straight out if there were problems at home. I'm a proud woman Vicky; I wouldn't show that woman how her words and actions stabbed at me. Instead, I told her Alex was a very happy child at home and if she was seeing problems at school, then maybe school was the issue. I said it in the sweetest voice I could give. When all I wanted to do was slap the woman for her condescending words and bigotry. With my head held high, I walked out of there, but the meeting affected me. Made me more vulnerable than I ever felt before.'

'People are cruel.'

Cassandra shrugged. 'Not all. Teachers and priests had too much power back then. The church already shunned me; I hadn't stepped foot in one of them after the local priest refused to christen Alex because I was unmarried. That hurt. Knowing in the eyes of the Catholic church, if Alex died, the gates of Heaven wouldn't let him enter. No God I could believe in would shun a child just for the faults of their parents. I didn't want a part in that church. Alex was three years away from communion age, in the schools they were already preparing for it and Alex had already started talking about it. I didn't have the heart to tell him he couldn't be involved. In the end, I couldn't take the pressure and let his father back into our life. That was my biggest mistake. After we married, the priest happily christened Alex and allowed him to have his communion. Yes, socially and financially, it took the pressure off, but marrying John wrapped a noose around mine and Alex's neck and, as time went on, it squeezed tighter and tighter. I didn't know what to do. My brothers wouldn't speak to me for getting back with a man who abandoned his child. Divorce didn't exist in Ireland back then. John made it clear the only way I was kicking him out of the house was in a coffin.

'Things changed between me and Alex after John moved in. What I was hoping for by having a male presence in the house was the opposite of what I got. Instead of more love, the house grew pungent and oppressive. We began to tiptoe around. John didn't like us "talking in corners" as he called it, so Alex retreated. Spent more and more time away from the house playing with his friends. And forgive me, but I was glad when he was away because that brute couldn't harm him.

'When John was out or sleeping off the drink, I taught Alex about

Greek Gods and Celtic mythology. I taught him about David and Goliath. About heroes standing up to bullies, about the need to be brave, cutting out real-life underdog stories from the paper. Or explaining about people who had to learn to be submissive to survive, then who rose above and fought the evil oppressors. It was important he knew this, having the type of father that he had. Having the type of father I allowed enter our lives. Education was key, I'd say to him on repeat. It was the key to independence from eventually being able to escape his father.'

'Your husband, when did he die?'

'Years ago. Alex was only turning nineteen.'

'Were they close?'

Cassandra blinked slower than normal. 'Alex idolised his father.'

The woman was lying.

'How did your husband die?'

Cassandra straightened. 'I found him at the bottom of the stairs. Accidental death. Lost his footing at the top. They said he would have died instantly.'

'Was he a good father?'

Cassandra looked Vicky in the eye and this time answered with the truth.

'No.'

Vicky nodded.

'Can I ask you something, Sergeant Fitzgerald?'

'Fire away.'

'What does asking questions about a man who died years ago have to do with finding my son's murderer?'

Vicky shrugged. 'It's just the way I've always worked. I find asking all the smaller questions eventually leads to the bigger answer.'

'I don't see how his father dying when he was barely an adult can have anything to do with it.'

'Nor me. Yet. That's why I'll keep asking until the answers add up.'

Chapter 18

Almost there. Reaching climax. Nearly at that moment of bliss. Needed after some rough few days. A hand grabs my throat. My eyes open, I stop moving, not sure what to do.

'Keep going.'

Soft at first, just a hand resting there. Even though I don't like its position, don't like the threat of it, or the intention, I try to ignore, fall back into the rhythm of our bodies. It is nothing to worry about, I soothe myself. The hand is just resting there, just for balance. I push it out of my mind and concentrate on the pleasure. The heat rises. Close now. Until the hand tightens. The grip firms and my last fragment of air escapes. Breath goes. And even though I gasp, nothing comes. The movement keeps going, up and down, faster. The grip tightens. My head becomes light, dots appear in my vision even with my eyes closed, breath still doesn't come. This time, I think, I might die. This time, I promise, after, I will leave. If I survive, this time I will find the strength to go. Before I pass out, I orgasm. Pleasure mixes with shame.

I won't leave. I never do.

Chapter 19

A slim, brown-haired woman in her mid-thirties, Carole O'Sullivan, looked like she was taking in every detail of the interview room, including the layer of paint that was peeling away in the corner by the door. Vicky stopped her eyes from rolling.

'You wanted to talk to me about the case?'

'That's right. I wanted to see if you had any leads yet.'

'Carole, if you've come for a story for the girls in the gym, you won't be getting anything from me.'

Carole wrapped her arms around her chest. 'That's not why I'm here at all.'

'No? You wouldn't be one for gossip now, would you, Carole?'

Carole's chair screeched against the linoleum. 'If you want to mock me, I'll go now. I'm just sick of seeing those news reels and from what people have been saying, it sounds like you are getting nowhere. You were good to me that time with my brother Phil; you got him out of a tight spot so I just thought if I could offer you a bit of information I would.'

Vicky held her hands up. 'Sorry, you're right. I'm frazzled from the pressure. If you think you have something for me, I'm all ears.'

Carole sat back down then, after getting comfortable, leaned in. 'You remember how close Alex and Saoirse were back in the day, right?'

'Yeah, the whole of Knockfarraig knew.'

'Well, maybe you talked to her already then and I'm only wasting my time.'

'We haven't been able to reach her.'

Carole lit up with this news. The girl almost salivated. 'But you saw her at the funeral, right?'

'What? You did?'

Carole licked her lips, enjoying the power now. 'Sure did. She tried to hide down the back. The huge black glasses didn't help. Especially when she couldn't stop the tears. Made a holy show of herself, if you ask me.'

'How would you even recognise her? It must be fifteen years since you saw her.'

Carole flicked her hair back, then examined her nails, relishing having something else. 'Yeah, but you see, that's the thing. I recognised her because I'd only just seen her a few days before. And guess whose company she was in?'

It was Vicky's turn to lean in. 'Alex Hayes?'

Carole pointed a magenta-coloured, manicured nail at Vicky. 'Bingo.'

'Where?'

'This is the mad thing. You know Triona Joyce, from up near Crookstown?'

Vicky waved her hand to carry on.

'Well, we were on her hen night up in Dublin. She'd booked her last wedding dress fitting in this fancy place where the veil prices start at over a grand, so she made the weekend of it and had her hen at the same time. Decided the city wouldn't be grand enough for her so made us fork out for this boutique spa hotel in the sticks. Give me a nightclub in Dublin City any day. At least there we would have had a laugh. More money than sense, if you ask me.'

'Carole?'

'Oh yeah, sorry. Anyway, I was walking down the road from my hotel. In a place out in the middle of nowhere you'd think they could at least sell fags but no, there I am walking down some dead-end lane trying to work out exactly what direction the shop is that the pimply dope in reception told me to take, when I came near this house all by itself. Next of all, I see Alex Hayes rushing out of it. When I saw him, I ducked into a bush, more worried at that stage that he'd lamp the state of me, but also, I was interested in what he was up to. He was carrying a heavy bag and threw it into the front of the car. Seemed to be in a rush. He looked both ways, as if checking the coast was clear and, 'cos I ducked down, he never saw me. Then he rushed back in and came out almost carrying a woman. Cradling Saoirse Thomas as if she was a child. At first, 'cos I was hungover, I thought I might be in the horrors, seeing things, but by the time they drove off I ran until I was near the window. The woman covered her face when she saw me but it was her alright, that I'm positive about.'

'What day was this?'

Carole looked at the ceiling, thinking. 'Seventeenth of this month.'

That was the day before Alex was murdered.

'How can you be so sure?'

'When she covered her face, I saw her wrist. She has a tattoo of a house martin on it. I know because I was there when she got it.'

'You remember the address?'

'Get out maps on your phone and I'll show you the exact house.'

Chapter 20

'Fitzgerald, what's going on with this case? Ballinroe are ready, spitting at the bit to take it over.'

'Mara, don't even go there. No one else is touching it; isn't it bad enough I've Barratt shadowing my every move?'

'Doesn't seem to be making a difference. If you don't make headway fast, it won't be your case any longer.'

'There's headway. Plenty of it.'

'How? Give me one proper avenue of investigation.'

'I'll give you three.'

'Go on then.'

'One, the ex-wife. There is a strong suggestion that with Alex having the majority of custody, she would have good reason not to have him around anymore.'

'Seriously? You're going down the hitman route?'

'Maybe. Second avenue following the same trail as the first, with the current wife, Melinda Hayes is lying about some things. There is a strong suggestion that she may have been controlling. His mother Cassandra is pretty adamant that she might have something to do with his death, so I definitely plan on investigating more into her. Then there is a woman I have yet to locate, a woman Melinda believes he was unfaithful with. A possible affair gone wrong maybe? Might be connected to a previous girlfriend.'

'Someone with a grudge?'

Vicky shrugged. 'Everything so far points to him being a stand-up guy. Story checks out. From what his friends have said, Alex was a relationship guy, not into flings or one-night stands. I'd like to talk to Saoirse Thomas, the previous girlfriend I just mentioned; they were close but according to his family and friends, they hadn't seen each other for fifteen years. Until a few minutes ago, every avenue led me to a dead end with her. A witness came forward today saying she spotted her and Alex the day before he died leaving a house on the outskirts of Dublin. According to her, they looked in a rush.'

'You get an address?'

'Have it in my hand right now. I was planning to leave straightaway and check it out.'

'Why go all that way when we have Gardaí in Dublin we can deploy for that? It would take you at least two hours to get there and then two hours back. Stopping for a bite, finding the place with all their one-way systems, could take you all night. That's at least six hours you could use investigating something else.'

'You know how I work, Superintendent, I like to see for myself.'

'All too well I know how you work, Fitzgerald. Send me the address and I'll get a Garda to check it out.'

'But what if she's there? What if she sees the uniform, panics and runs? Nearly everyone I've interviewed has dropped her name. What if the woman Melinda saw at the funeral is Saoirse? What if she holds the key to this whole thing? You telling me some twenty-year-old fresh out of Templemore is going to sprint after her or will know how to ask her about Alex?'

'Nobody can do it except you then, Fitzgerald? That's a pretty obnoxious belief, even for you. When are you ever going to give it up and trust a colleague? They trained the same as you.'

'Don't give anyone a job if you can do it better. Also, I knew Saoirse back in the day, maybe it might soften her enough to get her to open up to me.'

The superintendent sighed. 'Fine. Go to Dublin, but wait until the morning, pointless making a house call at night. Just give Barratt something to do while you're gone.'

'Thank you, Superintendent.'

'So, let me get this straight, the strongest lead you have is that the man who killed Alex Hayes was hired, is that what you're saying? Not a road rage incident anymore?'

'No, I'm keeping my options wide open. Road rage is still looking most likely, but if that's the case, where is he? The car still hasn't been located. Until we find that, we can't figure out the licence plate, so can't trace the man who drove it. Barratt was on to the image guy and he's promised to have the clearer footage ready tomorrow. As soon as we have it we'll release the images to the media. Until we have a weapon or the car, we have no prints. As much as you say I jump to conclusions, I'm not ruling anything out. It's just, no one has come forward to say who this man is. It's like he's nowhere to be found. I've ran through every person at the funeral, and I can't find anyone matching his description. It's like he vanished. Someone wrote that note that was left at the crematorium; there's a limit to who could have put it there. Nobody has so far matched the handwriting. If one of the women wrote the note, it would make sense if it was a hitman.'

'There are tons of media on this, Vic. I can't fend them off much longer.'

'I get it. Just give me some time.'

'Any sign of where he went after the attack?'

'Not yet. On the CCTV we see the suspect return to the car and drive off. The last visual is of the car entering along Knockfarraig woods. Three hours later on the footage there is still no sign of the car going in any direction.'

'It can't have just vanished.'

'No. Barratt walked the circumference, but he couldn't find anything. I'm not convinced, though. After checking out the house in Dublin, I was planning to take a spin out there and look for tyre tracks. I'm wondering if he abandoned the car somewhere in the woods and walked from there.'

'Is this too much to take on, Fitzgerald?'

'What do you mean?'

'This case. It's high profile. People are calling my office every second, asking why we haven't released proper footage of the attacker.'

'Well, tomorrow they'll get to see him.'

'Right, I'm sending over four Gardaí from Ballinroe. Brief them in the morning before you leave.'

'Hold on now, Mara.'

'They'll be no holding on, Fitzgerald. There should be way more progress than what you have. This case is bigger than a small station like Knockfarraig can handle. Screw this up and it will be a lot more than your job on the line. Do you know how much pressure I'm under to close the rural stations in the budget cuts? The powers above suggested Knockfarraig's name in the planned cull a few times.'

'It's always the same, Mara. Government think the only place of importance is the city.'

'Well, let's show them why they need you, so. Look, Fitzgerald, I know you are capable of this. Don't let me down with the guys coming over. You're still in charge, no one is trying to dispute that. Just use them, have them run through the footage again. Let them sit for hours watching CCTV and marking notes each time a car passes. Get them to trail every inch of the woods with Barratt tomorrow while you're gone. Throw every bit of admin at them so you don't get bogged down with the tiny details.'

'That's the problem though, what if they miss something?'

'Back to this. Every time, every case, it's the same thing with you.'

'That's not true. You haven't given out to me in over a year.'

'Let go, Fitzgerald. There has to be some delegation.'

'What if that's the essential piece, though? I need all the information in front of me.'

'Well then, instruct them to take notes and run through them each day.'

'And spend all night trying to decipher what they meant?'

'In any other branch, the sergeant would be grateful for extra hands. Not you, Fitzgerald. You're the only person I've met that has a problem with help.'

'What can I say? I work different.'

'Different isn't necessarily right.'

'Not necessarily wrong either.'

'Fitzgerald, if I hear even a whisper that you are giving hassle to the Gardaí I send down, this case will go to Barratt, you hear me?'

'Loud and clear, Superintendent.'

Chapter 21

Once a school, every time Vicky approached the entrance of Knock-farraig Garda Station, she expected a bespeckled principal with a bun in her hair to greet her. Looking more like a bungalow from the road, if you were a newcomer to the area, you could walk past the building even when you were searching for it. Only the sign gave any indication of it being a station.

The walls were thin and old, ensuring you needed to keep your jacket on in the winter, with the ceilings low enough to wish you could strip to your underwear in the coolest of summers. Just off Main Street, if the phone wasn't hopping, or no one was in asking for passports to be signed, Vicky could hear the sea. A small enough building, there was a basement with two cells which were more often these days used for storage, the powers that be preferred to send groups of detainees to the bigger, newer station of Ballinroe. There were another two cells on the ground floor, which served its purpose well if Vicky needed someone to sleep off their hangover or cool off for the night. Those two cells and a little kitchen, an office and a reception area where Phyllis sat as if she was on a throne. The largest single room was the interview room, used to be the old school hall. And that was it. Small enough for the higher powers to consider it insignificant, Vicky liked to think crime in Knockfarraig was at a minimum, with a little help from her. It wasn't a city station that was for sure, and the funding was never there; a pay rise was out of the question, and for a small town like Knockfarraig, the residents still found some way to keep her working way past her scheduled shifts. Still, Vicky loved the place. Except for Phyllis and the constant callers, Vicky was pretty much left to her own devices.

Usually.

Today, four Gardaí stood waiting for her at the entrance. One pimply male didn't look old enough to sit his Leaving Cert, let alone have completed four years of Garda training. Vicky grunted as she passed them. It was way too early for small talk.

After a minute of fiddling with keys, she walked straight to the small kitchen, then pouring water in the kettle and flicking it on, turned around to see she had an audience. She squeezed the bridge of her nose, the first niggle of a headache.

'Lads, I'll start the introductions in a minute. First, coffee. Any takers?'

There was a nod from one who looked about as young as the first guy. She held an empty cup up to the others to indicate she wanted an answer. One held up his cup, a takeaway from Ahearne's.

'Good choice,' Vicky said. 'Better than this instant shite.'

The cup holder was older, at least thirty, which perked up her mood, for he could keep the others in check if they didn't have a clue.

'No other takers so,' she said, pouring.

'Have you tea?' a female asked.

Vicky turned, pointing to the cupboard by the woman's head. 'Barry's finest in there.'

She had to step on her tiptoes to reach. Vicky suppressed an eyeroll. It wasn't the girl's fault if she was small. As long as she spoke up for herself, being brave was more important than how big you were. *She'll learn or she'll leave*, Vicky thought. As a woman, you couldn't survive in the Gardaí unless you could handle yourself.

Once the coffee hit her bloodstream, she addressed the room.

'I'm sure Superintendent Mara has explained about the case to you all?'

There were nods all around.

'That's good. I'm hoping he also told you I like to run things alone. Barratt will brief you, or come to me if you have any information. Time is important in this case though and Knockfarraig is under scrutiny, so I will take your help but I'm warning you all, if I give you a task and you only half arse it and I find out later you missed some crucial detail that costs me time and embarrassment or lets the murderer get away, I swear to you I will make your life a living hell. And when I say a living hell, I do not mean I will file a complaint or make your job uncomfortable. By that I mean every time you turn around, I will be there. Not only that, I will send so much red tape your way, you will never get up from behind your desk. Do you understand me?'

Vicky waited until they all acknowledged what she said. No one spoke, but a nod of the head or a look straight in the eye was enough for her.

'Right then, who have we?'

Chapter 22

In Dublin, the door knocker was missing when she went to knock. Not only that, but the wood of the door lay beside it in two halves. Hand hovering over her taser, her senses on overdrive, Vicky stepped inside without knocking or calling out. From the fresh smell of paint in the hall, at one time someone must have cared for the house, everything else in there screamed the opposite.

Vicky sniffed the air. Apart from the smell of paint, there was no scent of blood or rotting flesh. She tried to calm her breath.

Saoirse, don't be dead in here.

Glass shards from emptied photo frames lay in piles dotted around the floor. Shredded clothes shrouded a broken sofa, cracked straight down the middle, leaving the two ends facing up, making a V shape, its cushion stuffing splayed out as if the sick couch had vomited up its insides. Nothing was unbroken. There was no sound, no indication of movement, no creaks. The beat from the blood thumping in her ears was worse with silence. Every noise she made set her on high alert for she didn't know who was listening. Vicky edged into the next room, a kitchen. Mosaic splash-back tiles scattered on what was left of the counter and floor where someone had smashed a discarded flattened saucepan into it. The house wrecker ripped the sink from the wall, too. The marble counter spread out in shards, cracked like an egg. With downstairs clear, she ascended the stairs, careful to mind the spots that looked like a blunt object similar to a sledgehammer attacked it. She counted three bedrooms and a bathroom upstairs. Each door ripped from its hinges and smashed to smithereens. With caution, she edged to the first. A bright room, once coloured in different shades of green, left nothing to investigate. Flattened to the ground, with springs popping out from each side, lay a double bed. The busted-up wardrobes were only good for firewood. Expletives: WHORE, SLUT, BITCH, covered the once turquoise walls.

There was nowhere for Saoirse to hide.

A room once full of books had turned into torn pages on the floor. Springs, fluff and wood frames the only proof of a pull-out sofa's existence. The other bedroom might have once been a child's. It's purple walls with flowers indicated it possibly belonged at one stage to a girl, but Vicky knew those kind of assumptions could cost you. A chill went up her on seeing nothing had been spared in that room either. The bathroom only showed more disaster but no person. No Saoirse. The place was empty.

Vicky turned in a circle, surveying the mess. At worst, she had hoped to find some type of paperwork or memento that would give a clue to Saoirse's life, or even better, find Saoirse. Not only were all signs that someone had lived in the house destroyed, now Vicky worried Saoirse's life might be in danger.

'Where are you?' she asked the empty room.

Chapter 23

Stick thin and regal in appearance, Bernice reminded Vicky of Morticia Addams. In all the time Vicky came across Bernice, the woman wore only black, in what must have been a self-imposed uniform. The woman didn't seem to like colour at all.

Vicky tried to take people as she found them, but it was hard not to make assumptions when you saw people each day going about their business, unaware she was even watching them. What she saw of Bernice throughout the years was less than impressive. When Alex had married Bernice, it shocked Vicky. She just couldn't see the match at all. Bernice was beautiful, no denying that, it was just that Vicky couldn't recall a more miserable-looking woman than Bernice. Only after she heard the rumours that the girl miscarried did she understand the need for a quick wedding.

Bernice now wasn't acting like the woman she witnessed around town, as if forgetting that Vicky saw her almost daily. Thawed out completely, all trace of the coldness Bernice was known for had disappeared. Vicky wasn't one for buying acts.

'How've you been, Bernice?'

Bernice placed a hand on her chest. 'Shocked as you can imagine. I don't know how we'll ever get over it.'

Vicky made a point of flicking her notepad to the correct page. 'You divorced over four years ago, right?'

Bernice dropped her hand and threw Vicky a withering look. 'That's right. Nine years together is a long time. You can still miss someone you loved once.'

'Yes, you can. The kids must have been young when you separated. Lily must have been, what two?'

'Three. Kenneth was seven.'

Vicky took a breath. Why did this woman get under her skin so easily? 'Why would you say you divorced?'

Bernice adjusted her face again to the stance of victim.

'It is hard to love a man who doesn't love you.'

'You don't think Alex loved you?'

'I know he didn't. At the start, he convinced me, but that pretence disappeared quickly.'

'Are you saying Alex misled you into a relationship? On what grounds?'

'You'd have to ask him that.'

'We both know I can't, so I'll have to settle for your version. Why do you believe he pretended?'

'Alex still loved someone else when he met me. He forgot to tell me that going into the relationship. You can't fall in love with a woman when your heart has no room left.'

'Did he tell you this?'

Bernice scrunched up her features. 'No. He talked in his sleep. Once is just a dream. Night after night calling out the same woman's name, made me take notice. Alex was never a liar, I will say that; as much as he tried to hide it during the day, he couldn't maintain trying to love two women at once.'

'Did he have an affair?'

Bernice looked horrified. 'God no. Nothing like that. Although, maybe if he had, it would have saved a lot of hassle in the long term.'

Vicky wondered if the hassle Bernice spoke about were her children.

'No, it was the worst kind of infatuation. First love.' Her face turned as if she sucked on something sour. 'How can anyone ever compete with that? Our relationship was never good enough. Eventually, we gave up. It did surprise me, when he got with the other one. That wasn't the direction I thought Alex would take. I often wondered if Melinda heard him in the middle of the night, too. If she handled him loving another woman better than me. Or maybe he tried rekindling that flame with Saoirse and she sent him packing.'

She grinned, then remembered who she was talking to, changed her expression to sad again. 'Maybe he had gotten over the woman who ruined us.'

'So, that's what you put down to your marriage split, a man still in love with a woman who he wasn't having an affair with?'

Bernice didn't answer.

Vicky made a quick note. 'Do you remember me? I called to your house one evening.'

Bernice shifted her back away from Vicky. 'I'd rather not talk about that.'

'Considering it was a domestic violence incident, and your ex-husband died in violent circumstances, I think it's pretty important, don't you?'

'Like I said, Alex couldn't love me. When you live with someone but you want to be with someone else, it must get frustrating. Sometimes he would get angry.'

'Why didn't you make a statement that evening?'

Bernice's shoulders raised. 'I'd had a drink and foolishly brought up about Saoirse. Alex didn't like that. Didn't like the way the conversation was going.'

'How was the conversation going?'

'I told him if he couldn't forget her, I would have to leave. He said I could go, but I would have to leave the kids. I wasn't leaving them. It got heated.'

Vicky pictured Bernice that night. Her cheeks flushed. Strands of hair sticking out from her ponytail. Embarrassed, more than scared, although that in itself didn't mean much, for Vicky knew women could become experts on how to hide domestic incidences. Once the Gardaí left, unless the court forced one of them to vacate the premises, the couple still had to live together. Which meant, if a woman spoke up, they would be in more trouble after.

Bernice checked her watch. 'I actually have a work commitment I have to obligate.'

'Since I'm here, can I talk to the kids?'

'Kenneth isn't here; he's at a sleepover.' Bernice stared at her for a second, contemplating. 'But chat away to Lily if she'll talk to you. Just go up to her room, first door on the right. No need for me to go with you, is there?'

Vicky hesitated. Most parents would stand watching over their child if a guard wanted to speak to them.

'No, not if you don't want to. Or I could wait until after your call if you'd prefer to be present?'

'This work thing is important, if you could keep her occupied for ten minutes so she doesn't come down interrupting the call, I'd be able to get it done. Just a warning, though, the girl is shy.'

She said it like it was an affliction. Vicky suppressed a shudder. All her life, her hunches never let her down. Even in grief, there was something not right about Bernice.

Chapter 24

When Melinda described Lily's blonde hair being almost white, she wasn't lying. The long tendrils cascaded down her back as if dipped in milk. Coupled with round blue eyes, she was nothing short of angelic. The child had the looks and temperament to change even the most diehard anti-children campaigners. Even Vicky would stop birth control if she could guarantee birthing a child like Lily Hayes.

Her bedroom was floor to ceiling pink. Fluffy stuffed unicorns in every variation sat on the bed and windowsill.

Vicky leant on the door frame. 'Which one's your favourite unicorn?'

Lily, afraid but still polite, smiled and chewed on her lip at the same time.

Walking in, Vicky picked up the one closest to the girl's pillow.

'See, if I was to take a guess, I would say this is the one.'

The girl's eyes lit up; her mouth slackened with surprise. 'How did you tell?'

Vicky shrugged. 'It's my job to figure out things.'

She didn't add that the odds were in favour of the most threadbare unicorn being the most hugged, especially if it lay next to the spot the girl slept.

Vicky pointed to the floor. 'Okay if I sit?'

The girl nodded. Vicky didn't waste any time. She sat on the floor beside Lily.

'You understand what I need to do, Lily?'

Lily nodded again.

'You ever play with jigsaws?'

Lily nodded more vigorously this time.

'You like them?'

'Yes,' Lily answered.

'Imagine, that's like my job. When something bad happens, it's like all the facts get broken up and it's my responsibility to find all the pieces and put them in the right order. For a while it means I have to gather a lot of information and sometimes the questions I ask may seem weird, but they all help me figure out if they slot in. Does that make sense?'

'Is what happened to my dad like a jigsaw puzzle?'

'There are lots of little pieces I'm trying to figure out, yes.'

'If you catch who did it, will they go to jail?'

'I should hope so, yes.'

'When me and Kenny do little bad things, we get in trouble. What happened to my dad was a huge thing. They will be in trouble for a long time.'

'Is it alright if I ask you to talk about your dad?'

Lily nodded.

'I promise if you want me to stop, I will. Was your dad fun?'

Lily nodded animatedly. 'He said I'm his best daughter, and it's funny 'cos he only has me.' She held up a hand. 'Dad's number one in my top five.'

'Five dads?'

Lily hid her laugh behind her hand. 'No.'

'Who are the other four in your top five?'

Lily touched each finger as she reeled them off. 'Dad, Kenny.' She flicked her eyes to Vicky. 'He's my brother. Nanny Hayes, Mel, and Daisy who lives two doors down because she's named after a flower like me but also because when I was sad the other day over my dad, she gave me her Jammiedog, which you can't even get in the shops and said I can borrow it till I feel better.'

Lily scrambled onto the bed and scooted back to show Vicky a fluffy knitted teddy.

'I've heard about these guys; they're sold out everywhere. Daisy must really like you to trust you with one of hers. Your mum isn't on the list of your top five?'

Lily's mouth formed an O. She darted her eyes to the door as if worrying her mother might hear. 'I just ran out of fingers,' she whispered.

Vicky leant in. 'There's no wrong answers, Lily. Remember missing jigsaw pieces? As long as you're telling me the truth, you can't get it wrong.' She whispered then. 'No one needs to know except me.' Then louder. 'Will you tell me what you loved most about your dad?'

'Daisy's dad split up with her mum and she never sees him. Not like my dad, he's always there. Annabelle in my class is scared of hers.' She looked up wide-eyed. 'Her mum says, if you don't do your homework, I'll tell your dad. My mum never said that. She's the scary one.'

Vicky chuckled. 'Sounds about right. Did your dad let you get away with lots, then?'

Lily shook her head. 'When we stay at Dad and Mel's we go to bed way earlier but I don't mind 'cos we get story time and Dad makes up stories and they have a ball with a light thing on it that goes around and around so the room has loads of spinning stars. I'm never scared there.'

The hairs on the back of Vicky's neck rose. 'Are you often scared at home?'

Lily looked at the door, then shook her head. 'Dad always listens. He always tells the truth, like you said.'

Lily covered her face with her hands, but Vicky already spotted tears.

'You miss him?'

The girl nodded. When she lowered her hands, Vicky understood why Melinda called the girl sweet. Lily looked at her full of trust.

'It's all my fault. I think I got it wrong, the message.'

'What message?'

'He said he would come for me, that I wasn't to worry, he would find me. I waited at home all day but he never came. I think I got it wrong 'cos I went to the wrong place. My dad wanted to meet me, then he died.'

Chapter 25

'Lily, why did your dad ask you to meet him?'

She shrugged, her eyes big with worry. 'Dunno.'

'Was it usual for him to ask you to do that?'

There must have been an insistent tone to her voice. Too forceful for a child. Lily looked like she was about to cry.

'I don't know.' It came out whiney.

'Melinda told me your dad gave you a secret phone so you could ring him. Was it on that phone that he contacted?'

Lily nodded.

'Did he ring you or leave a message?'

'A message.'

'Can I listen to it?'

Lily shook her head. 'Dad told me to delete all my messages 'cos that way I can't get in trouble. That way I can just say I found the phone on the street or something.'

'Don't you worry that you'll get in trouble for hiding it?'

Lily shrugged, wary but no longer upset.

'Mum says it's fine to have secrets. Sometimes I think I have too many. Like if Santa knows everything, and lying is wrong, won't he know that I'm hiding something? I don't think it's fair if I don't get any presents at Christmas 'cos of them. A lie is always a lie Dad says.'

Lily lowered her voice. 'Kenny says, Mum says it's okay to lie when the secret is hers, but when it's me or him keeping a secret, she isn't okay. Most of the time, she thinks her secrets are just her secrets, like we don't see them at all when they are right in front of us. I didn't like the frown Dad got on his head when he was worrying.'

She wagged her finger, imitated a deep voice.

'"A lie is a lie. If you help hide it, it hurts you too." Kenny says there can be good lies too. Ones where you stop the fights from happening. Ones where no one gets hurt. Kenny looks out for me all the time. He's the best brother ever.'

Chapter 26

'Melinda, I can see you through the glass. Can you let me in?'

The woman who answered the door was not the same woman who sat opposite Vicky in their first meeting. With not a scrap of makeup and her hair looking like she hadn't brushed or washed it since before they spoke and wearing a huge t-shirt that hung to nearly her knees, covered with splatters of bleach or paint, she bore no resemblance to the elegant woman at the church. At four in the afternoon, Melinda Hayes looked like she'd just risen from the bed.

'Sorry about the state of me,' Melinda said and for a second Vicky saw the armour drop. She much preferred that woman to the one she had interviewed days earlier.

'If you need longer to get ready, I don't mind.'

Vicky wasn't lying. She could use the time to do a little snooping.

Melinda shook her head. 'Get ready for what? There's nothing I need to get ready for. Is there news? Did you catch someone?'

Vicky rocked back on her heels.

'No, nothing like that. Sorry if I got your hopes up. A thought just came to me as I was driving. I don't like to fester on a question if I can get an answer quickly. Should have called ahead first though and asked if it was a good time, sorry.'

Melinda raised a shoulder. 'It's not like I've a huge schedule. Just another long night of misery planned. Come in.'

They settled on opposite chairs. Melinda waited for Vicky to speak, but when no words were forthcoming, she filled the silence.

'The question?'

Vicky dabbed her eyebrow. 'Sorry, I don't know what is it with me today. Going through my notes, I never asked about Alex's work colleagues. Was there anyone he had an issue with? One woman mentioned a guy called Jefferies; do you recall any problems with him?'

Melinda's eyebrows knotted together. 'His name isn't familiar. How long ago was that?'

'Ten years approximately.'

Melinda shrugged. 'Maybe he moved on or retired or something. Alex didn't mention him to me.'

'Did he ever talk to you about troubles at work?'

'Ester Wilkins, the head of the ward, and Alex had some run-ins over patients over the years, nothing you'd call a reason to fall out though. More like a difference of opinion. Alex respected her, he often said she was just doing her job and was just as frustrated with the situation as him. She had to follow the rules, and make sure the others followed protocols. Whereas Alex, he liked to bend the rules sometimes.'

'Like?'

'Nothing sinister. Nothing that would get him into major trouble. Alex just despised unnecessary rules. He used to fume over the red tape that often threatened to bog them down and get in their way.'

'I agree with him there.'

'The patient always came first for Alex. He was never a fighter, but he would remind anyone if they were putting the paperwork first. Sometimes he needed me to reason it out. If they didn't complete the admin, the powers above would replace them with someone else who would. Ester had to find the balance to keep all happy. I respected her for that. So did Alex.'

'So, no issues with Ester?'

'No issues with Ester or anyone in the hospital. As far as I know. Wouldn't you be better off asking at the hospital?'

'We did. My colleague did, I just wanted your take on it.'

She didn't add that she didn't trust Barratt's competence.

'I mean, there were times when Alex came home and couldn't talk. Not wouldn't, not odd with me or anything to do with us. It was like he couldn't get any words out at all, that whatever happened in work rendered him completely numb. When he was like that, I didn't push him. Early in our relationship, Alex warned me it could happen, like on days when a patient died or he had to give a person a terminal diagnosis. He called them cloud days, because he said those days were like those clouds that loom, darkening the sky, ominous and full, ready to unleash the rain. The only way he could cope was to take cover, to wait for them to pass, or rain on you. Left alone, he could grieve them, then watch them pass on. Some days I would hear him cry before he fell asleep and the next day he would wake up, still a little shaky but ready to start again. On reflection, maybe some of those days weren't cloud days. It got to the stage where I didn't always ask. I would just make him a cup of tea, lay it down on the side table and give him a kiss on the cheek. On the clouds days we worked out a sign, where he would just tap my hand in thanks. If it wasn't a cloud day, or if he had processed it enough, he would look up and we would talk.'

'How often were these cloud days?'

'Not very often. Most days, Alex loved his job, came bouncing in. In the weeks leading up to his death, he had been quieter, sat away from me, didn't look up, which I assumed were cloud days. After seeing that woman at the funeral, I'm not so sure.'

'You think he may have been avoiding you?'

'Alex was a terrible liar. From my past relationships, I'm an expert at digging out the truth. If Alex needed to hide being unfaithful, the only way he could have done it was to avoid me.'

She waved her hand over her nose as if trying to prevent a sneeze. 'I'm sorry, it's a lot to process.'

'Take your time.' Vicky took out a packet of tissues and handed Melinda one.

The woman took it gratefully. 'You'd think there would be no water left in my body.'

'Crying helps. Believe it or not, the tears will stop and when they do, you'll wish you still had that release.'

Melinda parted her lips, about to ask a question, but Vicky cut in before her.

'You probably won't like hearing this but I have to talk to you about it, okay?'

Melinda nodded, then prepared herself.

'Melinda, I spoke to Cassandra. Your mother-in-law has a different view on some events in your marriage. She mentioned witnessing some friction. On one particular occasion, you walked out of a restaurant?'

If Vicky was expecting hostility, Melinda didn't give it. Sitting back in her seat, it was like all the air in her body deflated.

'I wondered if Cassandra would bring that up. It wasn't what she thought. Yes, I reacted terribly that night, and I shouldn't have walked out and left them or, even better, I should have said exactly what was bothering me. It was wrong to make such a scene; I know this and it mortifies me now. Before we even left the house, I was ready for a fight. The woman coming over in the restaurant sent me into overdrive. I regret never explaining it to Cassandra afterwards, I was embarrassed. After I confronted Alex and he proved it was a misunderstanding, I didn't know how to explain or smooth things over. It changed things between me and her after that. Which was a real shame because Cassandra was more like a mother to me than my own.'

'What sent you into overdrive?'

'It was a poem I found in his bedside locker. Written from another woman to Alex, to my husband. A piece of paper full of proclamations of love. That night when he arrived home, I threw it at him. Alex didn't even flinch. Didn't show any shame. He said we all have a past and that letter was part of his. That his past made him the man I fell in love with. He explained the girl wrote it over fifteen years before and she had moved on. A different life, he said. He held me after that, kissed my hair, said, "My poor, Mel, men really did a number on you, didn't they?"

'That was all I needed. My jealousy is irrational, I know, but it isn't unchangeable. Once he answered my question, I never brought it up again. Actually, I framed the poem because I wanted him to see I wasn't afraid of either of our pasts anymore. It hangs still in the hall.'

'That hall there?' Vicky asked, pointing.

'The very one.' Melinda pointed to a frame. 'Work away if you want to look at it.'

Cushioned between two large elaborate canvases, made from different mediums, both of a man strikingly similar to Alex, hung a smaller frame. Sure enough, it was a poem.

When the world was against me,
You became a shield.
Your kindness, your laughter, your love,
Turned into a torch that lit my way.
In the bleak days after,
The darkness could never fully ascend
Because your light lodged inside,
A reminder I once had a friend.

Vicky sat back down. 'Did you paint those?'

'A long time ago.' She pointed towards the canvases. 'That's my retirement wall, if I become homeless, which now is likely, they'll guarantee I eat for a few months.'

'Homeless?'

Melinda shrugged. 'Alex brought in the steady income. When I was single, I used to budget my money, was super frugal, but having security, I lapsed. So, if you are still wondering if I'm a suspect, just know financially, it is the death of me. Sorry, that's melodramatic. It will mean moving, though. There's no way I can afford the mortgage here on what I bring in.'

'What about life insurance?'

Melinda looked like the thought hadn't even crossed her mind.

'Alex looked after all that. Maybe, I don't know.'

'Out of interest, how much would you get if you sell those two pieces?'

Melinda shook her head. 'Not sure and I won't find out because I'm not doing it. You saw them, they are both of Alex. They were a wedding gift from me to him. I'll never sell them.'

Vicky wiggled her pen. 'Didn't you hold an exhibition a few years back in town?'

Melinda blushed. 'You remember that?'

'I do. It was of different sunsets, right?'

'That was one of them, yeah, when I first moved here. Seems like a lifetime ago now.'

'Why? You don't do it anymore?'

'Haven't picked up a paintbrush in years. I moved away from that medium. Mostly, I work with fabric and paper.'

Vicky stayed silent, encouraging her to speak.

Melinda shrugged. 'Having Lily and Kenneth four days a week, cooking, wanting to spend all my available time with Alex, my work took a back burner. The fabrics were a different way of looking at life, but I've never been happy enough with them to exhibit. The prints from before I met Alex still sell but new work, I don't know, I just lost confidence putting myself out there, I think.'

'Because of Alex?'

'No way. Alex was always on to me to paint and show off my work. It was me. I didn't want to be away from him. Working on a piece took over my whole being and I didn't want it to compete with my relationship. Maybe that's where I went wrong. Maybe if I'd concentrated more on my interests, Alex would have still seen me as an interesting person.'

'Here's a question. Did you ever poison Alex?'

Melinda's jaw slackened, and her cheeks darkened. 'Cassandra's wrong. It was another misunderstanding. Whatever she's told you, I did not try to poison him. Did Cassandra imply I did it on purpose?'

'She mentioned ye had been arguing before it.'

Melinda let out a huff.

'Not arguing, just ignoring. Alex started acting differently. He acted distracted when I spoke. Affection stalled. I'll admit I was hard work, needing constant reassurance, too much, I think. In the early days of our relationship he understood the need, understood how it healed me. Along the way he stopped. At first, I tried to ignore it, but then when his disinterest continued, I retreated too, until we were barely talking. I poisoned him through a complete lack of communication on both our parts.

'When I think about it, that is the reason I stopped painting. Subconsciously, I must have blamed it for my husband getting sick. Working from home, I used to get up late, potter around the house, cook, read, then go to my studio at night, often working on a piece until morning. It doesn't suit every marriage, but it suited us. Most days, especially if Alex was working, I would leave a dinner for him. Around that time, as we were mostly ignoring each other, I didn't know exactly what time he finished. I thought about not making him food at all but it felt like I would be the person in the wrong when we hadn't actually argued. So, I cooked some rice and left it on the hob with some curry. That day an old friend from art college had an art exhibition in Dublin, so I left a note saying it was there. How could I know he was on a double shift and wouldn't see the note until the following day? Or that brown rice left like that could kill you? The first I knew of it was when Cassandra rang me to say Alex was in hospital. That was hard. To hear that my husband was so sick he couldn't tell me himself. Or that we were in such a dark place in our relationship that the first person he picked up the phone to call for help was his mother, not his wife. That hurt. You asked before if I remembered why Alex lost his temper with me, well, it was over that. When he got better in the hospital, when he woke up, he flipped. Never before had he even raised his voice, but that day he accused me of trying to kill him. He honestly believed it. When he let me speak, I explained my side. The amount of bacteria in the rice was colossal, I don't blame anyone for thinking it could have been on purpose. My stupidity floored me. I couldn't believe my lack of concentration, my carelessness, could have killed my husband. Nearly losing him changed me. That day it all came out, how I felt his pushing away, about how I was afraid I was losing him. What scared me most was that he didn't deny it, didn't reassure me. It hadn't been paranoia; I was losing Alex. My behaviour and lack of trust was leading me straight to a divorce. I begged him for another chance. After that I dropped the attitude, dropped the accusations because wasn't I lucky just to still have him around? I saw how easily life could change, how quickly you can go from having everything to then having nothing. Not only could I have lost Alex, but it would have been my fault. Alex forgave me once I laid out my version of what happened. No matter how much I tried to explain to Cassandra, it wouldn't register. Ask her if I left my husband's side the whole time he was in the hospital. I haven't painted since then; I couldn't because it felt to me like my art caused the man I loved to nearly die. Instead I concentrated on the kids and Alex. Would someone who wanted their husband dead do that? I loved Alex, I wanted him around. You have to believe me. Do you believe me?'

'It doesn't matter what I believe. It's the facts that mean anything.'

'So, I'm a suspect?'

'Everyone I meet is a suspect until I solve the case. It's the only way I know. Hunches stay as hunches until I find hard evidence.'

Melinda raised her hands, then dropped them.

'Who even knew brown rice could poison someone? I swear to you I didn't. You asked me and I admitted I was a jealous person, but I never hurt Alex, never, ever intentionally. I used to fire up sometimes, but I always calmed down. It never turned into being like them.'

'Like who?'

'Bernice.'

'What did Alex tell you about their relationship?'

'He didn't go into any detail at all. He just made it very clear that if I went any further, pushed further I mean, no matter how much he loved me, he would walk away. There was a line he would never cross again. He said he would not tolerate my behaviour, which was fair. The way he said it scared me.'

'Did he say any more about Bernice?'

'Whenever I tried to prise it out of him about why they finished, he would just say, she is the mother of my children, Melinda, leave it be. There was a vulnerability with Alex, people are so closed off normally yet he wasn't afraid to show me that side to him. When I met him, my trust in men was lower than the floor. Looking back, that's why we worked, we were both damaged people searching for a partner just to be kind. From the outside, my jealousy must have appeared terrible, but it was only because I knew what we had, how special it was, that I was terrified of losing him.'

Vicky looked at the side view of the canvas. It was the spitting image of Alex.

'What will you do now?'

'After I tie up loose ends, move. That's the positive thing about being an artist, you can create anywhere.'

'Move away from Knockfarraig?'

'From Ireland probably. There's nothing for me here. If I have to survive on what I earn, it would make sense to move somewhere with less expensive overheads, and make the money stretch, somewhere inspiring. I've always wanted to travel. We planned to do it together, once the children were old enough to trek with us in the summer. Alex dreamed of seeing the world.'

She trailed off, her features drooped.

'You miss them?'

She nodded. 'Nearly as much as I miss Alex.'

'Have you asked Bernice if you could see them? Surely, she wouldn't prevent you from visiting?'

Melinda looked her square in the eye. 'Then you don't know Bernice. That woman would love nothing more than to slam the door in my face. I have no rights to those children now at all and I will be damned if I give her the opportunity to gloat. Anyway, they look just like Alex. Saying goodbye to them would feel like losing him all over again.'

Vicky flipped a page in her notebook.

'Did Alex ever mention a woman called Saoirse Thomas?'

Melinda jolted, but Vicky knew it could be a reaction to any woman being mentioned in relation to her husband rather than the name.

She shook her head. 'I don't think so.'

'Alex dated her in his teens. Their relationship was, how should I put this? Intense. According to Cassandra, it ended all of a sudden. Did Alex ever mention anything about it?'

'He told me his heart broke before Bernice. That he rushed into their relationship trying to forget. Why? Do you think she has something to do with his death?'

'Just trying to gather all the information. We have an old picture;

can I show it to you?'

The picture was old. Melinda caught her breath. A young girl, unbroken, unlined, with glossy hair and brighter eyes, stared back. Alex's arms wrapped around her waist. Melinda's cheeks flushed, and a bead of sweat formed on her lip.

'Who gave you this photo?'

'Cassandra.'

'Course she did.'

If she wasn't already sitting down, Vicky thought Melinda would have to. She looked like she saw a ghost.

'This girl was the same woman at the crematorium.'

Chapter 27

Hands on hips, Vicky paced the floor of her office, her focus never leaving the huge board that ran the length of the wall. Staring at the pieces of paper pinned up, trying to make sense of it, trying to decipher any link. She had added the notes which Derek, Colette, Nevan, McAuliffe and Barratt had briefed her on earlier, trying to hide her disappointment in front of the other gardaí. Take Colette for example, she had given her a simple task of entering the image of the SUV to decipher what make it was. From there she had wanted her to find out what model it was and how many years it was manufactured for, so they could narrow down the year. Colette came back delighted. It was a BMW X1. When Vicky asked when it was first introduced, Colette's face dropped saying she forgot to check. In a few seconds, Vicky had been able to add to the board that the SUV was bought from 2009 onwards. Not great. She had asked Colette to look again to see if there was any obvious differences between years.

What was she missing? She stared at the faces on the board. Apart from the man they had yet to identify, none were official suspects, not yet. From Vicky's perspective, all of them were. No one was safe from doubt as far as she was concerned. All had reason. Bernice, Melinda, the mysterious and effusive Saoirse, Cassandra, and the things she didn't say, and that was only the women. A number of men looked out at her from the wall. The names she already ran through with Melinda of the men that carried the coffin. Could the murderer be one of them? She fingered the photocopy of the note they found. The reason they, no, she, believed the murderer was at the funeral. The reason she had been thorough in finding out who carried the coffin.

Please forgive me. I didn't want to kill you.

Like her, the person must have believed that the crematorium cremated the body immediately. Only someone close enough to the coffin could have wedged it in.

Vicky closed her eyes, picturing the order of the day. Bernice and Melinda, Lily and Kenneth lined the row. Who else was there? Ernest. Cassandra's family from Galway. A few of his work friends that all had alibis including Ester. By the time the music played, people packed in to every available spot of the crematorium. Impossible to remember everyone there or even to have seen them all. The room was small enough, with only enough seats for a hundred people at the most, so others, after paying their respects, escaped the palpable claustrophobic pain inside and lined the walls outside, standing for the final goodbye. Vicky still knew nothing, but one thing she was sure of was, the person of interest they were looking for, the man on the CCTV arguing with Alex, was not present in the crematorium. The person who wrote the note wasn't him. So, who was? Could the possibility a woman might have hired a professional be correct? Even though Mara thought that was the line of inquiry she was following, it didn't ring true. A hitman wouldn't leave such a mess or stand around arguing. Still, someone could have hired a novice, someone inexperienced who didn't act straightaway. Her hunch was that the murder was impulsive, carried out in anger. She wasn't completely buying the road rage story, either, though. Yet so far, she couldn't find any connection to the men. *When in doubt sound it out,* she thought.

'Bernice is hiding something, I'd put money on that,' Vicky said. She stood over the image of Bernice.

Was not wanting her children away from her a few days a week enough of a motive? What if she had just wanted a guy to rough Alex up, threaten him to stay away? From what Vicky witnessed, children were exhausting, so surely a mother would welcome a father who wanted to do his fair share. Wouldn't it be in his ex-wife's interest to see no harm come to him? In a sugar-coated world maybe, where power didn't take over what was right. Or maybe she *was* the culprit. What if Bernice only planned to harm Alex, to have him need her help with looking after the kids more while he recovered? What if Bernice wanted him hurt but planned on keeping him alive?

And then there was Melinda. His present wife definitely had enough jealousy issues to fit the bill of a crime of passion. Melinda claimed she discovered Alex was unfaithful at the funeral and on this subject her body language seemed to tell the truth. Or the woman could be delirious; she had not ruled out either option. Alex might have been unfaithful. If Vicky believed Melinda, that she found out about his possible infidelity or his link to Saoirse after Alex's death, then that would eliminate a huge motive on her part. But she had said he was quieter than usual before his death, and afterwards she questioned this. In the same conversation, she told Vicky, what was it exactly she had said? *I'm an expert at digging out the truth.* If so, this wasn't a lady who was fooled easily. This was a woman who learned how to lie to decipher if she was being lied to.

Alex had met with Saoirse, according to Carole, who was not known for being discreet, maybe a rumour had reached Melinda?

Melinda hadn't mentioned it, but she jotted a note to check if Alex had life insurance. If she was the main beneficiary, if Alex's death meant she wouldn't have to worry about an income anymore, then there was another motive.

Even as she jotted that idea on a note, the idea didn't sit right with Vicky. Her instinct didn't light up for either of those women, and Vicky made a career out of following her hunches. To have a correct hunch, you had to have another suspicion, and Vicky wasn't there yet.

She stopped at another picture. Who was the man that attacked Alex Hayes? Not one person had identified him. Surely someone in the whole of Ireland knew of the man's whereabouts? Unless he was hiding low somewhere. Unless someone was purposely hiding him.

Barratt had received the image of the man just before he left this evening. Course he had checked his messages too late, missing the deadline for the news. They would have to wait until tomorrow to release it. For her, she had hid her frustration well because even Vicky knew she needed help with this case. No matter how hard she worked, she was no closer to the truth either.

She looked at the close-up again.

The grainy image now removed, the man's features contorted in rage. Light hair, light eyebrows, a nose that ended at a point, reminding Vicky of a bird. What motive could he have other than road rage? And where had he disappeared to? How could someone fall off the edge of Knockfarraig?

The sea, Vicky thought. That's how you fall off the edge of Knock-farraig.

Chapter 28

Now Melinda had a name.

Life made her jealous, this she understood. Alex hadn't been the start of it, hadn't been the cause, but having something real with him definitely highlighted the possibility of his loss, definitely triggered her fear and insecurities that she could lose him, because even in the early days she knew that he was capable of hurting her even more than anyone ever had. It was a continual bugbear between them, something she had been trying to combat. When he threatened to leave, she promised to work on herself, work on trusting his love, trusting she was good enough. His death sent her into a spiral, all her self-work for nothing. Because what had she been working towards except their happiness? Who did she need to improve for now?

And then, at the funeral, she had seen all the different women. On reflection, it was only grief triggering her old reactions, and she regretted making those comments to Sergeant Fitzgerald. Many of the women had come forward since, knocking on her door with flowers or a dish of food, or sent her a handwritten note, or email, explaining how they met Alex and her cheeks had burned at how innocent it had been. The hospital had even dropped over a box with mementos and cards from patients who didn't know where he lived. Both hard and beautiful to look at, for it just amplified what she had lost, proving how kind, how caring Alex was with people. After reading those letters, her jealousy seemed ridiculous.

Except for that one woman. That woman at the crematorium. Unlike the others, unlike her usual spikes of jealousy, Melinda had *known* this woman was different. This woman had loved Alex. Not only that, but Alex had never mentioned her name, let alone told her how much she meant to him. She had known he had loved a woman years before, but Alex had reassured her it was his past, and she, Mel, was his future. Cassandra had not once mentioned her, let alone shown her any photographs.

And now she had a name.

Chapter 29

Being called to attend a will reading when you didn't know your dead husband made one was a step too far. A hard enough feat to rise from the bed as it was, Melinda dreaded sitting in a room listening to Alex's last wishes. It was too final. At least when she slept, she could pretend he was just on shift. She could pretend he would join her later and coil his body around hers. The worst was the thought she had to continue on, had to keep breathing, keep moving, keep answering questions about her husband when all she wanted was him there with her. She missed him. Missed his smile. Missed the socks on the bedroom floor that she scolded him for not picking up when the laundry basket was beside the bed. She missed the sound of him humming in the shower. Or the way he placed the top back on her glue if she fell asleep before doing it. Most of all, she missed having another human care about her. It hurt to think if she died, the person who would have missed her the most was gone.

The will reading came at a time when she could only cope with tiny decisions like what to wear or whether to eat. The prescription her doctor gave her helped take the edge off overthinking herself into a grave. It covered her grief in a hazy cloak, shielding her from feeling, shielding her from caring. By the time she arrived at the law office, the pill turned Melinda's steps weightless. She floated on soft clouds, where dead husbands and murderers evaporated into nothingness.

Separate words flowed by, flicking sparks in her consciousness that registered on the periphery but never fired up, while the rest rushed past in aural waves. Cassandra entered the room after her, and if the pill hadn't taken such effect, Melinda might have, she *would* have, slighted when the woman sat on the opposite side of the line of chairs. Instead of cutting herself up about the obvious scorn, Melinda wondered if the doctor would give her enough pills to take them on a more regular basis. Numb was definitely a better feeling than the churning pain that swirled in her stomach and head since Alex's death. She frowned. No point getting her hopes up, for she already knew what his answer would be. He had only given her the prescription for a small blister pack on the promise she wouldn't ask for another saying, 'Eventually grief will always catch up on you. It is better in the long run if you allow it to take its natural course.' *Condescending bastard*, she thought, wondering how hard could it be to change your general practitioner.

She closed her eyes.

Go someplace better, Melinda. go someplace where you were happier.

She pictured Alex lying in the bed. The sunlight hitting his cheek. His dark–blond hair brightened almost white, as if a halo surrounded him. Stroking her arm. His laugh, an easy to make sound. God, she loved that man more than her own breath. She had lived to love him.

When the man in the suit raised his voice, she sat up. He used a word similar to her name. On second thought, it was her name.

'Melinda, are you listening?' he repeated.

She smoothed her hair.

Don't annoy the important man, Melinda.

'Yes, yes I am.'

'Right then, I will read Alex's note now.

"Melinda, I hope the day never comes for you to have to hear this but I have enclosed photocopies here of my life insurance. Please find the originals in the desk drawer in the spare room. Money was always tight for

us, and I know it was never what you needed most, but I promised I would always look after you. In the event of my death, I cannot physically keep that promise, so financially will be the only way I can ensure you will at least be secure. It was the best policy I could find or afford. Please note, in the event of my death, I have named you as next of kin and at the time of evaluation, was told the payout would be at the very least five hundred thousand euros. Also, as my wife, with joint ownership of the house we bought together, you already own half. I have divided my share into three. One third for my mother Cassandra and a third each for my children Kenneth and Lily. You are free to keep the house and buy my family out of their share at the market value or sell it and divide it."'

As much as the pill numbed her, it couldn't turn her to stone. Melinda couldn't feel the wet on her face, only noticing the tears when they dripped onto her blouse. She slumped in the seat. 'Are you sure? Alex didn't have any life insurance.'

'The paperwork here proves he did,' the man in the suit said. Then unflustered, he read on.

'*"For my mother Cassandra, I have left a lump sum of ten thousand. There is a private letter for her to read."'*

'What is in the package?' Melinda asked, pointing to a yellow envelope on his desk.

The man in the suit slid the envelope nearer to him. 'Mr Hayes instructed Brooks and Belmont to send the contents of this envelope to the local Garda Station.'

'What's in there?' she asked.

The man in the suit didn't respond.

Cassandra smiled at Melinda for the first time since before Alex's death. Whether it was the pill or the circumstance, Melinda couldn't tell what type of smile it was, whether full of contempt or genuine pity.

'I don't know either, Melinda, but I guess we'll soon find out.'

Chapter 30

According to the CCTV footage, they lost visibility of the suspect's car right at the start of Knockfarraig woods. Exactly in the spot where she now stood. Barratt and the other Gardaí assured her they'd scoured the whole area, but there was still no car. With no other leads, it just wasn't in Vicky's nature to take anyone by their word, especially four novices barely out of nappies and a disinterested one like Barratt.

Anyway, they didn't know those woods, didn't know its nooks and crannies like a person who grew up there. Generation after generation, Knockfarraig woods was a rite of passage for the youth of the day. Over by that log was where Vicky had her first drunken kiss with Sean Sully. She shuddered at the thought. Sloppy lips Sully, she'd called him after that.

There was no plan. Only follow the path until something struck her not to.

It didn't take long to notice the dip in the grass, the indent of tyre tracks veering off across the field. Unheard of in Ireland but there had been no rain since before Alex died. Weeks with only the sun shining had about as much chance of happening as seeing a unicorn. Yet here they were, entering their second week of sunshine.

For half a mile, she followed the tracks, weaving around trees with barely enough of a gap between the trunks to fit a car in. A tight squeeze, but definitely manageable. Until the grass reached a gravel area. No more marks. No more places to track. The gravel area panned out to three other areas. Vicky stood at a crossroads. One way led out of the woods and onto a road. Once the woods hit tarmac, CCTV covered the road and had showed no signs of a car so she could dismiss that direction. The opposite way led to the beach. To the right was an overgrown area, where the weeds met closer-set trees and overgrown bushes became a fortress of foliage. The other way brought her back along the path she had already taken. Vicky stared off into the distance. There was no going back. *If you wanted to hide a car, where would you go?*

She headed towards the overgrown area to the right.

At first, there was nothing. No sign of movement, no track marks in the grass. Something stunk, though. The prickles rising on the back of her neck were her sign to keep going. Despite scratches, she pulled at shrubs and bushes looking for any clue. She tapped on one particularly dense bush and it moved more easily than she would expect. In fact, it came away in her hands. Setting part of the bush down and lying on the ground, she noticed between the long blades of grass that black rubber peeked out. Scrambling to her feet, Vicky shoved at weeds and grass, ripping skin on her hands and fingers. Some moved, some didn't, but she didn't stop hacking until she uncovered a tyre underneath. Not just one tyre. And not just tyres. And not just from any car either. This one had a licence plate covered in what smelt like manure.

'Thank Christ,' Vicky whispered. 'Finally, a break.'

With cautious steps, and without touching the car, she peered in the window. No sign of life. No sign of a body inside it either. The low shrubbery covered the front and the roof, meaning she had to contort her body to see in. On the passenger seat, loose coins spread out over the fabric, along with a packet of cigarettes and a lighter. A corner of a burgundy stub peeked out from the pocket of the driver's side of the car; if Vicky was a betting woman, she would put money on it being a passport. The item of most interest though, above all others, was the bloodstained knife almost waving at her on the dash. After putting on gloves, she tried to open the doors and the boot. All of them were locked.

Hitting the dial button on her phone she rolled her eyes when it went straight to voicemail. So typical when she wanted to gloat.

'Mara, just found the suspect's car. Hidden in the woods that five of your Gardaí already signed off on searching. And then you tell me I have a problem with trust.' She tsked loud into the phone. 'He's not inside, unless he's in the boot, but it doesn't smell like he is. Oh, and by the way, the possible murder weapon is inside. So, I need you to sign off on getting a locksmith out as I don't want to jeopardise the case by breaking the window. The car will have to be moved to get in, so if you can set those things in motion, that would be great.'

Then she rang Phyllis. 'Can you tell the lads they dropped the ball. When I get back to the station, we'll have to have another meeting about how I like things done.'

'What did they do?'

'What did they not do is more like it. I found the car in the place they spent all day searching.'

'The eejits.'

'Incompetents would be better than eejits, Phyllis. Give them the heads up to scare them, will you? Also, tell them I want a report from each one of them about what leads they have been looking into that they forgot to mention or take note of.'

'Will do. Before you hang up, Vic, there is a package that arrived for you.'

'What makes it any different from the tons of others, Phyllis?'

'I had to sign for it. Not by Tim, the usual delivery guy. You know Kieran the boy of the O'Sullivan's originally from Passage, who opened the card shop last year?'

'I know Kieran, Phyllis.'

'Well, he works at Brooks and Belmont,' she said it over pronouncing the B's. 'He came up to the door all suited and booted and smelling lovely and just handed it to me, saying make sure you give this to Sergeant Vicky Fitzgerald. You know that fancy lawyers in town, the one off of Plunkett Street?'

'I know the lawyers, Phyllis,' Vicky said, pinching her nose to fend off the start of the headache that always niggled when Phyllis started gossiping.

'There's a pen or something inside. Do you want me to open it?'

'No. If it's addressed to me, then I'll open it.'

'Fair enough,' Phyllis said, the disappointment obvious in her tone.

'Can you leave it on my desk and I'll get to it as soon as I get back? I'll be here awhile and after that I have to pop to Cassandra Hayes' house before heading to the station.'

'Will do.'

Chapter 31

Not expecting the drop in, Cassandra didn't appear surprised or put out with the visit. With a smile, she let Vicky enter, walking ahead towards her living room.

'Cassandra, thanks for seeing me. I just wanted to run over a few things with you.' She pointed at the mantle place. 'Are those Alex's ashes?'

Cassandra's perfume wafted when she moved towards the mantle place, placing a hand on it. Pink lipstick frosted her lips. Mascara slicked her eyelashes.

'They are. Melinda didn't want to divide them up. When the time is right, we will release them somewhere.'

'Not bury them?'

Cassandra gave a scathing look. 'I told you already how I feel about the Church. Alex was traditional, though. As much as I hated religion, when he fell in love, it was very important he marry in a church. That wasn't from me, that was all Alex.'

A sound came from the other room, a whoop from a child.

'Is there someone with you?'

'Yes,' Cassandra said, her features lighting up. 'I have the children for the day.'

'I thought you seemed brighter. Can I say hi?'

Cassandra shrugged. 'Bernice might not be happy about it, but I haven't seen my grandkids since the funeral, so I don't really care what that woman says.'

The kids were leaning over a jigsaw in the dining room. On entering, Lily waved. 'Hi, Vicky.'

Kenneth, not used to her and probably intimidated by the uniform, recoiled.

'Hey guys, what's the picture going to be?'

'It's really hard. It's Nanna's flowers,' Lily said.

'Corners first always helps me. Kenneth, it's nice to meet you.'

Kenneth looked up from the puzzle, two pink patches formed on his cheeks. He nodded.

'He prefers Kenny,' Lily said.

'Ah right, sorry, Kenny.'

He shrugged. 'It's okay, I don't mind.'

'You've both had a tough time. If there's anything I can do to make life easier for you, please come to me. I want you to know I'll do everything I can to help find who did this to your father.'

Kenny sunk lower in his seat, his eyes welling. Embarrassed, he turned to Cassandra. 'Nan, can I go? My friends are coming online now.'

She patted his head. 'Of course, honey. Only an hour though, okay? Dinner will be ready about then.'

'Okay,' Kenny said. 'Nice to meet you, Vicky.' About to exit the room, he backed up and faced Vicky. 'There's nothing you can do. Even if you find the man, you can't bring him back. Even if he spends a hundred years in jail, my dad is gone.'

Vicky took a step closer. 'You're right. I'm sorry you had to go through this. What happened to your dad, I can never erase. The only way I can help is to give you the answers about what happened. I hope you can understand that?'

Kenny nodded. 'It's not your fault. I just miss him.'

'How about I make us a tea or coffee?' Cassandra asked Vicky.

'Coffee would be a lifesaver,' Vicky said. 'Cassandra would it be alright if I just have a quick word with Kenny?'

Cassandra hesitated, then nodded. 'Go easy on him though, he's very cut up.'

Vicky followed the noise up the stairs, finding Kenny just about to enter a bedroom.

'Kenny, is it alright if I ask you a few questions?'

His cheeks turned puce and looked like talking with her was the opposite of what he wanted. Yet he nodded.

'I just wanted to ask if there was anyone you had thought of that might have wanted to harm your father?'

He shook his head. 'Dad got on with everyone.'

'That's what people tell me. You are older than Lily, it must have been hard for you when your parents decided to divorce.'

Kenneth stared at the ground. 'I guess.'

Vicky leant against the wall. 'Having both around then all of a sudden one is gone.'

'They were still in our lives and my mam and dad were better apart. I told Lily this.'

'She told me you're the best brother ever.'

Kenny grinned. 'She did?'

'Yes. I think you have really helped her through this. Are you doing alright?'

Kenny bit his lip. 'Not really, I keep wondering if I could have done something. I miss him. And I miss Mel. We haven't seen her since the funeral. This was the first time I saw my Nan since too.'

'People's heads can be all over the place when they are grieving.'

'It's just my mum. She doesn't like us to visit Nan.'

'Why?'

Kenny shrugged, looked to the floor. 'My mum doesn't like her.'

'Kenny, Melinda mentioned your dad gave you a secret phone.'

Kenny scowled.

'Don't worry, I won't tell. I just wanted to know if your dad contacted you before he died?'

'Not that day. The night before he sent me his normal text.'

Vicky waited.

'Every night we were away from each other he sent me a text saying goodnight and that he loved me. I deleted it not knowing it was his last message. If I'd known I would have kept it and now he's gone and I've got nothing.'

Kenny sobbed. 'Can I go?'

'Please don't. I didn't want to upset you.'

'It's not your fault. I just want to forget it for a minute. That's why I wanted to go online with my friends.'

'I'll leave you alone. But Kenny, will you promise me you'll contact me if you remember anything?'

She rooted around the backpack she carried everywhere with her, and pulled out a card with her number on it.

'Or if you just want to talk, okay?'

He stared at the card, his eyes still glistening with tears he was trying so hard not to spill.

'Okay,' he said.

Back in the living room, a sheepish Vicky smiled at Cassandra then stepped nearer to Lily. 'Can I help you with this?' she asked, pointing at the jigsaw.

The kettle clicked off the boil, and Cassandra busied herself making coffee. Lily picked up a jigsaw piece and tried to slot it in a different-shaped hole. 'Okay.'

'I think I just made your brother sad.'

Lily shrugged. 'We're sad all the time now.'

'Were you sad when your dad left your mum?'

'Not really, 'cos we knew we would see him all the time. Dad had to go.'

'Why do you think your dad had to go?'

Lily looked up towards the kitchen. 'Because of the bruises.'

The hairs prickled on the back of Vicky's neck.

'Someone got hurt?'

She nodded her head. 'It happened all the time, so he had to go.'

'Did you ever see your dad hurt your mummy?'

Lily bit her lip, then studied the pieces.

'Did you ever hear shouting from them?'

Fear crossed the girl's face. She shook her head with force.

'How did you know your dad hurt your mum? Did someone tell you?'

A shake of the head again.

'Did you see the bruises?'

Lily lifted her head. Bingo. Vicky lowered hers to be nearer the girl's eye level.

'Lily, did you ever see bruises on your mum?'

Lily scowled. Melinda was right, Lily looked adorable when she was angry. Crossing her arms, Lily clamped her mouth shut.

Go easier, Vicky thought.

'Sometimes the people we love can make mistakes. Everyone gets angry from time to time. Parents can too.'

Lily eyed her, the trust coming back a fraction.

'You know my job is to find out what happened to your father? We want to make sure the bad guy won't hurt anyone else. But to do that, I need the whole truth. I need to find out everything. Remember what I said about the jigsaw? If we slot the wrong piece in somewhere it shouldn't go, it won't work. All the pieces have to fit and if you are hiding the middle piece, it can put a stop to finishing it.'

'Will the guy go to jail?'

'If I can find him, yes.'

In a low voice full of sadness, Lily said, 'I don't know who he was.'

'I know that, Lily. All I want is a little help. I have most of the edges, but until I join the middle bits, I can't figure out the puzzle. Is it okay if I ask you some more?'

Lily nodded.

'Did your father ever hurt you or your brother, like when you were naughty?'

Vicky rarely cowered from anyone, but Lily gave her such a withering look, it made her edge back. This look was far from cute.

'It isn't telling on your dad. You won't get him in any trouble.'

Lily dangled the crayon in her hand. 'How can my dad get in trouble? He's dead.'

'That's why I'm here. We only want to work out what happened to him. If he had a history,' she stopped. Simplified it. 'If your dad hurt people before, then he might have tried to hurt the other man or the man might have wanted revenge for something. We need to know in what way he hurt your mum.'

Lily covered her ears as if trying to block out noises. 'He didn't.'

Vicky suppressed a sigh. 'Remember when you said your dad left because of the bruises? Can you tell me how your dad made them? Or where they were on your mum?'

Lily moved away from Vicky and the jigsaw. Instead, she picked up a crayon, then coloured hard on a piece of paper. Deep red lines made gashes on the picture of an apple. For a minute, Vicky thought Lily was going to ignore her.

'Dad didn't give my mum any bruises.'

Vicky looked up at the ceiling. It had been a long day.

'My mum gave *him* the bruises.'

Chapter 32

Hearing Cassandra getting ready to come back in. Vicky hurried up the conversation.

'Did your mum hurt your dad?'

'He said it was just playing. Mum said they were having fun but she went too rough.'

'Did you believe them?'

Lily shook her head.

'Where were the bruises?'

Lily looked at Vicky with confusion.

'What body part?'

Lily pointed to her thighs.

'Your daddy had bruises on his thighs?'

Lily nodded.

Could Lily have misconstrued Alex's injury? Could it be a case of rough play like they said? Vicky had seen it in friends' relationships. Consensual rough play was not uncommon. Still, though, Lily's conversation worried her.

When she was leaving, she asked Cassandra if she could walk her out.

'Cassandra, did you ever witness any violence between Alex and Bernice?'

Cassandra raised a hand to her chest as if struck. 'No, never. Why?'

'It's something Lily said there. She mentioned Alex had bruises. Look, when I get back to the station, I'll do a background check to see if there were any alerts from social services.'

'And I'll keep a close eye on Bernice. Maybe the kids will open up to me later.'

'If so keep me informed, yeah?'

Vicky walked into the station a little wearier than she left it earlier. Just as she reached her desk, ready to grab the envelope, her door opened behind her with a racket.

'Fintan Clancy,' Garda Ryan said, grinning, with his head half in and out of her office.

'How are we sure?'

He raised his finger with each point. 'Ran the plates. The locksmith got the compartment open and his passport confirmed it. And as soon as the news ran the clearer image this morning, over ten people rang in to identify him. They all say he's Fintan. From the sounds of it, he was a right prick.'

'Good to know. Can you note everything the callers say and give it to me before you leave?'

'Will do, Sergeant.'

'Derek?'

'Yes, Sergeant.'

'Don't forget this time, okay?'

'No chance.'

He bumped into Phyllis as he went to leave the room. Vicky rolled her eyes. The two of them were like something from a comedy act. Or her nightmares, it depended on the day. All she wanted was to open the envelope.

'Phyllis, if you were a dog you'd be panting. What is it?'

'There's a woman out in reception looking for you. She says she needs to talk about Alex Hayes.'

Vicky wrote down the name Fintan Clancy beside his picture on her wall.

'Take her name and number and find out what her relationship regarding him was. If it sounds important call me. If not tell her I'll give her a ring. Or if she insists on speaking to someone today, get Barratt or Derek or any of the others to sit in. It's probably some patient of Alex's telling me how he saved their husband or brother-in-law. What I need now is to concentrate, not waste time.'

And open this envelope, she thought.

'Vic, I don't think this woman wants to wait. She seems very jumpy. She says she has to get back.'

'Did you take her name?'

'I did.' She held up the notepad Vicky insisted she carry.

'Hold on, I have to find it, I stuck a post it note on to keep the page, those bright pink ones thinking they'd be brilliant for being able to find them quickly but it turns out the stick isn't that good on them and they keep falling off, oh hold on, I have it here.'

Vicky rolled her eyes and silently counted to five.

'Got it. Her name is Saoirse Thomas.'

Chapter 33

The room is dark when I enter. I flick on the light. It is not empty at all. There in the corner is my partner in life, the one I swore in front of all my family and friends that I would love for the rest of my life. Now, they stand there waiting to kill me. A knife glints in their hand.

Chapter 34

She wore her hair half up and down, with loose strands framing her face. A thinner face than when Vicky saw her last, with little fine lines around her eyes and mouth. It didn't make a difference. Saoirse was as beautiful as Vicky remembered, even though fifteen years had passed. Even with the hint of bruises around her eye socket.

'I came as soon as I saw the news.'

'Come in,' Vicky said, leading her into the interview room. She pointed to the seat, the harsher light giving a full view of the woman's profile. 'Sit down.'

Saoirse grimaced as she sat.

'Are they bruises?' Vicky asked.

Saoirse touched her eye, as if only remembering.

'Can you tell me how you got them?'

Saoirse hugged her body, bent nearer, as if the truth physically hurt. All too often, Vicky came across this, came across women hiding the pain others inflicted. She wouldn't push with this line of questioning. It was too early, too triggering.

She held out her hand across the table. 'Sorry, I should have done this straightaway. Let me introduce myself; I'm Sergeant Vicky—'

'Fitzgerald. I know. I remember you from around Knockfarraig. You used to hang out with Gerard Deasy's sister, didn't you?'

'Cara, yeah. She lives in Perth in Australia now. Haven't seen her in about ten years.'

'Funny how time goes. The days back then seemed to go at a different speed. Or maybe it was that I remember every detail. Maybe it was because I was more present, I don't know, I'm probably not making sense.'

'You're making perfect sense, Saoirse.'

'You know me too?'

'Sure do. I've been looking for you.'

'For me?'

Vicky scrutinised the look Saoirse gave her. Was it fear or genuine bafflement?

'You are aware of what happened to Alex?'

Saoirse's eyes watered. She nodded her head vigorously, over and over, as if the motion might stop the fact.

'I can't believe he's gone.' She smoothed a strand of hair behind her ear.

'Look, Saoirse, I'm not known for my tact and in an important case like Alex's, I won't change. I know why *I'm* looking for you. What I'd like to know is why you're looking for me.'

'The person on the clip, the one you released today on the news saying he was the main suspect in Alex's murder, that man is my husband.'

Chapter 35

'Fintan Clancy is your husband?'

Saoirse hugged her body, nodded at the ground.

'Do you know where he is right now?'

'No. I haven't seen him since the morning before Alex was murdered.'

'Where would Fintan go, Saoirse?'

'I don't know.'

'Has he family here?'

'Not here. His parents retired to Spain. His sister lives in New Zealand.'

'Could he have ran away to them?'

'Maybe, I don't know. They aren't close, he never really spoke to them in all the years he lived with me.'

And his passport was in the car, Vicky thought.

'What about friends?'

Saoirse shook her head. 'Fintan's very proud, he wouldn't be the kind to ask people for help or want anyone knowing his business. He knows lots of people, acquaintances more than friends. Most of the people he's closest to, he fell out with over the years. There's none that I can think of that would hide him when he is being wanted for murder.'

'Why did they fall out with him?'

Saoirse avoided her eyes.

'Fintan has a temper.'

'The bruises, Saoirse. Have they got something to do with Alex?'

She shook her head.

'With your husband?'

She nodded.

'Did you report it?'

Saoirse shook her head. 'Not to the guards. I'm staying in a woman's safe house.'

'Was it the first time?'

Saoirse didn't look up. Stared at the brown desk. 'The first time he hurt me? No.'

'Where do you think your husband is now?'

'I'm not sure. Should be Dublin, where we were living.'

Vicky walked over to the wall and checked her notes. 'At Sycamore Drive?'

The shock on Saoirse's face was the kind you couldn't fake. 'Yes. How do you know that?'

'Like I said, I've been looking for you. You've had no contact with your husband since you left?'

'If I had, I wouldn't be able to have a conversation.'

Vicky sighed.

Saoirse's eyes welled. 'You don't get it. You're wondering why I would stay with someone like that and I don't blame you. Now that I'm away from him, now I know what he did to Alex I can't understand either. I didn't know how to leave him and survive. You don't leave someone like Fintan unless it's in a box, he made that very clear. It wasn't my first time trying to get help, I just could never go through with it, so I fooled myself that staying with him kept him in check. I thought I was smoothing the waters by not running. And I was right. Because look what running did?'

The hairs raised on the back of Vicky's neck.

'What do you mean?'

'Maybe if I hadn't ran away, Alex wouldn't be dead. Fintan was probably driving around acting half crazy. I don't know how he found out about Alex or where he would be, but it's my fault. Alex would be alive if I hadn't come into his life again.'

'You think Fintan came looking for Alex?'

'Well, yeah, he must have.'

'According to the CCTV footage, Alex bumped his car into your husband.'

'Alex did?' Saoirse reeled back, her lip quivering in shock. 'Do you think he did it on purpose?'

'That's what I'm hoping you can help me with. On camera it looks like Fintan was going to break the red stop light but all of a sudden he stopped. Alex didn't stop in time.'

'Did he crash into him?'

'More a bump than a crash. Enough to make Fintan get out. Would he have known who Alex was?'

'The two of them never saw the other. Knowing how jealous my husband is, I never kept photographs of Alex.'

'You said you came into Alex's life again? When?'

Saoirse looked around the room as if making sure no one else was listening. 'If I'm going to tell you about me and Alex, I'm going to have to go back to the start. To understand what we went through together.'

'Then that's what we'll do.'

She stood, about to call Phyllis to make sure she wasn't interrupted. 'Before we get into it, is there anywhere at all you can think of where Fintan would hide?'

'One time, he disappeared for two weeks. When he came home he told me he slept in his car. Find his car, find Fintan, I'd say.'

'We found the car. Fintan wasn't there.'

Saoirse screwed up her nose. 'Then I don't have a clue. I'm sorry.'

'Why would he obscure his car? His licence plate was covered in manure.'

Saoirse's hand went to her mouth. 'The day before Alex died, I left Fintan. Alex found a women's shelter in Cork, drove me and my daughter all the way from Dublin so Fintan wouldn't find us. As soon as he walked in to our house he would have known we were gone. Fintan wouldn't have taken me not being home well, I was never allowed to run more than thirty minutes over my time even if there was a school run or shopping needed and if I wasn't there when he got home from work, well, I can't tell you, I never dared. You've been to my house, you said? Well, there's a dirt road and next to that there's the farmer's fields edged with bushes and trees with a stream that leads to the main road. It was raining heavily the night before I left; he probably drove through the field looking for me thinking I would hide there. Normally, you see, I wouldn't have any money to run, Fintan made sure of that. Made sure I had no friends around so I wouldn't have a place to go either. He wouldn't have expected me to run to a shelter, wouldn't think I had it in me. He probably drove up and down those fields like a maniac thinking I was hiding in a ditch. Maybe he was in such a rage he decided to smear it on so if he hurt me he wouldn't be identified easily? I wouldn't put that past him, he told me repeatedly if I ever left him, he would kill Laurie first, then me. He was probably running around livid, ready to hurt me, when Alex crossed his path.'

She covered her face in her hands. 'I'm so ashamed.'

Vicky sat on the edge of the desk. 'Don't be. These guys go for the kindest of women. The most loyal. You cannot be ashamed for wanting to see the best in someone. You carried too much guilt around as it is from the sounds of it. Will you tell me about you and Alex?'

Saoirse dropped her hands. 'I could talk about Alex all day every day.'

'Then do. Start at the beginning. Do you want a drink of something?'

'Water would be good.'

'I'll just pop out and let the others know, then I can talk to you all day if you want.'

'I have to leave at two.'

Vicky smiled at Saoirse. 'You're not under arrest. You can leave at any time.'

'Maybe I should be. Maybe you won't think I'm so innocent by the time I finish talking.'

This time Saoirse looked her right in the eyes. What was held there wasn't defiance, anger, or fear. It was resignation, and it scared Vicky more than anything else.

Chapter 36

'As a kid, I moved all the time. My mother could never settle, so we never stuck long in one spot. In every school I moved to, I was bullied. It's easy to pick on the new kid, even easier to become an outcast in a classroom where no person knows who you are. These days, the teachers know what to look out for, how to handle feelings and emotions. They use talking circles and make them watch videos on bullying and ask how it would make them feel. Back in my day, it was each to their own. The playground was the place I dreaded most.

'It was hot the first day I started at Knockfarraig primary, not unlike the kind of weather we're having now. I was seven years old. When the bell rang for lunch, a crowd formed at the door, desperate to get out of that stifling room and breathe some air. As was my usual, I hung back as I never wanted to make a scene or draw attention to what I was doing. It was always better to blend, to slink into the shadows. A book and a corner were my ideal lunchtime companion. On bad days, in many schools, I sometimes hid in the bathroom, hoping the teacher wouldn't do a headcount and hunt me out.

'Too hot to stay in the classroom any longer, once the entrance was clear, I ran to the light of the yard. As I ran out, a leg kicked low and I went flying, landing on my knees. Being a hot day, the tights were left at home, so when skin and concrete met, my knees were skinned back, red blood mixed with black gravel. Determined not to let them see me cry, for I had learnt the hard way that only made them worse, I bit the inside of my lip. All I could hear was laughter. A crowd formed, cutting off the teachers' view but it wouldn't have mattered anyway. On lunch most of the teachers ate their food inside with only two patrolling the outskirts of the yard, with hundreds of children running in between us and them.

'A boy, Dean, leant over me saying, "Will I ask the teacher to call your mammy for you?"

'I sniffed, waiting.

"Oh wait, Your mammy doesn't care. My mam said your mam didn't even want you. Your mam said you'd be aborted if it was legal," Dean said.

'"What's aborted?" someone in the crowd asked.

'Dean loving the attention, licked his lips, then said, "They stick a sharp thing up the mammy and scoop the insides out."

'Gary Lynch hovered over me and said, "She musta hated her giving her a name like that. Seesaw, is it?"

'"What are you on about?" another piped up. "Her name's easy. Shitsa. With a silent t," he said in a fake posh accent.

'I closed my eyes. The stinging knee forgotten, for all I wanted was to get up and run away and for them to stop. The place went silent. I opened my eyes, expecting to see a teacher near or one of them getting ready to attack. Instead, there was a boy, about my age, who had broken the circle and was standing above me. His hand extended out, waiting for me to catch hold. I didn't know if it was a trap, if he was just looking for a laugh from his friends, or if he would snatch it away or drop it if I went to take his or drop me back to the floor. But he was looking straight into my eyes, his mouth serious. The other's weren't laughing; they seemed in shock. I took a chance, I took his hand and the boy pulled me up. The movement broke the stunned silence of the crowd, kicked them back into action. As the circle surged forwards, led by Gary, the boy stood in front, tucked me behind the surge.

'"What are you doing?" Gary shouted, moving close to the boy's face.

'"It means free," the boy said, with almost a bored expression. Certainly not scared. I had never seen anything like it. Gary was a full two heads taller than everyone else in the class and wide with it. No one confronted him. Not used to someone standing up to him I'd say, Gary looked like he didn't know how to react. He gawped at the boy first, then me.

'I bit my lip to stop from smiling; it would not help matters if Gary thought I was getting saucy.

'"What's free?" Gary asked, not with his previous bravado though.

'"Her name. Pronounced Seer-sha. It means free or freedom and was popular when the Irish were fighting for independence. My mam says those people were fierce brave, and it's 'cos of them we have our freedom in the south."

'Gary stepped back as if he didn't really know what to say. I discovered later he was never really the quickest with his retorts, which was probably why he resorted to using his fists all the time. Dean nudged him. "Do something," he said. Gary straightened, rising to the challenge. Another boy edged through the crowd, standing alongside the boy who helped me.

'"Touch him or her and you'll have to go through me."

'The boy, I later discovered was Ernest Morley, was tall, almost as tall as Gary. He grinned at me. Gary and Dean slunk back closer to the crowd.

'The blond boy took my arm. "I have tissues in my bag if you want me to help clean the cut up?" he asked. He was a nurse even then.

'I took his arm and looked at this beautiful boy, with his ears that pointed and a strand of blond hair that stuck out from the side of his head and before I even discovered his name, I fell in love with Alex

Hayes.'

Chapter 37

'Being in a new school, living in a new town, and the small detail that I was only seven years old, there was enough to worry about without concentrating on the fact that I had just met the love of my life. But I tell you now as it is significant, because that is the moment my life first changed. The words or feeling weren't recognisable enough to call it love back then but I knew I liked him. Alex Hayes had a smile that would spread across his whole face. I had never seen that before, someone so unashamedly happy. It drew me to him. That and the fact he and Ernest were the only people to stick up for me, like ever. What drew him to *me* I have no clue, maybe it was the need to fix my sadness that appealed. I don't know, you'd have to ask him. But you can't.'

She stopped speaking as if that sentence only just hit her.

'Sorry, you're stuck with only my side of the story. I promise to keep it as close to the truth as I can. One thing that can be said about me is I'm a very honest person.'

Vicky smiled and sipped on her coffee.

'Whatever his reason was for liking me, all I can tell you were his actions. All I can give you are the facts. As he cleaned my cut he said, "you're going to be my friend."

'Normally I flinched when touched, but not with Alex. Never with Alex. Because the way he touched me was different, never threatening, always with that smile. I swear, Alex broke up fights with that grin. It was his secret weapon.'

She frowned.

'I told you only a few seconds ago that Alex was unashamedly happy, but I discovered the more I got to know him he had more reason to be miserable than I did.'

'How so?'

'Home,' Saoirse said.

'His parents?'

'Cassandra, his mother, was lovely. I didn't meet his father until years later, I think Alex purposely made sure I visited when he wasn't around. As a child who grew up with a mother who seemed to pick the worst type of boyfriends, I recognised a few things.'

'Like?'

'Bruises. Limps. His hair styled to cover a cut on his forehead that he could never completely hide. Alex was sickly too. Often pale or coughing. Thin as a twig. But he was good at sports and somehow able to chat away with people which I struggled with. When his dad was at work, his mother didn't mind him playing outside. My mother didn't even notice where I was most days. Only living two streets away made sense for us to hang around, but not having a friend before, I would have walked miles to meet. And then having two, because Ernest hung out with us whenever he was around. We were so young. People think you don't know about anything when you are that age, but I've never understood that. What I knew then was clearer and purer than any age since. For the first time, I knew what it felt like to have a friend. And once I found him, I didn't want to let him go. Free to do whatever we wished for two months in the summer; we used to run down to Knockfarraig woods and play by the tree swing until later in the day when the teenagers would rise from their sleep ins and hunt us away. For about a week we built a fort, finding old cardboard boxes and sticking them together, securing them to some trees. I've never been as proud of something I created. Actually, that's a lie. It was my second best. My first will always be Laurie, my daughter.'

Vicky scribbled. 'How old is Laurie?'

'She isn't Alex's, if that's what you're asking,' Saoirse sighed. 'She's eight.'

Vicky stopped scribbling. 'Continue?'

'It surprised me the fort lasted that long, really. A week is a long time in Ireland to not get some type of rain. After a downpour overnight, we rushed over there to find the cardboard turned to sludge. We didn't have the energy to try again. And it didn't seem that big a deal when we thought we had forever to make another one. Little did we know then that we would only get a year.'

'What happened?'

Saoirse pursed her lips.

'My mother was a mover; she didn't like to get stuck in one place. That's the reason she'd give to anyone who asked, but I knew it was because she burned her bridges with the people she hung out with or borrowed from or cheated on. It was like she pitched a tent and lit a fire and when the flames got too hot, she stomped it dead, packed up the tent and moved on. Most times, I wasn't around long enough to make an effort with my classmates. Ernest was lovely but his family were very sporty and went away camping a lot and I was shy around him. It wasn't until later that we grew close. Alex was the first real friend I ever had. When we moved on from Knockfarraig, he was the hardest one to get over. Mam gave out to me for that, for how long it took me not to mope, but I couldn't help it. A year is a long time for a kid. In a year you can make bonds for life. You can start to be convinced your mother has finally settled and it's permanent. A year is enough time to forget to worry about leaving. To forget what life could feel like without someone like Alex in it. For twelve months, someone smiled when I looked at them. Someone cared to cry when I told them I had to move. I still can picture Alex, with dirt on his cheek, and his hair sticking up, bruises dotted the length of his shin, chasing after our car, not even trying to hide the tears that lined clean tracks across his skin. I still see my hand against the window, as my mum screamed to sit back in the seat, the exact moment my heart broke for the first time.

'Afterwards, I went back to being Silent Saoirse, hoping I wouldn't be noticed enough to be picked on, or singled out. Throughout the years, I never forgot him. So much so, one time when Mam started her shifty ways, and I knew a fresh move was brewing, I suggested we head back to Knockfarraig and I swear we'd been to enough places for her to forget she was ever there. Even if she didn't blank it out completely, enough time had passed for her to welcome the notion. Ten years was enough time for her mistakes to be forgotten. So, I braced myself, excited to see my Alex again. Thinking I was ready but I could never have been ready for what was to come.'

Chapter 38

'I won't pretend the time away was fine. No point sugar coating any of it. A year of meeting a friend doesn't change your outlook enough, especially when that person isn't around to remind you. But it was enough for me to know life could be better; it was enough to spark a little hope. All my life people have told me I'm not good enough. As far back as memories go, people pointed out my flaws. Even my mam, the person meant to nurture and be my biggest supporter, told me how much of a waste of space I was on a daily, often hourly, basis.'

Saoirse flicked her eyes to the light, her tears in danger of spilling over. 'I don't know what it is, what quality I possess. If I did, I would stop it, stomp it into non-existence.'

She placed a hand on her chest, then met Vicky's eyes. 'I have tried; there are days I've stripped myself so bare there is nothing left. The fact is any person that took the time to figure out who I am, couldn't wait to tell me how worthless, how dumb, how wrong I was.

'Alex was the first person not to see wrong in me. After meeting him, I discovered that was all I needed to survive, to continue to live. One person to believe there was good inside. It didn't matter that *I* didn't believe, his conviction carried me through the years.'

She smiled then, an unseeing the present smile, lost to a memory.

'We were nearly eighteen years old when we saw each other again. Time transformed our features to almost unrecognisable, yet as soon as I saw him, and witnessed him see me, I knew, nothing had changed. Alex didn't even pretend not to recognise me, didn't even pretend to hide his thrill in coming over.'

Saoirse straightened. 'I can't tell you what that felt like. To have years of not being seen and then the person you prayed would, did.'

Vicky nodded, bit the inside of her lip to stop from showing how much that sentence affected her.

'When I asked to return to Knockfarraig, I didn't know how I felt about Alex. At eight, what I had felt for him was not romantic. Before I left, I was a child with a friend, a child with a lifeline. All I could go on was that draw, a calling to see him again, wondering how his life was panning out was constant in my thoughts. As soon as I saw him, I knew he was exactly the same as the boy with the kindest eyes who once cared about who I was.

'On the outside, everything was different. The boy had grown. In my search for a boy I loved, I discovered a man. In my teens, I usually avoided the opposite sex, I think because of the poor relationships my mum had, I was terrified of relationships.'

She smiled at Vicky. 'Or maybe I was just waiting for Alex.'

Saoirse laughed. 'As soon as I saw him, for the first time I wanted to run my fingers through a man's hair. To get as close as I possibly could to his face in order to see every colour in his eyes. To stroke the fine hair on his top lip. Sounds like typical teenager behaviour, but I want you to know what I felt was more than some crush. It was all in. Every inch of me. It was bigger than any feeling I'd ever felt. Terrifying and thrilling, all at once. As soon as Alex stood in front of me again, it all made sense; why I had pushed to come back to Knockfarraig. On the return of a look, I knew. Alex was the first man I would love, the first man I would sleep with.'

Saoirse blushed. 'It wasn't just lust. When someone sees you and still likes you, when you were forced apart and then you see each other again and you know, just by sight that they *still* see you, when no one in all the years apart never gave you a look like that, never even got close to understanding who you were, there was nothing more to do or say, I was taken. I was his.'

She shook her head, fiddled with her fingers. 'We didn't even kiss. "You came back," he said.

'"I came back," I replied, my breath catching with each word.

'And without saying anything else, he pulled me into a hug. And when we broke apart, Alex couldn't completely let go. Taking my hand in his, he smiled at me.

'And then a girl called his name.

'His eyes widened, and he whispered, "Jessica." Then, he dropped my hand and said, "Give me some time."

'She ran over, did not even look in my direction, even though it was obvious she saw me, that the whole reason she ran was because of me. Her kiss caught him short; he shifted his face away turning what should have been a passionate kiss to a peck on the cheek instead. I caught him looking at me, saw the confusion, and understood he didn't have a clue what to do next. And I knew right then Alex Hayes had the power to break my heart again.'

Chapter 39

Saoirse cupped her mouth. 'I can't believe he's gone.'

'Do you need a break?'

Saoirse took a few breaths with her mouth covered then dropped her hands. 'No. I'll keep going. If what I tell you helps you understand, it's better you know. At least it helps me feel like I'm doing something.'

'Did he break up with the girl straightaway?'

Saoirse gave a wry grin. 'He kept away from me for a couple of days and the longer it went on, the deeper my heart felt like it sunk to my stomach. Not that he completely ignored me, Alex wasn't the type to play games. He always waved or said hi but it was unspoken between us that he had to clear the way for us to be together. After waiting for ten years to reunite, I didn't want our beginning to start messy. Not that I knew what he wanted. That first night meeting him replayed too many times. Was it guilt that made him come over in the first place, then made him take my hand? Did he now regret what he said he would do? Or had he felt sorry for me and as sweet as he was just got caught up in the surprise of my return and just wanted to hug his friend? It felt like both ways. It felt like he looked at me and only realised something, only then thought of how I might feel. *Dumb Saoirse, I thought catching feelings for a guy who had none.* That would be typical me.

'And then, as I sat outside in the yard eating my lunch one day, Alex sat beside me, holding out a packet of cheese crackers. The offering meant more than a snack. It told me he was free. It told me he was ready.

'He said to me, "I don't believe in God but every night I told him he could prove he was real by bringing you back to me."

'And I said, "every night I planned how I could come back."

'His little finger brushed my thigh.'

Saoirse opened her mouth, then closed it, as if wondering if she should continue.

'As we talked, the more we talked, the more we reestablished a connection, the attraction grew stronger. But I was afraid. What if it ruined what we had? He hadn't actually kissed me. Maybe he only wanted to be friends?'

'What did you do?'

She smiled at Vicky. 'On the night Knockfarraig won against Ballinroe the whole of our year went to the woods to celebrate. I'll never forget the smell in the air, pine and grass, the tart stink of orange mixing with the sharp nostril burn of vodka; there was a weight in the air, denser, like just before thunder and lightning, a charge in the atmosphere. A force of energy you could feel tingling on your lips.

'Alex sat beside me. We didn't talk. I was afraid to, afraid of what words would do to the moment, would do to the static between us. It would break this new feeling somehow, even though it was words that bonded us all that time. The energy was too thick. I could feel the particles of him, as if his skin was vibrating, as if they had voices of their own and were screaming at me to touch him. I wanted to. That was all I wanted. I wanted him to turn to me, for his face to give me some indication that he felt the same. That he didn't see me as just a friend anymore or as only the little girl he hung out with. I wanted him to show he saw me as a woman.'

'Did you ask him?'

'The words were too big to say. How could I tell Alex I wanted him and change everything between us? You have to remember I was called Silent Saoirse for a reason. And anyway, I felt, shouldn't he know I wanted more?

'What did you do?'

Saoirse tilted her head and laughed.

'I shouldered away from him, the annoyance fresh. And then his breath was on the back of my neck.

'"Saoirse," he whispered.

'And I turned and his face was against mine and I tilted my jaw towards him, giving permission and I thought I'd die with want. Then his lips were on my lips. It wasn't rough or clumsy. It was soft. It was more feelings than I ever experienced in one moment. There was no clashing of teeth, no knocking of noses. With Alex, I didn't have to pretend I knew what I was doing, I didn't have to pretend that it wasn't new.

'After that, there was no more being friends. Once I felt his lips on mine, there was no way I could picture Alex as only a friend.

'We spent hours kissing. Hours and hours turning our lips raw. His stubble chafing my chin and jaw. Creaks in our neck from the awkward angles our heads moved at. Love bites there too. I would always stop when it heated up. Not because I didn't want to go further but because when you give a heart to someone that they stuck back together, you become terrified it will break again if something goes wrong. My mother taught me love didn't last, that relationships ran their course, sizzled out, became stifling or sparked and blew up. Even though I couldn't see that ever happening with me and Alex, I understood my mother had never wanted pain either. No one chooses misery over joy.'

Vicky nodded. 'That's very true. Chasing misery is learnt behaviour that creeps up on a person until it becomes a safety net. Until it's better to have sadness around then risk aiming for joy and losing. Because at least misery is reliable.'

'Exactly. They say young people know nothing but I knew everything there was to know about Alex. The length of his eyelashes. The slight dip in his right hip when he walked. The way he cleared his throat just before he would tell me he loved me, as if he needed to clear the path from his heart to his mouth. Or how it was unspoken that he would sneak into my house on a Friday night so he wouldn't have to be around when his father came home from the pub on pay day.'

'Alex was afraid of his father?'

'He avoided him at all costs. Some days he wouldn't say anything but I would just know he'd had a run in with him. His posture would change, as if he'd curled inwards and my heart would just ache for him and I would try anything just to turn his mood until he would smile.'

'Did you ever argue?'

Saoirse pursed her lips, as if trying to recall.

'One night, as we grabbed a burger, a girl from our class, Pamela, turned up worse for wear. Whether it was just too much drink or just the right amount to make her brave, she grabbed his arm.

'"Are you going to Farrelly's Saturday night?" she asked him.

'Alex smiled at me, bemused. "I don't know, are we?"

'I smiled back. "We are not."

'"We are not," Alex answered.

'Pamela gave me the once over, then turned to Alex, blocking me. "If you don't just want a prick tease, you know where I am."

'My breath caught. As Pamela walked away, Alex called out, "No, thanks." He grabbed for my hand but I pulled it away.

'"What's up?" he asked.

'"Why would she say that?" I replied.

'"She's drunk. Can you imagine her head in the morning?" he said.

'"Have you been telling people about what we do, *in private*?" I almost hissed.

'Alex looked confused.

'"About what we don't do?" I said, standing up. "If you want a quick shag, Alex, be my guest. Like Pamela said, there's plenty up for it but that's not what you'll get from me."

'I walked as fast as my legs would go, the blood rushing up to my head making me dizzy. Before I reached the end of the car park, he caught up with me.

'"Saoirse, come on. Don't act like you don't know me. There's nothing in any of this; she's just trying to freak you out," he said.

'"Have you told anyone?" I asked.

'"Why would I? What goes on between us is our business, no one else's," he replied.

'I kept walking.

'"Saoirse!" He stopped me by blocking my path.

'"You're better than this. What is this really about?" he said.

'Looking down at my feet instead of facing him, I answered, "I'm scared, Alex. We're getting closer and I want that but, I don't do one-night stands, Alex. I do forever. And I know that's probably unrealistic. It's probably outdated and old-fashioned and not cool but I don't care because it's true to me, it's who I am. And if you can't handle that, if you can't go into this thing with me believing the same, then get out of my way because you're only wasting my time."

'He took a step back.

'But then he stepped forward. "Forever it is then."'

Saoirse tilted her head until she was looking at the ceiling. She took a long breath as if trying to suck in the memory.

'To describe what Alex's love did for me is impossible. Only to say, I never thought I would have that kind of moment, the type where you read about the guy lighting up when he sees the girl. Those things didn't happen to me. With Alex they did. With Alex, his eyes lit up and his face beamed. Never before or never since has it been that way. Because with Alex, someone finally saw me. He saw me as I was and still loved.

'After that promise, forever didn't seem that scary. We both cracked ourselves open and didn't hide. That night I kissed him in the middle of the street not caring what anyone would say. Until we heard this loud laugh. Not the usual sniggers from the lads either, this was an adult laugh, full of scorn. Breaking away, a man stood a few feet away. With hands in his pockets, he stood staring at us, with a grin that didn't meet his eyes. Unnerved, I shuffled into Alex's chest.

'"You want to get in there while she's ripe," the man said. The way he moved his hips, it was clear he had an erection. It turned my stomach. Greasy haired and wobbly, with ruddy cheeks and bloodshot eyes. When I looked up at Alex to say something, there was this terrified expression on his face. I placed my hand on his chest and the touch brought him back to the present, brought him back to me.

'"Let's go," I said.

'Catching his hand, I tugged him away. Almost frozen to the spot, it took three attempts before his legs moved and he followed my lead. Even when we were half way down the road, I could still hear that man's hoarse sandpaper laugh. It still makes me shiver. When we stepped around the corner of the street, I hugged Alex, laying my head on his chest. "He's gone now. Are you okay?"

'His heart was pounding in his chest. "It's not okay."

'"He's gone. I'm fine. He can't hurt us." I smoothed back his hair.

'"Saoirse, that was my father."

'My hand stopped mid stroke dangling between hair and air. It doesn't matter how many times you're told stories about a person, until you see them for yourself you can't understand. Now I understood why Alex avoided his father. Now I understood why he would never want to introduce him to me.

'"He cannot harm us; we won't let him," I said.

'And then I kissed him. As I did the heaven's opened with a downpour that soaked us within seconds. Running for the shelter of the woods, we ducked between some trees. And whether it was the gratitude for having left the heaviness of what happened, something in us changed, like the first time we kissed, there was a force of energy in the woods. I wasn't going to let his father turning up ruin the perfect moment before. So, I made another perfect moment. Running to the spot known as the clearing, I whooped, jumping over little branches and twigs, careful but not really caring about catching my ankles on nettles or brambles.

'"Come over here," Alex said, pointing over to a cluster of trees.

'The clearing was the last place anyone would shelter, for the open space meant getting soaked again. Which was exactly what I wanted. No one would stay out in this weather, which meant we had the place to ourselves.

'Right in the middle, I stood, making sure Alex could see me from his shelter. I peeled off my sodden top, looking at him all the while. And then he understood. He pulled off his clothes and we danced naked to the tune of raindrops and the rhythm of our quickening heartbeats that rang in our ears. And then when the rain stopped, the cold set in, and we had to find another way to keep warm.

'For a girl who travelled the breadth of Ireland, the only place I wanted to explore was Alex. Knowing I would do anything, absolutely anything he asked of me. Knowing, like I knew my own name, that I was his.'

'Your relationship became sexual?'

'Alex was my first everything. First crush. First friend. First kiss. First lover. First person to stand up for me. First person to tell me I mattered. It is about a million times more than just being the person that got there before anyone else and took my virginity. He was more than just someone you experiment with or first in line.'

Vicky smiled. 'I remember you. I remember how in love you both looked.'

Saoirse smiled back. 'It's easy to fall in love in a place like Knock-farraig. Plenty of places for catching a quick kiss, for stealing glances, for whispering in corners. Many scenic scenes can backdrop a budding romance. There was nothing to hide back then. No one to hurt. We could love freely and we did. Alex wasn't afraid to love me, that's what I loved the most about him. He didn't care if people saw. Didn't care if he got ribbed about it. It unleashed me, made my confidence grow.

'No one ever came close to Alex. Maybe it was because of the way things ended. We didn't even get a year. There was no closure, no way of binding the loose ends together. When that happens, you spend your life wondering. *Did he know? Did he care? Did he ever love me?* On the bad days, on the days where I wished I could become someone else, when I wondered if I would be better off giving up completely, the thought of meeting him again one day, the thought that actually at one point in my life at least, someone had acted like or pretended they loved me, got me through. Those days I still held on to hope. Because both of us being alive, living somewhere out there, even if it was on the opposite side of the world, even if I didn't know where he was, meant the future could still hold some chance, that fate might one day intervene and allow us to cross paths. And now that is gone. There is no more hope.'

She let out a staggered breath.

'Not even with Laurie?'

'Laurie keeps me alive, Sergeant Fitzgerald. The only hope is for her life, that I don't ruin her upbringing like our families ruined ours.'

'Your families ruined your life?'

'Maybe not being able to forget Alex after I left had nothing to do with the way things ended and all to do with the way we began.'

'What do you mean?'

'For you to understand my actions after I met Alex for the third time, you have to find out about my life before. About *our* life before we met again.'

Chapter 40

'When I left Alex fifteen years ago, I kind of gave up. Not kind of, I did, I did give up. Don't get me wrong, I dressed and washed and shopped and worked and ate. All of it went on as if they were happening outside of my body, outside of my brain. It was like, I emptied. Just a hollowed out carcass of all the good inside me. When I woke each morning, before I even opened my eyes, my first thought was of Alex and my heart would do a little flicker and then my stomach would churn at the realisation of what happened, when I would remember we were no longer us. Could no longer be us. Being without him broke me. I look back now and still wonder how I survived. The only thing that kept me upright, kept me from going into a black depression was the hope that love would find me, that one day I might see him again, when the timing was right. This time I can't do that, so I don't know how I'm going to keep going, I don't know if I can survive losing Alex again.'

'You don't?'

Saoirse's breath caught, juddering her chest. 'The first time, I could survive knowing I might one day see him again. The second time I reasoned I had to let him go so he could live. I lost him to circumstances, to time, to impossible to navigate problems. This time I've lost Alex to death. There will be no more chance meetings. No more serendipity. No more right or wrong time.'

She covered her face with her hands. 'So much time wasted. So much of our life wasted.'

Vicky handed her a tissue, then waited for Saoirse to calm. She dabbed at glistening eyes that brimmed but never fell. She took a deep breath and seemed to gain strength from it.

'When Alex looked at me, I'd feel myself go weak. That's what I used to think, that I weakened, that loving Alex, dropping my guard with him caused me to become weak. There is such beauty in vulnerability, though. Being unafraid to show love, to be that free, to strip off naked and dance in the rain, to tell him without worrying about him not feeling it back, to light up like that. It strengthened me, made me grow. I learned with Fintan that it is the wrong type of love that weakens you. Now Alex is gone, I can never do that again, can never love anyone that way, become that raw again. Even with Alex, when he entered my life once more, I tried to give a more subdued version, a more careful one because I knew how much he could hurt me even when he promised he wouldn't. So dumb to think I could protect my feelings. Broken is broken. There aren't different levels to a broken heart. I wish now I had given him everything, that I hadn't held back anything at all. Hadn't been afraid about other's opinions or about other's feelings.'

'Like his wife?'

Saoirse straightened, looked Vicky straight in the eye and for the first time in the whole interview, uncertainty left her face.

'If I knew what little time we would have, how that was going to be it, or how good it was going to feel to be near him, if I knew we would never see each other, or never be with each other again, I would have clung and begged him to stay, I would have taken that knife and plunged it in my own heart. How many moments end before we know they will be our last?'

Vicky sat back in her chair. Saoirse had hit a nerve.

'You asked if I'd thought about his wife's feelings, it might come as a surprise but I have never wanted anyone to get hurt. But, let's be clear about something Vicky, after a life of everyone else insisting their joy came first, when it came to Alex, there was no negotiation. He was mine and I was his. Time would never change that. If I could rewind and change meeting Fintan, and erase Alex meeting Bernice and Melinda, would I? Yes, if it was just about me. I would suck up all that time wasted and live it without a second thought. But it isn't just about Alex and I. Our life included three other important people. Laurie, Kenny and Lily. So, there is nothing I can change about the years in between, all I can do is accept it.'

Saoirse fixed the position of her earring, a plain diamond stud. Doing so Vicky spotted the tattoo on her wrist. A house martin mid-flight, the v in the tail pointing towards her arm.

'What's the significance of the house martin?'

Saoirse traced the wings with her finger.

'Alex used to sneak into my house sometimes at night. In my housing estate, house martins made nests on the walls of every house. I loved them. Loved the way they swooped down to play when I stepped outside. My neighbour explained they returned every summer. Knowing how my mum loved moving, Alex called me his house martin. That when I left him when we were eight, he'd always known I'd return. I got the tattoo as a surprise, I showed it to him at the Grads, but it didn't go down the way I hoped.'

'The night of the Grads, isn't that the day before you left?'

Saoirse flinched.

'What happened?'

'When I showed Alex the tattoo, he wasn't happy. Alex wasn't a drinker, the most I'd ever seen him drink was one can of beer. So, when he took the vodka shot one of the lads handed around, I thought it was strange but put it down to the night it was, that he was just celebrating. Exams over, school finished, time to relax before the results came and we had to worry about getting accepted to college. When he started necking it back, that's when I worried. From our parents' history with alcohol we usually preferred to stay sober. From the way he seemed to ignore me I could tell he wasn't happy but wouldn't say why. He continued to drink. At one stage I went to the bathroom and when I came back Bernice was sitting on Alex's lap.'

'You knew Bernice?'

'Yeah she was in our year.'

'Were you friends?'

'Far from it. She made it obvious she wanted Alex any chance she got. Alex was drunk, the drunkest I've ever saw but that was no excuse. When I approached, he didn't shove Bernice off. I stood near him, not trying to make a fuss, even though I felt like bursting into tears. We had looked forward to the night for months so I didn't understand. When he wrapped his arm around her waist, I knew for sure he was trying to make me jealous. There was no fight in me, so I made my excuses, saying I was tired and would head home.

'Alex stood up, said no, he'd go because I had already ruined his night. I followed him. Half a mile up the road he turned and said he was angry at me. He didn't make sense. He picked up my wrist, said I should never have gotten the tattoo, that my skin had been perfect as it was, I didn't need to ruin it with ink.

'I told him I got it for him, so he'd know no matter what I'd return.

'He swayed from side to side. "You *are* planning to leave me then? Well go now."

'"I'm not," I told him.

'"Go on," he said again. Then louder. "Go."

'When I didn't answer, he said, "fine then, I'll go."

'And he did, he left. I didn't follow him, wanting to give him space and to be honest I wasn't sure I wanted to talk to him when he was acting so out of character. I sat on the kerb and sobbed. And when my tears dried, when I'd given him enough time to calm down, and hopefully sober up, I walked to his house. But when I got there Alex wasn't there. Only his father was.'

'What did Alex's father do?'

Saoirse bit down hard on her lip showing teeth.

'I will not talk about that man. I will not darken how far I've come with thoughts of him. If you're asking me, then you know. I will not add to it. He ruined our lives, isn't that enough? Please Vicky, don't make me add to it. Don't make me relive what he did.'

Vicky placed a hand on Saoirse's shoulder. 'I'm sorry. No more questions about that night, okay.'

Even though it made her want to ask a million more.

Chapter 41

Vicky poured the coffee in the kitchen, taking her time. Apart from the constant need for caffeine, she wanted to give Saoirse a few minutes to compose herself.

Saoirse smiled at Vicky when she handed her a cup.

'You're probably waiting for me to talk about Fintan. Wondering why I'm talking about Alex when he's the one dead and not the one you're after.'

'I wasn't wondering. I knew you'd get there when you were ready.'

'The dead don't have a voice. It's important you heard how much I loved Alex before I talk about the man who, from the looks of it, murdered him. I can't believe Fintan might have.'

'You don't think he is capable?'

'I'm not saying that.'

Her leg moved up and down. 'Crazy as it sounds, I met Fintan because of Alex. Walking down Grafton Street on a busy run up to Christmas, all I could see were heads bobbing as I shuffled along. It had been a gruelling day and I couldn't wait to get home and throw some noodles in a pot. Until one head stood out. A man, tall with the exact hair colour as Alex's. Without even questioning, I picked up my speed. Four years had passed – enough time for the pain of our breakup to abate, enough time to care more about talking to him than the circumstances that forced us apart. In that instant, it mattered that I talk to him again.

In that moment, I didn't care that he was married or had a baby son. I weaved through the crowds, getting nearer each time. The closer I got, the more panicked I became. How would he react? What if he ignored me? Still, I wouldn't stop, still I rushed to catch up. And then a woman with at least ten shopping bags twisted in the other direction, nudging me so I tripped, landing in a heap on the ground, banging my lip on the shoe of the walker in front, splitting the skin. When I looked up Alex was gone. A crowd stopped, more because they couldn't get past me rather than with concern. The lady with the bags helped me to my feet, apologising profusely. Taking a tissue, I didn't care about any of the pain; all that mattered was seeing Alex. But what direction? I rushed ahead, until I reached the traffic lights. Unable to cross, I looked down at my bloodied legs. The fall had ripped some skin off. Realising I was running in the wrong direction from home, for a man who was long gone, I let out a sob and sat down on a concrete square. As I did, the man with the same blond hair, the man I thought I was chasing, approached me to check if I was alright. And I cried right in his face. Because he was not Alex. His hair was the same colour, but his features were different, sharper than Alex. He took a tissue from his pocket and offered it to me, even though I already had one in my hand. And I shuffled to make space for him on the concrete square when he gestured to sit. It all broke out of me. All the frustration. The hope of seeing him. The admission to myself that I still wanted to when I had tried to bury my feelings since hearing he had married Bernice. Sobbing, I dabbed the tissue on my bloody knee and looked at this man, grateful for his kind gesture. Grateful that at least someone was looking at me with any interest.'

'I'm sorry people hurt you, Saoirse.'

Saoirse tilted her head in acknowledgement.

'When I think about it, I've been hurt my whole life. My parents weren't the best examples of love for a start. My father ran out when

I was two years old, leaving my mother to raise me. What father abandons his child without looking back? Not one I had any urge to find, that's for sure. He left me with a woman who reminded me every single day exactly what she had to sacrifice. When Fintan showed up, offering a second chance at love, I packed up my bags and jumped into his life. I went from a mother who couldn't care less, to a man who cared too much. Moved from a house without rules, who never noticed where I was inside its rooms, to a house revolving around rules and restrictions.'

'Where did Alex sit in the balance?'

Saoirse smiled. 'Alex loved me just the right amount. Fintan acted different from Alex and at first that was what I needed; my heart couldn't handle any reminders of him. In the shelter, they've taught me about love bombing, about how a man can make you feel like you are everything. Flowers and tickets to concerts on a whim, booking fancy hotel stays without checking if I was free. Fintan, with his big gestures and declarations, was the tonic I thought I needed. It was the complete opposite of what my family had been.

'After losing a love like Alex, doesn't it make sense that the wrong man found me? Growing up, my whole life thinking I was worthless and then the only person who believed in me and told me otherwise, turned out not to be forever like they promised. My heart never healed when we broke up. Love hurts way more than hate ever could.'

'How did you find out about Bernice?'

'It took me over a year to recover. Recover isn't the right word; it was more like I needed to adapt. Or pivot. I missed Alex. So much. As the months went by the pain of that night lessened enough that I could allow some hope in. When I contacted Ernest and he wrote that Alex's father had passed away, I started to see a way we could work. Without overthinking, I got the first bus to Knockfarraig the next morning. It was early when I arrived, too early so I sat in a coffee shop waiting until it was a decent time to knock on his door. I never got to. Before I finished my coffee, Bernice passed by the window. I hadn't seen her since that night and was embarrassed so when she entered I covered my face with my hair. Bernice chose a seat on the opposite end of the room so I was safe. She looked pale. Straightaway a bad feeling washed over me. Before the woman behind the counter asked how excited Alex was to hear he was going to be a father, before I saw the wedding ring on Bernice's hand, I just knew she was with Alex. I finished my coffee, walked to the bus stop, and left Knockfarraig.'

'Did you ask Ernest why he didn't tell you?'

'I think Ernest was hoping Alex would see me and leave Bernice. He knew if he told me I wouldn't even try.'

'Why didn't he tell Alex?'

'Because I made him promise not to. I was a child of a broken home, I knew what it felt like. Alex owed it to his child to try and make it work. Even after Ernest told me Bernice miscarried, I made him promise. Alex had moved on, and that was what I needed to do.'

'What was Fintan like?'

'He was lovely at the start. Aren't all relationships, though? Otherwise, why would any of them begin? Not the same as Alex, nowhere near, but I was already resigned to never having that type of love again. And broken people are weak. A half love was better than none at all, I figured. A love that he could rip away at any moment was still some form of love. Fintan must have known he had me entirely, that there was no going back or anywhere else for me. That there were no other options and even though I chose to go, to leave my mother, Fintan knew it wasn't a returnable situation. Whether he would have been like that anyway or this fact produced it, it became a game of control.'

'For just Fintan, or the two of you?'

'Fintan loved me but also despised me as if I was the worst person he'd ever met. I never understood that.'

'Did he hurt you?'

She nodded, picking at the skin on her hand.

'One time, we lay next to each other in bed. We'd had a fight earlier, well not a fight, just something I'd said, something I couldn't even remember and he wouldn't tell me what had annoyed him saying I should know. Anyway, when he'd suggested we go to bed, I ran, glad the fight was over. The unexpected intimacy nearly brought me close to tears. Afterwards, his eyes were closed, sleep was coming for him. I coiled my leg over his, snuggled in.

'"Happier?" he asked.

'"Yes." I kissed his shoulder. "Next time, instead of fighting, let's do this instead."

'That was enough to set him off. Even though he didn't move straightaway, I lifted my head at the mistake. Maybe his body tightened, maybe his breath hitched, but something changed in that bedroom, I knew it and I was right. First, from the sliver of light coming from the bathroom, his brow creased, then his jaw clenched, the shard of bone visible under his skin where his teeth clamped down. My heart started thumping. He ripped the duvet away. My skin puckered at the instant cold, my hands automatically covering my nakedness even though he could remember every part of me whenever he wanted; all he had to do was close his eyes and see me naked. If that had been it, if he'd finished there, I would be okay. It didn't finish there. Fintan flattened his foot. With a violent thud, he pushed me away from his body.

'I asked him to stop. Told him I was sorry.

'Another thud, catching me on the shin. Another on the thigh; I winced from bone meeting bone. Next, a two-legged shove, until I dangled near the edge of the bed. Again, I asked him to stop, saying I would fall.

'I grabbed a handful of the sheet to keep me from dropping. There was no stopping. He shoved at my thigh with that flat foot, until I landed on the floor. Our bed was high up, the floor hard wood. Even though I braced, my body reeled from the whack. I didn't shout out, didn't cry, because all those things in the past had heightened his anger more. Afraid to move, I lay there with his semen still inside me, trying to work out what I did wrong, trying to figure out how I could get up from the floor without triggering him again. When he didn't attack, didn't follow through with more, when I couldn't think of an obvious choice to work out my next move, I stayed where I was. Biting down on my lip to stop the chatter of my teeth from my shivering body. Until I heard light snoring. Until it was safe to brave standing. Then I moved, sloping out like *I* did something wrong; I tiptoed into the main bathroom and found my robe. For the rest of the night, I didn't dare return to bed. I stayed downstairs, drinking a cup of tea, then dozed sitting up where I waited, for him to get up, wondering if he'd gotten over it, my only thoughts on whether the outburst would calm him and he would greet me as if nothing strange happened or if it was going to be one of those long days that could turn into weeks when he carried the slight on. In later years I learned to avoid some of the anger by soothing, by keeping quiet, by doing anything to please, finding new ways to fall over him worked and I did it and hated myself more for turning into this submissive character, but still did it, anyway.'

'I'm sorry you went through that, Saoirse,' Vicky said.

'Me too,' Saoirse said.

'When did you meet Alex again?'

'Don't worry, Vicky, I'll answer all your questions. Me and Alex were not done. We are just getting to that.'

A phone alarm went off. Saoirse gave an apologetic smile. 'Sorry, I have to collect Laurie.'

'Can I get one of our officers to collect her so we can continue?'

Saoirse shook her head. 'Fintan could be out there. With the situation with him, I warned her not to talk to any stranger. If an officer approaches, it'll terrify the poor girl and she's been through enough. In the last few weeks, she's lost her home and school, her friends and her father. If I'm not at the school gates, she'll think she's lost me too. Don't worry, I'll come back.'

'When?'

'By the time I get the bus, and then there's her homework and dinner, it will have to be in the morning.'

'What if I get Barratt to give you a lift to the school? He can bring you back and Phyllis can get Laurie set up in my office with Netflix or whatever she'd like. Phyllis can help her with her homework with the promise to bring her to the shop and let her pick out an ice cream or something? I just need to know everything, Saoirse. Because the quicker I have all the information, the quicker I can find your husband. I want you to be safe.'

'I haven't felt safe in a very long time, Vicky.'

'Then let me help you change that. Please come back and finish your story.'

Saoirse thought for a moment, then said, 'Okay.'

Chapter 42

Vicky picked up the mustard package on her desk. Phyllis was correct, the package was light and seemed only to contain something the size of a pen inside. Opening it, a rectangular object fell out. A USB. Checking the rest of the package the only other item inside was a note. Scanning the sender address, she saw it was from the solicitors, like Phyllis mentioned. She read:

In accordance with the will of Mr Alexander Hayes, we have been instructed to release this to the acting officer of Knockfarraig Garda Station in relation to our client, Mr Hayes' sudden death.

Without reading on, Vicky picked up the USB, then fired up the computer and slotted it in.

It listed over two hundred different files.

One was titled: *Open First.* She started there.

It was a video.

Alex Hayes stared right at her.

Chapter 43

It was a strange sight to witness a dead man very much alive. When Vicky built an image up of Alex, formed an opinion on how he carried himself, it was jarring somewhat to see him have his own ways, some different, some spot on to what she expected. Witnessing Alex now, brought a tuck to her throat and a heaviness to her chest.

Facing the camera, Alex sat behind a desk, so only his top section was visible. For all his beauty, the man looked tired, his blond hair flopped over one side of his face, which he kept smoothing back. And then he started talking and the case exploded.

'If the Sergeant in charge of Knockfarraig Station, which presumably still is Vicky Fitzgerald ...' He leaned forward. 'Hi, Vicky, if it's you.'

Vicky smiled, then clamped her lips. This was not a happy occasion.

Alex straightened, serious again. 'Whoever is in charge, if they are watching this now, it means I have died in ...' Alex stared at his hands, his Adam's apple moved up then down. '... suspicious, violent or sudden circumstances, then the solicitors at Brooks and Belmont have been instructed to send these files to you.'

He rubbed his upper arm as if trying to self soothe. 'I hoped never to use this. I hoped there would never be a need. But as protection for my children, as proof of what happened, of evidence of the truth, my truth, I had to keep a record. If the worst has happened and I have been murdered, I need you to know my past. I want to help you with your investigation.'

He sat back in his seat. There was no hint of spite. *Reservation*, Vicky thought.

Closing the video, she opened the next one.

The image was of a subtly lit room. Two lampshades provided the light source on either side of a couch. A woman stood in the middle of what appeared to be a living room. Most of her body took over the screen, blocking any other view, her back to the camera. Vicky couldn't make out who it was. Next, the woman bent and Vicky saw she was leaning towards a man. The woman shifted her body and Vicky could make out a face.

The man was Alex.

He sat on the edge of the sofa, his body almost curled in, as if trying to make himself smaller. Vicky turned the volume up to maximum, and a crackle sounded. A voice spoke then, saying, 'You think you're smarter than me?' The woman waved a gin bottle. Her body language was threatening, drunk, swaying back and forth. With her other hand she pointed a finger. Alex didn't answer but as the woman whose face was still obscured stepped closer, his head hung low. Then lower. The more in his face she got, the more passive he became. Despite his retreat, the woman still swung the bottle. Vicky braced even though she had seen similar instances before. Classic intimidation. All threat with no action. The woman wouldn't go through with hitting him.

The woman hit Alex with the bottle, right in the face. Then the arm. Then the hand. He folded in, held his head, his face contorting in pain. First, he cowered. Then, when she didn't stop, he tried to restrain her hands. Not once did he try to hit her or even stand. If Alex stood, he would tower her, but he didn't, not at any time. Even to a hardened sergeant like Vicky, it was shocking to watch. The woman turned around, laughing. The woman was Bernice.

In the next clip, Bernice screamed, 'I'll tell everyone you hurt me.

No one will believe you. You're not a man. You're meant to be the protector – you couldn't protect a nit.' Her hands flailed. Her hair loosened from its ponytail, stray bits sticking out in wild angles. 'I'll make sure you never get the kids.' She stumbled forward, pointed in his face. Alex flinched but didn't grab the finger. 'You wait and see. You go tell and your precious kids will end up in care with some stranger, some paedophile.'

The next video was recorded in a different room; this time it looked like a living room. To the left of the room was a sofa. Alex sat on it. The rest of the room was empty; except for a few toys on the floor, the place was tidy. The lamp at one corner of the room was turned on which suggested it was evening but there was still some daylight entering from the window so, Vicky guessed it was summer, possibly later in the evening. Alex sat with one hand cradling his head. He looked worried. There was shouting coming from the next room. Vicky turned the volume up to its maximum but still it wasn't decipherable. It got louder and then a person appeared. Bernice, bottle of wine in her hand. Holding it like a weapon, she used it like one, landing it on Alex's thigh.

There were at least twenty similar videos. Except for a change of outfit, or lighting, or a different room, they could all be the same recording. Some of the images were obscure, while some were as clear as if they were standing in front of her. A woman different from the funeral, different from the composed woman who sat in front of Vicky after Alex died. The woman in the videos was dishevelled, her hair sticking up or scraped back in a ponytail. All were undeniably Bernice, standing over Alex, with some hard object in her hand. Anything was used to hurt. A piece of Duplo held in a fist. The legs of a doll. A porcelain cup that shattered on a jaw, slicing his ear.

After that assault, Alex picked up the shards while blood dripped down his neck after Bernice stomped away. Vicky stifled a sob when

Alex kept looking at the door, for she just knew he was checking so the kids wouldn't come in and cut themselves. In another video, Bernice punched herself in the face – not once, not twice but five times. After that, Vicky understood the woman was unhinged. The look of glee on Bernice's face as she then hit Alex sent shivers down Vicky's spine.

'Tomorrow I'm going to walk the town and make sure everyone sees my face and when they ask, I'll get all feeble and by the end of the day every single person I meet will testify you're a wife beater. Your name will be shit in this town. You'll lose your job. They'll take the kids from you. You'll never see them again.'

In another clip Bernice entered the room waving a hammer. As she paced the room, the light caught the blunt edge. She slashed the air in front of Alex. He didn't move, didn't flinch, cower, or beg but Vicky caught the fear in his eyes. There was enough evidence to convict her of domestic violence on that video alone.

After the videos, there were also hundreds of pictures. Bruises to the ribs, feet, every part of the body. Split lips. Black eyes. Every single one dated and timed.

But then, at the very end, there were other videos.

There, in person, alive and facing the screen, was Alex Hayes again, this time he didn't look tired, this time he looked ready. Speaking to the camera, he said.

'Now that you've seen my worst, I want to tell my story.'

Chapter 44

A wine bottle slaps against a palm of a hand.

Avoid eye contact.

Don't aggravate.

Don't instigate.

Stay passive.

Never take your view away from those hands holding that bottle.

Voice raised.

Pacing.

Unsteady on feet.

I watch the bottle, willing it to drop to the floor.

But the anger ramps up.

The bottle swings in the air.

Then hits.

My right eye bulges instantly.

My first thought is that I won't be able to go to work tomorrow.

When it should be, will Bernice kill me this time?

Chapter 45

He was so handsome Vicky thought. His demeanour was gentle, as if he was embarrassed to film. His gestures soft. Yet he looked straight into the camera, so not a push over either, not a doormat. He looked like he had become stronger. *Then again, there was no one standing over him waving a whiskey bottle*, Vicky thought.

'You have seen my darkest secret, the thing I planned to carry to the grave. The fact you are seeing this, means death came to me quicker than I hoped.'

He rubbed at his jaw. 'Looking at the footage, I almost can't believe I'm the man in those videos. You must wonder why I didn't fight back or leave. If it was a woman, I'd say run, but I am a man. It's different for us. My wife threatened to take my children from me. This society is made in a way that the mother is favoured with custody. What chance would I have to be believed if she said I abused my family? Can you imagine what that's like? Bernice knew this, knew I would do anything for my children, knew she had total control. Because, if you stood the two of us next to each other, who were they going to believe was the abusive one? The man over six foot tall or the five foot nothing skinny woman with bruises all over her face? After she threatened to get me jailed for abuse, I decided to get evidence. I had no choice. It was my only way to escape.

'After a few times turned into many times, I looked into hidden cameras. If I'd gotten the angles right the first few times, I would have much more footage but eventually I worked out the best spots, got the mics working right. Got pretty inventive with them in the end and had them hidden in every room.

'Once I worked up the courage to watch them, it was all I needed to leave. To see it for myself was enough, there was no need to report it.'

Alex raked his fingers through his hair and sat back in the chair, looking straight at the camera. 'Before I saw the footage, my head couldn't get around it, couldn't label what it was. In day to day life, Bernice was a good person, a good mother, how could it be abuse? She told me I made her crazy, she wasn't like that with anyone else so it had to me.'

He looked down at his hands, his voice low. 'I wondered if it was me. Wives don't hit their husbands. Or like she said, it's not like she could hurt someone twice her size. But that was exactly what she was doing. She did hurt me. She did intimidate me. Once I watched the footage, it was clear it was abuse. Her size didn't matter. Threatening behaviour is threatening behaviour. A weapon is a weapon no matter who is holding it. Seeing it for what it was, for the abuse that it was, freed me right on the spot.'

Alex leant towards the camera. 'Not from the trauma, you under-stand? But it was enough to pack my bags and go. As much as I didn't want to be around my wife anymore, I didn't want to cause any more hurt for my children. So, I warned her that if she hurt a hair on their heads, I would press charges. I never told Bernice what I had on her, just implied it, Bernice was the kind that would have set fire to the lawyer's office if she needed to. If something has happened to me, my ex–wife needs investigating.

'Now that you have watched the videos, I want to add some insight. I left Bernice in 2020. On the day they announced the country would go into lockdown. Being forced to spend every day in her company, without any escape, I couldn't do it. I removed myself and the kids and stayed with my mother. Bernice was fine with it for the first few months. Working in the hospital was hectic, but having the kids near, safe away from everything, it was bliss.' His face fell.

'Until lockdown eased and people could wonder again about other people's lives. Then, Bernice wanted her children back, wanted evidence of her perfect world. There was no way I could return and there was no way the children were going to stay in her custody full time. You may question why I let her even see the children again but as crazy as it sounds, all her rage, all her anger was directed at me. After months of not seeing her in person, the kids missed her desperately and I couldn't be the one to rip their bond. After time apart, my head was clearer, I felt stronger, so I confronted Bernice. I told her we could share custody but if anything was to ever happen to me, if she ever harmed the children or tried to harm me, I would reveal all. Although at first, whenever she had them, I stayed watching the footage all day and night.

'I could have sold the house, instead, I gave it to her, making myself effectively homeless. Paying custody and a mortgage on a house you no longer live in meant there was little left to get my own place. I didn't care. It kept her in check for the most part. When I met Mel, Bernice kicked off again, changing their visit days, making them late, all manipulation tactics. None of that affected me as you might think.'

Alex grinned. 'I was free. As long as my children were happy in life, as long as she wasn't making their life miserable, I would take her games. It drove Mel mad, she couldn't understand why I was so lenient with Bernice but these videos were my reasoning.'

He straightened. 'Knowing Bernice, she must have seethed that I had something on her. Over the years she tried to wheedle it out of me. I caught so-called friends on play dates snooping in my house, where they confessed Bernice put them up to it. I never told her what I had, never confessed to any camera or recording as I'm sure she would find some way with GDPR law or something to force me to hand over the evidence. It needed to be opened by you, even if it meant I would have to die first before anyone knew it existed.'

Alex closed his eyes, and breathed deeply, then looked at the camera.

'I hope this video is sitting gathering dust in a drawer. I hope you never get to watch it and what happened to me stays hidden. If I'm dead, do what you have to do. A murderer, an abuser, shouldn't raise my children. If I can no longer be the buffer to her anger, if I can no longer watch over Kenny and Lily, then she needs to be removed from their care. I have mentioned it in a letter to my mother in my will already, but for the record, I state that I want my mother, Cassandra Hayes, to have custody of my children.'

He stroked his cheeks.

'And if there is still any doubt about whether you should take away custody, I am going to show you this last one.'

His Adam's apple moved as if he was having trouble swallowing. 'Please just know, it was the only time I witnessed anything like that between her and the children. After that I never left Bernice out of my sight. I took her anger. Because at least if I was around, I could stop her. If we had part custody, I wouldn't be able to watch what she was doing. This was why I took the abuse for so long. I waited until the kids were old enough to tell me if their mum did something to them. If you are wondering why I would allow my children to live with someone who could be that violent, you need to know I left the cameras. Another reason why I gave her the house because that way I could keep a close eye on what she was doing. Bernice was a vile wife, but it was adults she seemed to hate, not children. Still, I would not take her being calm as a given. If I am gone, I will not play the game of chance with my children.'

He wiped at his nose, visibly distressed. 'The hardest part of it all was thinking I was less of a man. I knew if I told anyone they would look at me and not believe that someone half my size could bully me, could overpower me. I hope you understand now. If I touched her, if I harmed her, I would be just as bad. She was the mother of my children, I owed her so much, and she needed help and I tried, I swear I tried. Bernice refused to go to counselling or admit she had an anger or alcohol issue. It was like being in a cocoon, trapped in a cage of my own making without a key to the locked door. I couldn't find a way out. At that time, I contemplated giving up, doing myself in but the only reason I didn't was those two kids.' His voice caught. 'I'm so proud of them. With all of Bernice's anger, they still turned out perfect.'

Vicky took a deep breath before selecting the last video.

The video was older than most of the others. In it Bernice faced the camera. Lily, a toddler, was moving across the room. Bernice shouted something indecipherable at Alex. Then she surged forwards, scooping up Lily, then flipped the child upside down, catching her by one leg, Bernice dangled Lily in the air by her feet.

Alex took a step towards the child, trying to cradle her head. Bernice swung the child like she was a doll.

'Don't, Bernice. Please,' Alex begged. 'You'll hurt her.'

Lily screamed, her face turned red from the blood pooling.

'It'll be your fault if I hurt her,' Bernie screamed.

Lily was less than two years old in the video. Vicky pictured Lily, her face set in concentration as she picked out a jigsaw, her blonde hair falling over her cheek. The same girl who held the hand of her husband's grieving wife, recognising how much Melinda needed her. The same girl who in her own words told Vicky her mother abused her father and what had Vicky done? Except from checking social services and telling Cassandra, she had ignored her. Left her stay with an abusive monster. Vicky stared as the recording paused with Lily dangling in the air, her mouth wide open in a scream. How could that woman hold that sweet child like that?

There was a knock at the door. Vicky wiped her eyes.

'Vic, Saoirse is back.'

'Thanks. Phyllis, I need you to get the other guards to meet me in the kitchen for a quick briefing in about five minutes. After that you can send Saoirse into the interview room. Just give me a moment.'

Vicky dialled Cassandra Hayes' number.

'Mrs Hayes, can you go over to Bernice's and look after Kenneth and Lily?'

'Of course. Is everything okay?'

'No. I'm about to arrest your ex-daughter in law for domestic abuse and suspicion of murder.'

Chapter 46

Still shaky from seeing the videos and giving the brief, Vicky stepped into the interview room fully prepared to postpone. Wanting to be the one to arrest Bernice, she needed to talk to Saoirse at a different stage. Saoirse sat with her back to the door, holding her phone, looking at a photograph. A recent photograph of her and Alex.

'Dammit,' Vicky muttered. She stepped back out of the room.

'Barratt, can you handle it without me? I think I need to stay talking to Saoirse to see if I can find out where the hell Fintan is.'

'But I thought we were arresting Bernice?'

Vicky tilted her jaw while thinking.

'Arrest her for domestic abuse. If we go arresting her for murder, Mara will string me up. The abuse I have definite proof about, the murder, I'm still not sure. I still need the facts.'

'You're the boss.'

'Cassandra Hayes should meet you outside the house to take custody of the children. Do not cause a scene in front of them Barratt, okay? Make sure you remove them from the house before you arrest their mother.'

'Will do.'

In the room again, she closed the door loud enough for Saoirse to hide the phone. She smiled at her when she sat.

'You happy enough to proceed? Laurie's being looked after?'

Saoirse lit up at the mention of her daughter's name. 'She won't want to leave with the amount of junk Phyllis bought her.'

Vicky went to stand. 'If there's anything you don't want her to eat, I can tell Phyllis.'

Saoirse swiped at the air. 'No, leave her. Anything that makes her smile these days is fine by me. I haven't exactly been good company after hearing about Alex.'

'Grief isn't fun. Where were we? I'm hoping you were about to tell me how you met Alex again.'

Saoirse smiled. 'I'm ready. I want to.'

'Then the floor is yours.'

'I hadn't planned to go to Cork that day. Until I heard about Mrs Arcadia's funeral. She was nice to me, Mrs Arcadia; other than Alex and Ernest, she was the only person in Knockfarraig who was kind. When we moved to Knockfarraig the first time, she was my neighbour. She had this lovely way of knowing things without saying them, you know? Like, when Mum locked me out for the night because she had company, Mrs Arcadia came over to the front of my house and asked if I could stay with her because she heard a noise and was scared to be on her own. Like I was doing her a favour. Or she always had a dinner ready for me when I came home and my mum's car wasn't there. She knew. When I came back at eighteen, Alex and I made a point of calling to her once a week for tea, on her insistence. Mrs Arcadia was the closest I came to having a mother.'

'You didn't get on with Cassandra Hayes?'

'Didn't have the chance to. Alex kept me away from the house as much as possible. His dad, remember?'

Vicky nodded.

'As soon as I heard she died, I made the decision that whatever the consequences, I had to go to the funeral. When I mentioned it to Fintan, he refused. Said he couldn't take time off from work and there was no way I was going by myself. I agonised about whether to go or not but the woman meant a great deal to me. It was the bravest act I've ever taken. And it was exhilarating, making a decision like that. I asked a work colleague to ring me with the excuse I wanted a recipe from her. When she hung up, I carried on the conversation pretending she asked me to cover her shift, making sure Fintan was in earshot.

'That day, I left at my normal time and after dropping Laurie at school, I took the train to Cork. I'd already arranged a play date for Laurie after school and aimed to return to pick her up for tea. I don't know if it was the fact that I could never lie, or that he knew me too well, or maybe he always followed me and was just good at not being caught, but whatever the reason, when I stepped out of the train station after a two-and-a-half-hour journey to Cork, Fintan was standing in the car park. My stomach, my jaw, my hope dropped. With his hand on his hips and his face puce with rage, his eyes bulging until they might burst, I knew I would be lucky to make it out of the car park alive. And I was right; he nearly killed me. What I didn't know was how my darkest moment would be my saviour.'

'How?'

'This was how I found myself being treated in the hospital. This was also how I found Alex again.'

Chapter 47

'What did he do to you?'

'Do I have to talk about it?' Her voice cracked.

'Not if you can't. Just list some injuries, so I can understand.'

'Fintan tried to kill me that day. Only that a passerby pulled him off just before he was going to stamp on my head, I don't think I would be here to tell the tale. After the third or fourth blow I think I either passed out or my brain blocked it from memory. I was told he ran after that. In physical terms, broken jaw, bruised ribs, concussion, possible brain bleed.'

Vicky took a sharp intake of breath. 'You would have been hospitalised for more than a few days with that. Was Laurie okay up in Dublin?'

Saoirse snorted. 'Fintan didn't even text to check where she was. When I woke up at the hospital and I realised so much time had passed and she wasn't there, I freaked out. But they had called my last dialled number, which luckily, was Ernest.'

'Ernest Morley?'

'The very same.'

'You kept in contact with him?'

'A yearly email at most but when he emailed me about Mrs Arcadia, he left his number saying to message if I could come. I texted him on the train to say I was on my way and would see him soon. The hospital wondering who was next of kin, saw that was my last text and rang him. Ernest came straight away. As I slept, still unconscious, Ernest travelled to Dublin and brought Laurie home to his partner who still to this day I've never met and the two of them looked after my child as if she was their own.

Saoirse wiped at her eyes. 'Can you imagine? A person who I never met showed me more compassion than my own husband? I knew I had to make an exit plan. Every pore of my body knew. Every broken bone. Every bruise knew. Mentally though, I was still weak.'

'Did Ernest tell Alex you were in the hospital?'

'Not that I know of. Ernest was always good at keeping secrets. It was one of those unique things about him. He didn't tell anyone your business. If you confided in him, if you asked him not to tell anybody, no one would ever know.'

Vicky scribbled in her notepad. 'How long did you stay in the hospital for?'

Saoirse bit down on her lip. 'Five days. Even though I woke up shortly after being admitted they kept me in for observation. At first, they treated me for a concussion, then they worried about a brain bleed because I kept feeling faint when I moved. Until I had a scan, I couldn't leave.'

Saoirse stared at the ground. Shook her head. 'You'd think I would have told them then but I said nothing. The words were stuck inside me. I was so used to holding on to the secret between us, holding on to the shame. Witnesses said they saw me get off the train and this man had just attacked me. The fear, I can't describe it, in the hospital bed, even with nurses and porters around, I kept looking at the door, in case he snuck in to finish the job. My thoughts wouldn't stop; at night he could just charge in and attack; what if he knew where Laurie was and his plan was to hurt her while I couldn't protect her? I knew I had to get away, but my brain wouldn't stop; I couldn't sleep, I couldn't rest. I don't think I've rested since the first time he hurt me.'

Vicky recognised the truth of that statement, seeing it many times in other women with similar stories.

'Why didn't you say anything? The help would have been there.'

Saoirse tilted her head, disappointed. 'Would it? Most people, even nurses want to clock in and just survive the shift. They were kind to me; they treated my symptoms but they were rushed off their feet. It's the loud troublesome patients that garner the attention and there was at least three on our ward demanding twenty-four-hour service. The other patients were lucky to get fed and medicated. Even now, I wonder why I didn't tell them in the hospital who it was that did it. In my defence, it was too big to say. It hurt to admit how stupid I'd been. Or change the life I knew when I didn't know what would happen after. It is a hard sentence to say to a stranger, a person who is sure to judge, sure to not understand. And how could I expect them to when I couldn't make sense of it myself? Also I didn't trust they could help. Fintan knew people. No matter where I had ran in the past, he'd found me. So, I stayed silent, which by omission made me a liar. Made them think the man who attacked me was a stranger, was a random, evil person and not my husband. Not the father of my child. Not the man who was meant to protect me more than anyone else in the world. If anyone had asked me outright if I knew the attacker, I would have told them. By the time I regained consciousness, they had already decided it was random. I just agreed.'

'I'm sorry they failed you.'

'No. I failed me. I just want you to understand my reasoning, not issue blame.'

'You're right, the last thing I want to do is make you feel worse. I'm sorry.'

'Okay,' Saoirse said. The two women nodded at each other.

'On the second day, a porter wheeled me down for a CT scan as I was too dizzy to walk and left me waiting with the promise to come back after.

'A waiting room is an apt name in a hospital. There was nothing else I could do but wait. Immobile, with nothing to distract me, I waited. Sat and contemplated the mess of my existence and tried to ignore the stares of the other patients around me.

'It was just a tilt of the head. A person passing on a normal day. But it was that tilt, that angle, coupled with that dip of the hip; with a swing of an arm while he walked that made me bolt up. Brought me straight back to another time, to another life, another love. The way he walked hadn't been of any importance when I thought of him. Already passed, his movements brought more clarity than being struck. *I remembered.* Without even seeing his face I knew who it was, knew him. Little details make a person significant, make them unique. Alex's walk was unique. Yet, it was the least interesting thing about him. My reaction was involuntary, my body remembered him. I felt it in my stomach. Not like a punch. More like a flip.

'Alex was in the same room again. The person I spent years wondering about, dreamed of a possibility with, who I wished I would someday see once more. Now about to disappear down the corridor. I wanted him to look back but also prayed he didn't. In that chair for a few seconds, I transported to a different life, travelled back in time. Seeing Alex was more than I ever wanted, while being my absolute nightmare.

'Because I was not ready.

'Even though I had waited the entirety of my adulthood for the day, for the chance to see him, panic crawled up my body. I looked a mess; not like the movie meeting I dreamt of, certainly no meet cute. Not like the scenes I played out when I needed to escape my unwanted life. If Alex saw me, he would see the victim I'd become, see straightaway how weak I really was. Someone braver would have called out to him.

Someone cleverer would have thought of some witty remark. All I wanted to do was hide.

'Fifteen years.

'How had I survived all that time without him? Without seeing that walk? Before he even saw me, I was his once more. Whether he wanted me or not, I was his, because in that moment I realised I always had been. Believe me when I say, that's the way I was prepared to leave it: silently in love, carrying my unrequited awe like a comfort blanket. I couldn't handle his disappointment at seeing me, all that love evaporating into ambivalence. Better to keep the memory in case it turned out as another delusion, another fact I held on to that was wrong. Better to remember it as it was; a reminder that once I understood what it was like to be loved.

'The truth was, no matter what way my appearance looked, I would never be ready. Too much time had passed. What if the momentous love I felt was only a brief affection on his part? I couldn't do it. My want, even though it spanned years, was too big to ruin. If he had told the truth when he called me beautiful all those years ago, I couldn't tarnish the image he might have held on to, couldn't let my bruises and brokenness be the fresh memory he remembered.

'So, I let him go.

'Even though I knew I would regret him walking away for the remainder of my life. I let Alex go.

'But Alex, I don't know why, stopped in his tracks.

'And then he turned around.'

Chapter 48

'As soon as I saw his face, that was it. A glimpse of Alex was enough to strengthen my resolve. It was enough to confirm I would rather die that day than live another hour without the chance to talk to him. Without the hope of it. Do you want to know what I learnt that day, Vicky?'

She waited until Vicky looked at her, until she knew she had her complete attention.

'Time means nothing. Not when it comes to love. All the worry, all the stress that he would see me at my worst, was subservient. Alex cared, of course he cared, but his delight on seeing me, I would have paid a million just to see that reaction. Just from a smile I remembered what it meant to be loved again. There was no awkwardness. It was as if life had only been on pause, waiting for the moment we could return, until we faced each other again. He sat on an empty chair beside me and instead of trying to embrace me, his face clouded on seeing my bruises. He traced his finger along my bruised jawline.

'"You're hurt, Saoirse," he whispered.

'"Alex, we have to go," his colleague called back, checking his watch.

'He held his hand out to the guy, gesturing he was coming. "Do not leave," he said to me.

'"I'm about to have a scan, I don't know whether they are sending me for other tests," I explained.

'"I'll find you. Just don't leave the hospital. I might be an hour or so but as soon as I can, I'll come. Promise me, Saoirse."

'"Alex, come on!" his colleague called again.

'He stayed, didn't even look in the colleague's direction, just sat, waiting for a response, for the right response. Looking at me with eyes I could always read without words. Even with all the missing years between us I hadn't lost the ability and he hadn't lost his openness. Now, it held a million questions. *Why did you leave? What happened to you? Who hurt you?* There was a sadness in him I understood. Saying without words, *my life since has been painful, has yours?* There was promise too, in his eagerness to talk. Maybe it was just curiosity. Maybe I was just an itch that continued driving him crazy until he scratched it, until he found out what had happened all those years ago. There was so much we needed to say to each other. So much I was afraid to say.

'In that busy hospital, in a packed waiting room, with a colleague calling a fellow nurse, I wanted to reach out and touch the skin around his eyes, touch the slight indents that creased, because they were an unknown part of Alex. One wrinkle sparked a wish to discover all that had happened in between for him too. I knew he would stay until I answered, until I promised, no matter how many times he was called, no matter if he got fired.

'"I won't leave," I promised.

'As soon as he walked away, I wanted to rewind time back and share the same space again. With Alex, I wanted to freeze every moment just to prolong it. I've never experienced anything like that with anyone else. That need to draw in the same air, to see his lips up close, to feel the static between our bodies, drawing us closer like a magnet. It was as if the years in between became seconds. All that was left was this wanting, this same love I once held tightly. How could I ever have let it go? Even after fifteen years, how could the passage of time not change me? As I waited for that scan I knew, if he came back, if he spoke to me, if he showed interest, I couldn't, I wouldn't, say no. My answer would still be the same. In regard to Alex Hayes, it would always be yes.'

Chapter 49

When Vicky's phone rang, she knew she couldn't ignore it. Excusing herself, she stepped out of the room, then answered, automatically holding the phone away from her ear. It didn't help. Vicky waited until the superintendent paused for breath.

'Once I send over the videos of Bernice, you'll understand.'

'That isn't what I'm talking about. You know how much press is on this case and there you go now stirring the pot.'

'I thought you would be happy considering it shows the case is moving forward.'

'Moving forward. Have you established any link between the man in the CCTV footage and Bernice?'

'No.'

'Well then it seems to me your direction is unfocused.'

'That's where you're wrong, Superintendent, all I do is think about this case.'

'Maybe that's where you're going wrong. Maybe, you need a break.'

'Don't you dare. You're not taking me off this. How can you punish me for having a breakthrough? I have video evidence of Bernice degrading a man who is now dead. She is on camera saying she will have him murdered. They have children together. Watch the footage and tell me you don't support removing those kids from a house where someone can be that abusive. Not only that, but right this moment I am interviewing Saoirse Thomas, the ex-girlfriend of Alex Hayes, who also happens to be the wife of Fintan Clancy.'

Mara sighed. 'Well, that's something. Send the video's over. Fitzgerald, in the future, keep me in the loop so you don't give me a heart attack next time. You've had a rough few years, you sure it isn't too much for you?'

'I can handle it, Mara. Let me prove it.'

Chapter 50

'Did Alex ever confide in you about what happened in his marriage? His first one,' Vicky asked.

Saoirse nodded. 'When we met again, there was nothing we didn't say to each other.'

'Tell me.'

'Alex kept his word. Later, when it was almost evening, I was back in the ward, in bed, trying to close my eyes, and rest the jitters that hadn't stopped since seeing him. He drew the privacy curtains, and sat on a space on the bed, then he lifted my hand to hold it. As he did, the sleeve of my top rose up, exposing bruises on my wrist. I couldn't look at him, couldn't see his wondering why I would let someone hurt me like that. Pulling away, my first reaction was to go on the defensive.

'"It wasn't all his fault," I said.

'"It never is," he replied.

'I told him, "You don't understand. I know you're thinking I'm making excuses, and I am. Because my husband wanted all of me and I could never give him that. He always said I held back, that I kept a part of myself tucked away and he was right. It drove him crazy. Made him angry that I held on to secrets, made him believe I was untrustworthy. And, as bad as it got, I still couldn't share. A part of me could only be for you."

'Alex's voice caught. "You kept a part of you for me?"

'I couldn't answer. If I took it back, it would be a lie.

'Alex's finger circled the bruise on my wrist, with the lightest touch, bringing comfort instead of pain.

'He said, "It's easier to cope if you rationalise the behaviour. If you tell, it changes how people see you, or the relationship, or him. It doesn't matter what you tell yourself, other people will see him as a monster. They'll look at his actions and baulk. But you'll always see it from a different angle. You see your faults, your actions, the triggers that provoked. If only you were calmer, didn't poke, didn't answer back, didn't try to cover up, didn't try to protect. They are complex. They are vulnerable. They need our help."

'I looked at Alex confused. "They?" I asked.

'Alex nodded. His eyes were glassy.

'I said, "You know, don't you? I mean you really know. It isn't just sympathy, is it? It's been done to you too."

'Alex wiped at his eyes. "It's not like I didn't know I couldn't hit her back. Course I knew, I also knew if I did, I would hurt her. How can you hurt the one you love?"

'It killed me to think of Alex loving another, of that person taking that love and hurting him.

His voice came out in distorted spurts as he explained. "The first time she tried to hurt me I caught her hand just as it hit the skin. That night I broke it off. Bernice wrote me this huge apology letter and promised she would never do anything like it again. She was also pregnant. We got married and then she lost the baby and her emotions were up and down but she never hurt me then. When she did it again, over a year later, she was pregnant. Before he was even born I decided I wouldn't leave Kenny. No matter what, I would stay. She knew it too, knew she had me right where she wanted me. After that she got worse. Most of the time I managed to restrain her, then the insults flew. Ignoring her only made the rage escalate. I didn't know what to do. Financially, physically, I shouldn't have been afraid to leave. But real men don't get beaten by their wives, do they? There was so much shame there, Saoirse. The mother automatically gets the child, doesn't she? When she would flip, she would hurt herself too. She'd turn her wrists towards me if they turned black and blue from where I'd tried to restrain her. She would offer them up to me and say if I went to the guards she'd show them. During one argument as I rang the guards, she headbutted the wall until her face swelled. I hung up. Who were they going to believe? I was trapped. Until then, I knew she had control issues, knew she had a drink problem, but didn't know how much she was capable of, didn't know that she would do anything in her power to make herself the victim. Over the years, she would make a comment here or there, just little remarks that shook my whole world, implying she had set the scene that I was violent. She would mention how she bumped into so and so on the street. It was the way she'd say it, saying but not saying, until it would needle at me all day. Until it would come out later after she had a drink. Then she wouldn't leave it go, saying she hinted to them she was scared, that I was difficult to live with. It made me embarrassed to look at them, Saoirse, even though it wasn't the truth, because I knew what I would think of someone if I was told the same, I knew what they must think of me. It isolated me from everyone I loved until I had no one to turn to but her. And for a long time it worked. Until I left her and all those people were fine with me. She hadn't told them anything or if she did, they hadn't believed her. Bernice managed to get into my head. She used my own fears against me. You know my history, Saoirse, know me better than anyone. You know what way my dad was. There was always this blame I carried around, of not standing up to him. I couldn't believe I married someone like him. Everyone I loved ended up hating me."

'"I didn't," I told him.

'But he said, "You left me when I needed you most, without even a goodbye. Why wouldn't I believe you hated me too?"

'"Never, I could never hate you." I started to cry. "You don't understand, I had no choice, I had to leave."

'Alex shushed me, wiped the tears away from my cheeks. "It's okay, you're okay." He smoothed my hair back exactly like he used to in another life. I closed my eyes, not wanting it to end.

'He whispered into my ear. "That's all I need. You don't have to explain why you left, we've both done enough explaining to last us a lifetime. I'm just sorry I couldn't help you then, I'm sorry I didn't get to say sorry for the way I acted that night. All you've been through, it's too much. That type of life is exhausting and the way out narrows each time they hurt you and you give them another chance until it disappears. It can feel so closed in, claustrophobic, that type of life, but I found a way to get out, and if you want, I can help."

'"I am nothing like the girl you once knew," I said.

'"Do you know what I learned after I left Bernice?" he asked.

'I looked away, afraid to hear it.

'But he continued, "I am in charge. No one gets to decide what I should do. Same for you, Saoirse. You are in charge of your life. No one gets to tell you how to live. Or how to act. They can try. They can threaten you if you deviate from it. They can batter you into submission. But they are still not in charge. They cannot control what you don't allow. You have to allow it. When you take responsibility, it is both upsetting and freeing. But you carry that shame anyway, don't you, Saoirse? It's part of it, the feeling complicit, feeling like you play a part in the abuse. You think if you can only stop annoying him then you can fix the relationship. It will never happen. He will tell you he only acts that way with you, like you have magical powers that force him to lose control. When you know, for sure, you are the only one in control of your life, that every single person has control of their own decisions, then you are free from the contract of blame he made you sign. You are not accountable for his actions. Just step away. You do not need to change him or convince him. Remove yourself from the situation. You can stop it today. Stop it right now. You will not be alone. Until you step away from the relationship, from the house that surrounds you, from the cage you have locked, you are clouded. You have to leave. Only when you remove the possibility of abuse, when you take away the threat of it happening again, can you heal."

Saoirse sniffed, then met Vicky's eyes. 'I wish I listened to him. I wish I discharged myself that very moment and ran to a safe house. I wish I pressed charges because Fintan might have been in prison and wouldn't have been free to murder Alex.

'Over the years, I kept having a repetitive dream. It was of Alex and it was always the same. He sat on a wall overlooking a beach, the sun beating down. In a white linen shirt and khaki shorts, he turned and when he saw me, he smiled, with no surprise at all. As if he was waiting for me to turn up. And he had; he had been waiting for me all along. In the dream, I ran to him and said, "We wasted so many years, Alex." He smoothed back my hair and said, "But we still have forever."

'That dream got me through every beating. Every insult. Every putdown. Each time Fintan pulled me by the hair across the floor or spat in my face or kicked me while calling me useless, I kept Alex's dream words in my brain. Because of that dream there was always hope. Because someone somewhere, at one time at least, thought I was worth loving. Someone, somewhere, loved me and told me it would be forever. If I still meant my promise, which I did, then maybe he did too. Maybe someone, somewhere still loved me. And then we met and it was more than I could ever have imagined. It was bigger and better than my best dream. His love held a mirror to what I had allowed Fintan to do and like being under water, I broke the surface or waved away from the fog surrounding me. Reminded once more of what love should look like, should feel like, I changed, regained that strength I forgot I had. All the shit I put up with couldn't be taken anymore. I left Fintan. I finally made the step. Finally decided I would not allow him to hurt me anymore. And then Alex died and all hope of forever disappeared.'

Chapter 51

'Was Alex's plan to hurt Fintan?'

Saoirse looked shocked. 'No, nothing like that. Alex could never have confronted Fintan, he wasn't wired that way. If he'd tried, Fintan would have ripped him apart.'

'What happened?'

'Alex suggested I report him. I told him I was afraid they would take Laurie from me. What if they said I was an unfit mother? What if they ruled she needed to go into care. Alex understood, he suggested I document the injuries, to start with the truth of how I ended up in the hospital. I agreed, promised I would do it after his shift finished. And I meant it. An hour later Fintan showed up holding Laurie's hand. Ernest followed, raising his voice, saying he was sorry, that Fintan intercepted them as they walked in and if he wanted me to call the nurses or security he would.'

Saoirse gasped, struggling to take in a breath. 'Vicky, he held on to her so tight. He said all the right dutiful husband things. I didn't believe any of them. I just looked at Laurie. Her eyes wide with fear, asking me without words, *did my father hurt you?*

'I couldn't break her heart. I wasn't ready to admit to her what her father was capable of. Because I didn't believe I had the strength yet. If I'd had another few days to talk to Alex, maybe I would.

'Getting no immediate accusations, Fintan thought it was the same as all the other times. He could have won an Oscar for his role as the concerned husband. No big flowers or gestures. Just him, holding on to our daughter, while the tears ran down his face. Had all the nurses on side with this big story about searching for me for the last few days. He already knew he was safe, you see? When he acted like he didn't know what had happened and they told him a stranger attacked me, he knew then he had an opportunity to still get me to go home. He didn't promise the world. Because manipulation isn't as effective with huge statements, better if it chips away at you with small gestures. When Laurie went to the bathroom, and Ernest told me he would give us some space, Fintan swore he would get help, he would go to AA, something he refused to go to in the past.'

'You wanted to believe it?'

Saoirse shook her head. 'Once I saw Alex, I couldn't fool myself anymore. Fintan couldn't change, no matter what he promised. But I needed time. To get Laurie to safety, to find information on where to move, to gain strength.'

Vicky welcomed the lull in the conversation, wanting to gather her thoughts.

'Do you believe in coincidences, Saoirse?'

'No.'

'Yeah, I don't either. That's why it's bothered me that this attack was so random. Now, I'm here faced with the knowledge that your husband happened to bump cars with Alex. That the love of your life completely by accident bumped into him. Yet here was Alex knowing how this man was violent to you. Are you telling me he wouldn't have threatened him?'

'I never showed Alex a picture of Fintan.'

'He must have seen him at the hospital?'

'No, Alex was on shift when Fintan came in. I knew what time he was finished and made sure Fintan had taken Laurie to a hotel well before.'

'Come on now. Social media makes it easy to see every relation you have in four seconds tops.'

'Fintan doesn't post on social media. He's a prison officer, it's not safe to have pictures of him or his family on there. Too many prisoners holding a grudge can find out where you live. And knowing Fintan he probably made enough enemies there.'

'Which prison?'

'Mountjoy, it's why we lived in Dublin.'

Vicky scribbled a note to contact them as soon as she finished up with Saoirse.

'How did Alex take it when you told him you wouldn't leave?'

'He didn't show any surprise at all. It was like he expected me to change my mind. He held my hand and said to me, that this time I would know I wasn't alone. And then, he gave me another alternative. Cameras. He told me it gave him his power back, how, even though he never showed them to another soul, it gave him the strength to leave. He said when he watched some of them back, it was like looking at a stranger.'

'Did you install them?'

'Alex bought the cameras, showed me in the hospital how to set them up, all I had to do was position them. I was terrified Fintan was going to spot them in the house but they were tiny. One camera was a teddy bear I positioned on a toy shelf for Laurie.'

'Do you still have the footage?'

'Alex set it up that they automatically saved to my drive, so yes.'

A rush of blood rose up to Vicky's cheeks. 'That is important information. Can I see them now? See if your husband is at home?'

'You won't find anything on it. The last one is of Fintan as he wrecked the house on the day I left. He must have smashed the cameras. You can look though, no problem.'

'Are they on your phone?'

Leaning down, Saoirse scooped up her bag and fished around inside. Taking out her phone she tapped at it a couple of times then handed it over to Vicky. There were line after line of entries. Vicky selected the last one. At first she thought the man was Alex. The blond hair the same. When his face appeared, the men were nothing alike. It was Fintan, pulling a TV from the wall, then tearing down bookshelves until the camera turned blank. Vicky selected the one dated before. It showed a frantic Saoirse grabbing a number of items and running from the room. Not before Vicky caught a glimpse of Saoirse's face. One eye was completely closed, the skin swollen and purple. Blood oozed from her split lip.

'I'm sorry that happened to you.'

Saoirse sucked in a breath. 'Alex was right. As soon as I watched the first one back, I knew none of it was my fault. It was like stepping out of my own body and watching someone mistreat a stranger. I wanted to scream at the screen and tell him to leave me alone. I felt so sorry for the girl he was hurting.'

Vicky cleared her throat.

'I knew Alex. Although I was five years older, I remember him in school. When he started secondary, I was going into my Leaving Cert year. That day, I was nervous as hell, because I was asked to address the school at an assembly welcoming the new students. When I spoke, my voice quivered and I thought about running off the stage. I was about to when I looked down and there, dead centre, sat Alex. He gave me a nod of encouragement, like he was interested in what I had to say. His calmness calmed me. As if sensing my fear, he smiled. With no words at all I knew he understood how terrifying it must be to get up there. A smile telling me not to worry. All without words. All from a look.'

Saoirse laughed. 'That was Alex.'

'It blew my mind how a first year student could have his shit together like that. Over the years I kept track of him, like I do all the residents of Knockfarraig. With ye, it was obvious ye were the real deal, with Bernice, I always thought she was cold, that he could do better. I spoke to him only once in the years that followed and it was in a professional sense for a DV incident. An altercation between him and Bernice. It was shocking at the time for the guy I built up in my head would never have been violent. Bernice was drunk when I entered the house. Swaying and slurring, she fumed that he had made the phone call. He told me he rang to calm her that was all. There were no bruises, no scratches, no red marks on Bernice. Four long scratch marks ran the length of his neck but when I pressed him on it, he insisted he must have made the marks himself. The next day I returned to check if either of them wanted to make a statement but a very hungover Bernice replaced the venting one from the night before, insisting she was just drunk. That night, before I left, I said to Alex, women can hurt men too.

'"What can you do." He said it as a statement rather than a question.

'I knew what he meant. If it was a woman in an abusive situation, I could set up an escape. Give him details of a refuge. Move the kids with a police escort. There was no domestic refuge for a man. No judge would automatically offer him custody. He couldn't kick the mother of his children out of the house he paid for, couldn't make his wife homeless. I knew all this in his silence.

'I told Alex, "Accusations come very easy to someone who needs to lie. Evidence is the key to when there are two versions of a story. Protect yourself. There are cameras you can get now online that are the size of a thimble. They download straight to your camera. If I were someone tired of a situation, I would put things in place that would ensure my kids could never come to harm. Do you understand what I am saying?" I said.

'I remember Alex's kindness, Saoirse. I remember the scared look he gave me when we had that conversation. I should have followed it up, should have called to him again to check on him but a few months later, through the grapevine, I heard they split up. Throughout the stories I'm being told, I carry my own version of Alex. And now I understand it was me who gave him the idea for you both to stay in an abusive marriage and record it.'

Saoirse checked her watch. 'It's getting late, Vicky. I'll have to get Laurie to bed.'

'Can we continue tomorrow?'

Saoirse nodded.

Chapter 52

Anytime Vicky's thoughts were stuck, she got moving. Walking, she found, led to ideas. Vicky didn't know if it was the backdrop of sand and sea or breathing in the salty air, or the wind whipping at her hair or simply the action of putting one foot in front of the other, but some part of it changed her energy.

Whatever it was, Vicky knew she needed to get out. Being in the stagnant room in the station for too long had made her skin crawl. She took a deep breath, in through her nose and out through her mouth. That horizon stretched out beyond Knockfarraig beach never got old. Today the sea was calm but Vicky had been around the town long enough to know the other side of the sea's temper.

Tempers. There was plenty to think about. From the sound of it, Bernice and Fintan were one and the same. No wonder Alex and Saoirse reconnected. Forget about the bond they had at seven and then eighteen, in later life they were kindred spirits.

What are my instincts?

Vicky stopped.

The Saoirse and Alex she knew were decent people. Kind. It sounded like they had it rough for a long time. Could two decent people have concocted a plan to kill Fintan? Did it backfire?

She closed her eyes. Took in another refreshing salty breath. Did it matter if they did?

I need to know the truth.

Without knowing why, she trudged down to the beach, a feat in full garda uniform on a sunny evening. Vicky often got hunches, often got feelings to go in one direction or the other. It caused her problems with the superintendent as she couldn't explain them usually, but she never doubted them, never went against what she felt compelled to do, even if she had to suffer the consequences afterwards.

The only hunch she had to go on was the fact that other than the streets, one section of the woods, although dense, opened out on to beach. The only part without CCTV.

Even though it was nearly dinnertime, Irish people know you have to take advantage of a sunny day because another one like it is never guaranteed. The beach was still packed with sun towels and sunbathers, picnic hampers and people sitting on beach chairs sipping on cans, with many of their shoulders showing signs of sunburn. Vicky wiped the sweat off her forehead and salivated over a child's ice lolly. Noticing the lifeguard station, she decided this was her port of call. Basically, a little hut, with enough room for a chair and little desk, maybe a fridge. Terry Ivers was slumped on the lone seat, his sunglasses hiding whether he was watching the surf or fast asleep.

'Hey, Terry.'

The way he sat up made her think he was definitely snoozing. She frowned at the thought.

'Hi, Vic, I mean Sergeant.'

The guy was about twenty. He looked sheepish, which in itself wasn't anything unusual. *Probably has some weed in his bag and is worried I'll sniff it out,* she thought.

'Do you know if there was any unusual activity on June fourth, like someone running away, looking panicked?'

Terry thought. 'June fourth? Don't know who was on that day. We have a log book though; I can check it.'

He sloped off the chair and there, sure enough, open on the table was a log book. Trailing back a few pages, he tapped the book.

'Only thing out of the ordinary was they found some clothes that evening.'

Vicky's skin prickled. 'What type of clothes?'

'Patricia Rice logged it. Says here it was weird 'cos the beach was completely empty. The clothes were folded pure neat. Hoodie, jeans with shoes on top. No towel, no bag either. Says here she reported it.'

Vicky tilted her head, a sign for Terry to continue talking.

'We're taught to call it in to ye in case a body washes up or someone calls the guards saying a relative was missing.'

She would have to check the station's log book later. Bloody Phyllis or Barratt.

'Did she describe the items in the book?'

'No. But they're here. In the lost and found, I'd say. Hold on.'

Terry shuffled under the desk and popped back up holding a small box. Lifting the lid, he showed Vicky the contents.

'Bingo,' she whispered.

Fintan's clothes almost winked at her.

Chapter 53

Vicky played the CCTV footage again, this time with no interest in watching anything but Saoirse.

As the SUV appeared, Saoirse pointed at the screen. 'That's Fintan's car. By the way he's driving, he was in a temper, he always speeds when he's angry.'

The car stopped.

'Is that Alex in the car behind?'

Vicky nodded.

Alex's car bumped into the SUV.

'Fintan gave the driver behind no chance to stop. I know what you said about not believing in coincidences, but Knockfarraig is a small town, and they were both rushing in the one direction. Alex never knew what Fintan's car looked like. As far as Alex was concerned, we left my husband in Dublin without leaving a trail; there was no reason to believe he would travel to Knockfarraig.'

Saoirse quietened down when Fintan got out. Covered her mouth when she saw him pull Alex from his car.

'Stop it a moment. Rewind it back to the bit when you can see Fintan's face.'

Vicky did as instructed.

'See there. There's no recognition. Anger yes, but like I said, from the way he drove he was angry, anyway.'

Vicky played it again. This time Saoirse didn't say anymore; she watched the rest in silence, even when Vicky forwarded the footage to the part where Fintan drove off in his car.

Saoirse's hand shook when she smoothed a strand of hair back. 'It's my fault. If Alex didn't help me, he wouldn't have died.'

'You can't say that.'

'I can. Look at it. There is only one reason Fintan was in Knockfarraig, only one person he was angry with. He was looking for me. I know my husband and from that footage, I believe he had no clue who Alex was, because if he did, he wouldn't have given Alex a chance to run into that building. Witnesses didn't scare Fintan, he proved that when he attacked me at the train station. If he lost his temper, he didn't think of the consequences. If he had known Alex was an ex-boyfriend who helped me escape, Fintan would have stabbed him right there on the street.'

'Could he have spotted Alex in an old picture, or did you keep a diary? He trashed your place, could Fintan have found anything that led him to Alex?'

Saoirse thought for a second, then shook her head.

'Nothing would lead to Alex. I never told Fintan about him. Not even in the early days, when it seemed nothing I could do would annoy him or when we shared stories from our past. There was something in him I recognised even then, I think, that he might hold a jealous streak. When it came to anything about Alex, I stayed silent. Alex was my sacred story. A part of my life I had no wish to share.'

'Do you think Alex recognised him?'

Saoirse wiped at her face. 'I don't know. Maybe. No matter what way it was, I killed him. My husband killed Alex. It was my fault. Fintan killed Alex because he was angry with me.'

'Being angry with someone doesn't mean it's that person's fault.'

'Tell that to Alex's urn.'

'What would usually happen after Fintan hurt you?'

'What do you mean?'

'How would he act?'

'He'd go quiet. Or disappear. Sometimes for long enough that it would get to the stage where I would put aside what he'd done to me and worry about what he would do to himself.'

'Like self-harm?'

Saoirse nodded.

'He never did. For days, even weeks, he could ignore me until either I started a conversation, or he would come in from work and begin talking to me as if nothing had happened. When he did talk, there was never an apology. If I showed any hostility, he would turn it, making out like I was starting trouble and the silent treatment would start all over again. Or worse.'

'A life guard found the clothes your husband wore on the beach. Inside the pocket was his car keys. His passport was in his car door, not even hidden.'

'No,' Saoirse whispered. Her surprise seemed genuine. 'Do you think he went into the water?'

'I don't know. We haven't found a body, but that doesn't mean he didn't.'

Saoirse grasped the chair. 'This whole time I've been thinking he's out there, waiting to attack. But I swear, that day, this calm feeling came over me at the shelter, and I thought, he's gone, he won't hurt me any longer. This was before I found out about Alex. Before I found out my husband was involved and now you're telling me he might be dead too?'

She buried her face in her hands, and her body shook from sobbing. Vicky took some tissues from a box.

'Here,' she said, handing some to Saoirse, who took them with a grateful smile.

'You're probably wondering why I'm even crying for him.'

'No. He was your husband. Relationships are complex. Even in domestic violence situations it's hard to turn off your feelings.'

Saoirse blew her nose. 'All the things I've said point to him being an ogre. But Fintan could be kind and generous and extremely loving. Months would pass, years at one stage, where he was a model husband.'

'Because he changed, or you changed?'

Saoirse's mouth gaped open. 'When you say it like that, I did, I changed. I did everything I could not to anger him. He hated himself, I think. It was why he lashed out. Why he felt he had to hurt me or threaten me to stay.'

'Would Fintan be capable of killing Alex?'

'Capable? Yes.'

She shifted in her chair. 'As violent as he was, I don't know if he could live with himself if he murdered someone. And even if he could, there's no way as a prison officer he'd be prepared to go to jail and mix with the same prisoners he used to order around. He told me one time when I tried to ring the guards he'd do himself in before he'd end up in prison.'

Vicky scribbled some notes.

'The first time he hit me, I left. There were no scars that time, no swollen eyes or burst lips. No child either. When someone hits you, no matter what they say, no matter how hard they try to convince you, or how many promises they swear by, there is never one time, only a first time. Until that night I hadn't understood how dependent on him I was. I lived in a new town. With no friends or family. I had made this big thing of running off with him, I couldn't tell my mother I had failed.

'With thirty euros in the bank, I couldn't even afford a night's stay in the hotel nearby. There was nowhere to go. Instead, I wandered the streets, afraid if I stayed still, if I sat anywhere or rested for even a few minutes, someone would spot me, target me. Even though we lived in a rural area, it was still Dublin at night; not a place you want to be alone. With my heartbeat pulsing in my throat, I had never been more scared. Since then, I've learnt, there are many types of fear. You can be as terrified inside your own home as on the streets in the middle of the night. You can feel just as unsafe.

'Back then, I still thought there was a chance he'd change. He didn't try to ring. Didn't try to win me back. This made me question if my version of events were right. If he was the person in the wrong, surely he would try to get me to forgive him? Disgustingly, this made me want him back. Made me want to fix things between us. If he wasn't running after me, begging for my forgiveness, there must be an element of blame on my part. I hated my excuses. I hated how weak I was, loving a man capable of hurting me. When I found out I was pregnant, I cried. Because a part of me always imagined the father of my children would be Alex. It meant being tied to Fintan for the rest of my life. Before that day, I could just leave. After discovering I was pregnant, it would never be easy to leave him again.

'On one of the check-up visits at the maternity hospital, the midwife asked me to follow her alone to a room with an open door to take my bloods. The midwife asked if everything was okay at home. My eyes went to the open door. Through the wall I could picture Fintan sitting there, checking his watch, wondering why he couldn't come in, wondering why I was taking so long. How could I answer honestly when, if he strained, he could hear the conversation? I wondered about that exchange for years. If she had only asked me without him being in earshot, or if she had acted like she actually cared rather than just going through an obligatory box that needed to be ticked, maybe I would have told the truth, maybe she would have handed me the number with a safe place to stay. Maybe I could have shielded Laurie. Maybe my life would be very different.

'After Laurie was born, a newborn left me too exhausted to make any life-changing decisions. I swore I would never let him hurt her. He warned me he would kill us both if I ever tried to take her away, and I believed him. Leaving my daughter with him wasn't an option. Returning to work after maternity leave wasn't either. Childcare was not affordable with my earnings. Giving up work brought the control to another level. Fintan rarely gave me any money. If I asked, he would stay silent, until I went over and above explaining what I needed it for. It killed me to have to beg. Not working meant I had no money of my own and it became another level of control.'

Vicky handed her another tissue. Saoirse blew her nose but didn't cry.

'People wonder why a woman stays in an abusive relationship. It is so slow. Little by little you settle for less and less. You question your own opinion. They point out all your flaws. They magnify all the traits you hate about yourself. Gradually, continually, they scoop away bits of you, until you wake up and don't know what your beliefs are anymore, you don't know what love means, what safety means, what marriage means, and the first thing that crosses your mind is how much easier it would be to end it all. Until you see the only piece of relief, the only light, the only reason you will live sleeping next to you. Laurie kept me alive, Vicky. And the possibility that one day I might see Alex again.'

'No friends or someone to confide in?'

Saoirse shook her head. 'No one knew me and Fintan made sure it stayed that way. Out in the middle of nowhere, totally isolated. Even when Laurie started school, Fintan got me fired from every job I worked at.'

'What would he do?'

'Turn up accusing them of flirting or whatever else he could think of. Every time. Potential friends from the other mothers at school or work lost interest when I kept cancelling nights out or left them in the lurch at work, not knowing Fintan either locked me in the house or left bruises I couldn't go out in public with. He never hit me in front of Laurie. He didn't need to hit me. For the threat was there. Once I knew the possibility, once I knew what Fintan was capable of, I always kept a check on my behaviour. Never let go, never spoke out of line. No matter how hard I tried, I couldn't keep his temper at bay.'

Saoirse shook her head.

'How do men who hurt women know the exact limits of their love and stop a millimetre short? Is there some secret manual distributed around to these men when they come of age? Chapter one, how to gaslight. Chapter two, how to keep your wife from leaving. Three, how to give your wife just enough love to stop them running away. Four, how to spin their head so they spend their whole life blaming themselves. And I did plenty of that. If I'd been quieter, meeker, less confrontational. If I hadn't looked at him funny or sneered or did that thing with my mouth. Or breathed that way. Or, or, or, or. None of it changed anything.'

'Nothing would have Saoirse.'

'People don't understand when a woman doesn't leave. They say being homeless or begging for money would be better than putting up with that. They can never understand. You see a bird singing in the tree, flying from branch to bush to ground. That is the bird's life; it's all it has ever known. Capture that bird and shove it in a cage they will fly at the bars, gnaw on them, flap their wings. At first. If you cover the cage with a sheet, if you restrict food and water, if you don't talk to it for hours, the bird will go quiet, eerily so, to the point you will need to check if it is still alive. Do that often enough, repeat that treatment consistently and you will weaken the bird until you can open the cage door and it won't even notice. Then you can leave the door open all day and night, and it will never try to fly away. Because the bird remembers what you can do, what you can take away. The bird will only think about the punishment, not the freedom. Until the bird can't remember what it feels like to fly. Until it forgets it even has wings.'

Chapter 54

'Did you and Alex enter into a relationship again?'

'If you are asking if I was unfaithful, then mentally, absolutely. Physically, that's different.'

'Saoirse, it's important for this case that I know. If you and Alex had an affair and Fintan found out, that would definitely give a motive.'

'Affair? There was no affair. Both of us couldn't do that to Melinda. We couldn't start a relationship together out of lies. We had to both be free. Even if I had cheated, the person I was cheating with was Fintan, you understand? Alex came first. Alex was first. Once I remembered what it felt like to be loved by Alex, even if it meant Fintan would kill me, I would rather die.'

'So, you're saying the relationship wasn't physical despite how attracted you were?'

'Alex helped me. Once he knew what I was going through he supported me. Alex didn't push, or hound me to leave Fintan, he just planted little seeds every day. Fed me information. Gave me the confidence to believe I could leave. Vicky, these things will be hard for his wife to hear. I don't want her getting unnecessarily hurt.'

'Unnecessarily?'

'If we hurt her when he was alive, at least there was a reason. Now the only outcome is he is gone. If I tell you everything, it will be on record. Can we not just let her believe he still loved her? Sorry, that isn't right. Alex did still love her.'

'Alex still loved Melinda?'

'Yes.'

'But he was planning to leave her?'

'Remember I told you about Jessica, the girl he broke up with when I came back to Knockfarraig when I was eighteen? That's who Alex was. He would never have started another physical relationship while in one already.'

Vicky nodded. 'Understood.'

'Which was why he told me the night before he died, just before he left me at the shelter, that he was going to ask Melinda for a divorce.'

Chapter 55

Phyllis knocked on the door, then opened it carrying two steaming cups.

'Oh you're a lifesaver.'

Phyllis left the room leaving the door open but before Vicky could close it, the woman entered again with a plate of biscuits. 'Can't have ye collapsing with hunger now.'

Vicky shoved one in her mouth. 'Thanks, Phyllis.'

Once the door was shut and Saoirse had nibbled on a biscuit, Vicky carried on.

'Will you tell me about the day before Alex died?'

Saoirse sipped her coffee. 'Fintan flipped over an electricity bill. He told me we had to restrict our use, when I asked how, he attacked. After he left, as I lay on the floor, staring at the ceiling, I thought, *enough*. Then I rang Alex. He got straight into his car and drove as soon as I sent him the address. When he rang to say he was outside, I panicked. What if Fintan was waiting and found him in our house? He would kill both of us.

'It was hard to stand. From breaking a rib before, I knew it was at the very least bruised. I tried to ignore Alex looking over the broken glass, the hole in the wall, the perfect fit for Fintan's fist. He sat me on the couch and looked me over. "Do we need to go to the hospital?"

'I said, "Later. First, I have to go. I can't stay any longer, Alex."

'He smiled as if he was waiting for that sentence. "Good girl."

'"I'm sorry to ask this of you," I told him.

'He replied, "I was waiting for the day you would. Where's Laurie?"

'I explained she was at school. Fintan was waiting for me after I dropped her off. I thought he was at work.

'Alex asked me if I packed an exit bag, like he suggested. I covered my face with my hands, then asked him where could I even go.'

'"Come to mine. Stay with me," he said.

'I touched the band on his wedding finger. "I can't do that; you know I can't."

'He said he'd explain things to Melinda.

'The name was like a scratch to the face, or a kick in my bruised ribs. I couldn't even imagine how much it would hurt to see them together.

'I told him, "You don't know Fintan. Taking Laurie, his child, will tip him over the edge. If he finds out I've left him to live with an ex-boyfriend, it won't matter that your wife is there, he'll kill all of us."

'"You cannot stay. I won't let you," Alex kept on.

'My finger still touched the ring. I dropped my hand, let skin rest on skin. "It's better for everyone if I go to a refuge."

'Within minutes, Alex arranged a shelter. As we pulled up outside Laurie's school, before he left to go inside, he took my hand and kissed a welt on my fingers.

'He said, "I'm going to make this right."

'But I had to ask, "Right for who, Alex? Does your wife even know you're here with me?"

'As soon as the words were out, I regretted it. Alex recoiled.

'I apologised, "I'm sorry, that's unfair. You're being a friend and I'm taking it out on you. It's just, I don't know what we're doing here, Alex?"

'He looked in pain when he said, "No matter what I do next, someone will suffer. All I know is that it won't be you, you've done enough suffering for a lifetime. Mel will get hurt; I know that now. I crossed that line the day I saw you again in the hospital. You have my heart, Saoirse, you always have. Forever, remember?" he promised.

'"Forever," I said.

'Then he went inside the school and asked if the principal could come out and talk. Once she saw my bruises, she understood. The principal already knew the procedure, she explained the shelter would contact her, that I wasn't to worry about filling in paperwork about relocating. Her kindness, her familiarity with those issues brought the tears close. When they brought Laurie out, I felt such relief, I nearly dropped to my knees because I knew we were on the last hurdle to safety. Nearly there. Poor Laurie, my heart went out to her, she didn't know what was going on. Imagine meeting this fella for the first time and there he is moving her away from her father and everything she knew. She didn't react like I thought she would. Even though I was bashed up, she was chatty and cracking jokes, but as I was sitting in the back with her like Alex suggested, she grabbed my hand and squeezed it. Not in a way that said I'm scared, more like you did it. My daughter was ready to leave before her mum was. In Cork, Alex stayed with us until they were ready to move us. The shelter won't allow any men inside. While we waited, Laurie fell asleep on the chair next to me, with her head on my lap, and Alex's hand held mine.

'In the shelter, I huddled in the single bed with Laurie cuddled into me. The blanket was scratchy against my chin. A woman sobbed through the wall. It was pitch dark, with noises of the night surrounding me from every direction. I didn't cry, for I believed there were no more tears left. That night, what I felt was hope, like I was taking my life back.

'Out loud, I said. "I'm in charge. I control my life."

'And because Alex told me it was true, I believed it. You know what scares me the most, Vicky?'

'What?'

'If Alex knew he was about to die. What if he sacrificed himself? For me.'

Vicky stayed silent. Waited for Saoirse to continue.

'Alex saw my bruises, he knew from what I told him how much of a hothead Fintan was. If Alex knew what Fintan looked like, did he say something so he'd lose his temper? What if Alex made sure my husband could never bother me again? What if Alex died on purpose to save me?'

'There's no proof any of that is true. Don't beat yourself up about what might have been.'

Saoirse opened the button on her shirt pocket that sat by her heart. She handed Vicky a folded piece of paper.

'He left me this, the night he dropped me at the shelter.'

It was a letter.

When I first met you, you knew the true meaning of love. You knew how to allow love in. You knew how to give it freely – without being afraid to hurt. Remember these things always.

Remember what you always knew.

Remember how much I love you, even when we can't be together.

Vicky took a picture of the note then handed it back.

'You said before there was no way Fintan could know what Alex looked like but I saw yesterday a picture of Alex on your phone. Are you sure Fintan didn't see it?'

'He couldn't have. We took it that night, as we waited for the shelter to tell us they were ready.'

She scrolled through the phone and showed Vicky the picture. Saoirse's eye was swollen but her and Alex smiled at the camera.

'He wanted to document my new start. He said whenever I got scared, I was to take out the picture to remind me of how brave I am. When he was leaving he said to me, "It has to get harder before it can get better." His last words to me were, "Remember I love you, no matter what." Vicky, I think he was saying goodbye.'

Chapter 56

Vicky sat at the desk with her head in her hands.

'Job done. The kids are safe with Cassandra. Bernice has been interviewed and charged with DV. She's already been released on bail and is in District court bright and early tomorrow. What's up? I thought that would help you crack a smile at least?' Barratt asked.

'I have no case.'

'That's not true. There's lots of leads. If Bernice was capable of beating up her husband, murder is only one step away.'

'So, what are you saying? Bernice hired Fintan Clancy, a prison officer who just happened to travel to the town where his wife was hiding?'

'Stranger things have happened.'

'No offence, Barratt, but you don't know what you're talking about.'

'How's that now?' He stepped closer into the room, folding his arms.

'Times running out. All I have is one jealous wife, one abusive one and an ex-lover whose husband is the murder suspect.'

'That's something, no?'

'What have we got?'

'The car.'

'A car with no one in it.'

Barratt dabbed at the air. 'We have a murder weapon.'

'We do have a murder weapon. But no murderer to charge. Fintan has disappeared. We have his passport so travel shouldn't be easy. Not one sighting. Not one bank transaction. The prison said he hasn't been in contact since two nights before Alex died. Fintan's parents and sister insist they've had no contact, and even if he did turn up they said they would turn him away. Same with his work colleagues. They all say there has been no contact.'

'There's motive?'

'According to Saoirse, there's no way Fintan knew Alex. It's too coincidental.'

'Do you think she's lying?'

Vicky sighed. 'No. That's the thing. She seems to be telling the truth. Something isn't sitting right at all. What am I missing here, Barratt?'

'I don't know.'

Vicky rubbed at her face with rough strokes. 'Christ, why am I asking you?'

'Why aren't you asking me? That's you all over, Vicky, thinking you're above us all. Each one of us are losing sleep over this case. It's not just you out there trying to figure it out.'

'Yeah, but it's only my neck on the line if it gets screwed up. You'll go back to Ballinroe, and I'll get fired.'

Barratt stayed silent.

'I can't fail him. Alex deserves justice. Since I came on this case, I've messed up. Those women distracted me with their stories. I haven't paid attention to the little details. And then there's you.'

Barratt shifted. 'What about me?'

'Because of our history, I got distracted.'

'I distracted you?'

'Sort of. Instead of thinking clearly, you set me off kilter.'

Barratt smiled. 'Do you like me, is that what you're saying?'

'Get over yourself, Barratt. That's not what I'm saying at all. You being around has made me forget questions.'

'So, it's my fault?'

'No.' She gritted her teeth. 'Just proof I'm better off working alone.'

Chapter 57

The house was too quiet. Like being able to hear the dripping of the bathroom tap from upstairs, quiet. Melinda had never coped with silence. Alex had changed that, shown her how to sit in her own company, how to make peace with her thoughts. Shown her she was actually an okay person. Alex had changed a lot of things. Now that he was gone, none of the ways seemed to work anymore. She was coming undone.

In every decision, she was stuck. Not wanting silence, but she couldn't bear to hear some voice from the TV, even as background noise either. Music was the same; some sad tune would only make her feel worse, something cheerful would only remind of happy times that were no longer hers. It must be the shock. The constant shake of her hands would one day go, or the way she kept coming back alert to a room, not through waking, rather from zoning out, was part of the process. Protection, she supposed, for a brain couldn't cope with that amount of grief. Grieving was such a small word for the experience. She pined for Alex. Craved him. Longed. Missed. Wanted. Ached. Mourned. If you added them all up, then the magnitude meant *something*, yet the words still didn't tip the surface of what she felt. She knew she should move, get something to eat, get dressed, brush her hair, but it all seemed pointless. If you asked her how long she had sat in the one spot, she couldn't answer. It felt like she had always sat on that couch.

Days, weeks, months: it was all the same. Time only mattered when you had somewhere you wanted to go, someone to spend moments with. Nothing awaited her. So she sat.

The only thing that animated her thoughts was the rage that came when she thought of Saoirse. She kept seeing the woman inside the crematorium. The way she had smoothed her hair behind her ear, shy, as if embarrassed to be standing in her company. And so she should. Why was she there if it wasn't untoward? Her love for Alex showed in every line on her face, in the fear in her eyes, in the wobble of her lips.

When Sergeant Fitzgerald had mentioned the woman's name, had there been a hint of a smirk? Did Vicky think she had Melinda summed up? The guard could think she was the jealous wife all she wanted, as long as she followed up on who Saoirse was. And she *was* jealous; she knew that and why wouldn't she be? Her worst fears had come true, for she had lost Alex.

She wished she could take back all the accusations, all the nights she forced Alex to explain where he was or what he was doing, but you can't erase time, only waste it. She had wasted those nights. Instead of picking at him, why hadn't she taken him to bed, wrapped her legs around him and just held him there? That's what she missed. The fresh sensation of loss flowed through her blood, chilling her body. It made her want to vomit. Made her want to give up.

It might be different if she had friends in Knockfarraig that were her own and not an appendage of Alex's. It was too hard to meet them now, for they were all reminders of time spent with him.

When Alex asked if she wanted to move to Ireland, she packed up without a thought or glance behind at the friends she was leaving. Now, the years that passed meant she couldn't exactly ring them up again. How would it look? 'Hi Diane, how are you? I know I didn't bother to call you before, but you'll never guess what happened to my husband?'

No, that wouldn't be happening at all.

Diane would be fine with her if she did; she was a good friend back in the day. It was more than that. Melinda was not ready to talk about her husband in the past tense. She was not ready to explain what happened or the circumstances that meant she was alone.

She closed her eyes and tried to settle her breathing. The sadness was unbearable. Rage was much better. She took out her computer and typed in one name and scrolled.

Saoirse Thomas did not want to be found. Hidden away from social media for sure. No Saoirse going by that name matched the profile of the woman at the crematorium. Who was she? Not knowing made it worse. Not knowing meant Alex was automatically guilty when he probably, knowing Alex, wasn't.

She wished he was with her.

Because Alex understood her insecurities and he never got mad, no matter how much she did. No matter how much she raged, he waited and reassured after calming her down. Most of the times she wouldn't even have to say it, wouldn't even have to bring forth her accusations, for he would know. He would look at her and say, with a tilt of his head. 'Who is the woman you're worrying about now? He would make her laugh about it. His transparency reassured. His transparency evaporated with his death and left only doubts. Left only anger.

Melinda didn't know who she was anymore. The woman she had been, the possibilities for what she could do in the future, had all changed overnight with his death. Mainly, she admitted, the possibility of having children. With Alex, it had been certain she wouldn't get pregnant. There was no way Alex was having more children. Before Alex, having children had always been on her list of things she wanted from life, she had felt that ticking clock like every other woman approaching her forties. Alex having two children, softened the thought of not giving birth. Being around the kids filled the want in her, and she convinced herself it would always be enough. Honest to God, it would have been. But now they were gone. Alex was gone. And with it, any chance of motherly duties. What would she do, though? The thought of being with another man was a non-starter. Adoption? Wouldn't every committee believe she was just trying to fill a gap, a huge, Alexless hole? She was, of course, she was. Maybe she needed to get a dog.

She picked up a pen and notebook from the side table. She headed it:

All the things I can do now that I couldn't when I was married to Alex.

Then she wrote:

Have a baby.

Travel the world

Take a teaching job

Buy a place out in France or Spain and hold art retreats there.

Her pen hovered over the page. Four massive sentences. Every one of them would've been impossible when Alex was alive. Not that he wouldn't have supported her. The baby wasn't an option – he had a vasectomy at Bernice's insistence. The travelling the world and or moving to Spain wasn't either because he would never leave the children and she would never have asked him.

The doorbell rang. By the time she scraped together the energy to move from the chair and make herself look decent enough to face the caller, the delivery guy was gone and only a box remained. Addressed to her, she tried to remember if she ordered anything recently. It was heavy.

She placed it on the table and paced. Would the hospital post his belongings from his locker? She didn't think they'd be that heartless, but you never knew, did you? Not ready for that type of closure, she peered closer at the box, trying to determine if she could gather anything from the postage label. Stamped from the UK, relief flushed over her.

'Just open it, Melinda,' she said.

The package contained canvases, paintbrushes, palettes of water-colour and gouache, and acrylic paints that she wondered about trying but wouldn't splurge. When she saw the name on the invoice she slumped onto the kitchen floor; her back up against the cabinets. The tile ice-cold against the back of her thighs.

Alex bought them for her.

On the day he died, Alex had thought about her. There was a gift note enclosed. It said:

I keep seeing you pick up your paintbrushes and place them down again. You used to get lost in your art and it was beautiful to watch. This is your sign to start again.

Love Alex

And because it was Alex telling her, without a tear dropping, she walked to her studio with the contents of the package. Dumping the items onto the desk, Melinda tore the plastic from one canvas. Before she had time to think, she opened out the paints and squeezed the first tube straight on. Grabbing a paintbrush, she stabbed at the blob of colour, then slapped at the canvas with strokes left and right. Before she knew it, she was screeching at the piece, her chest heaving, she couldn't see the canvas through her tears. Selecting another paint, she emptied it onto the canvas and discarding the small paintbrush, she laid her palm right in the middle of the mass of paint. She smeared, smushing the paint into every corner. Messing it and smoothing with no care to make the piece pretty.

Here's your paints, Alex. I'm doing what you want.

She found the black and blobbed some into the middle and, with the side of her hand she rubbed it in a circle. Round and round and round until she was in danger of tearing the canvas or giving herself a friction burn. She sat back, gasping for breath. She admitted, for a moment, there was some release, some relief.

Covered in paint, she left the room, needing to get out of there to settle her breath. Upstairs she paced, shook out her paint-smeared hands, then lay on the bed. There, she jittered. She could not stay still. Jumping from the bed, she took the stairs two at a time.

The canvas leant against the desk just as she left it. It made her catch her breath. Grief on cloth.

'All that it is missing is a little hope.'

She selected white from the packet and painted little squares at the outer edges. Rummaging in another palette, she found a gold. On the very edge of the white, she painted the thinnest line. She stood back, thought for a minute, then approached the canvas again, paintbrush in hand.

This was what saved Melinda Hayes.

Chapter 58

People thought of art as escapism, or a way to freedom. As random strokes, that evoked emotions. When others pictured artists, they imagined someone wearing floaty fabrics, free and one with nature. Definitely not Melinda. There were many mediums she liked to work with but in recent years, discarded scraps of paper or fabric or plastic were her favourite. Flowers were her speciality. Even though she could create landscapes, portraits, animals, and scenes, the subject she came back to were flowers. She structured and meticulously planned the layering of paper or fabric. It was not freeing at all. Time consuming too, for one flower could take a day to construct. And the hand control, the precision, would cause an impatient person to throw the piece across the floor. Which was exactly what drew her to such work. It gave her control when the world wouldn't comply. The structure was not loose yet the act loosened her. It took layers upon layers to finish a flower. If she were lucky, it would take up an inch of canvas. Over the years, she had worked on those flowers, stockpiling numerous pieces but hadn't completed any to the point of being satisfied to show them to anyone but Alex. Now the worst had happened, getting a piece perfect didn't matter so much, allowing her the space to see each piece objectively, to recognise what had been missing. Correcting and adding, she had declared three previous works as finished in as many days. Since the delivery of the paints, she had become obsessed again with her work.

Returning to paint had been a revelation.

Spending hours in the art supply store, Melinda bought canvases in various sizes, some as large as a wall. Colour washing first, colouring the canvas meant more than just removing the cream background. It was the basis. The setting. The intention of what the piece would become. It was the most exciting part. Before disappointment that one section wasn't exact or questioning whether she should add more in or the sadness that came from finishing a piece.

She settled on a new blue, a colour from the set Alex bought. A sea-green colour, more turquoise, for it was unlike any sea-green seen in Atlantic waters. That sea-green was dark, a threatening of coiling seaweed underneath. Not the type of sea-green this palette promised. There wasn't an inch of seaweed near this type of sea-green. Melinda closed her eyes. Tried to imagine being in a place where the water was clear and the sand shone through. Waking up in a sea hut in the Maldives, her bare feet hanging over the wooden slats, dipping her toe in the water. One day she would see it for herself, she hoped.

Before Alex died, she went through a stage of creating art installations from recycled fabrics. Sounded simple, but that's not how anyone would describe them if she allowed them to see. Because of her use of fabrics, she was always interested in scraps. On days when creativity was at a standstill, she had rummaged in charity shops, or haberdashery's, looking for inspiration. Sometimes it was the colour that drew her, sometimes the way it felt against her fingers. Sometimes the pattern. If it resembled a skin or bristles of hair or the softness of a lip. Melinda never knew until she laid eyes on it, or until she touched the fabric. One room for her art was her only requirement to moving in with Alex. She sat in that room now. Alone with her many fabrics. She felt sorry for the woman who once sat there, full of a future, finally reassured. Melinda wanted to go back in time and leave her a note, to tell her to go, to leave before Alex broke her heart, to run before she discovered there would never be a happy ending with him. That her worst fear, him leaving, would come true. That the promise he made her to stay until they were both grey never happened. The scraps mocked her now. The canvas was huge, the size of a large wall. Only half done. One half as blank as the day it came home. The other half peaked out from the edge, a half-formed woman, one leg bent as if stepping out of the picture. One side of hair cascading down her shoulder. There was only one eye, only half a lip. Left as it was it could be a self-portrait. It would be an apt depiction for she felt half formed. Melinda sat and stared and decided she didn't want to finish it. She didn't want to add bits of fabric to the canvas when she couldn't do the same to her soul. She held back the tears, for they helped no one.

What would help her was figuring out who the woman was at the crematorium. Not who, for she knew she was Saoirse Thomas. The real question was whether she had rekindled with Alex before he died. Why had he never mentioned her if he didn't have anything to hide? He had confided about his ex-wife, so why had he kept his history with his ex-girlfriend a secret? An ex-girlfriend whose husband, according to the phone call from Vicky, might have been angry enough to murder her husband.

She wanted to believe nothing happened, that Alex had always stayed true, but she couldn't turn back a lifetime of believing men cheat and hurt the women who cared for them.

Surely, if he loved Saoirse, he would have kept keepsakes, some record of his love. Where though?

In the spare bedroom they both used as an office, she combed through every drawer, placing pieces of paper on top of each other in little neat files on the top of the desk. Tax items. Medical documents. She almost congratulated herself for how calm she was being. Her shaking hands told otherwise. With each page placed on top, she gained a little more faith in her husband. With the last piece, she sat back in his chair with a thud. Instead of satisfaction, the feeling she was missing something grew stronger.

If her husband truly didn't want her to find something, he could have left any belongings in Cassandra's. Should she call around? The very thought of it was enough for her to jump out of the chair and run straight to the kitchen. If she was going anywhere near her mother-in-law, she'd need wine. Apart from the one visit in the hospital the day of the funeral, and the will reading, Melinda hadn't seen Cassandra at all. Whose fault was that? Maybe the woman was feeling as upset about Melinda's absence as she was. It was just unbearable. Whenever she met Cassandra, Alex was beside her. To do it alone would mean accepting his death. Accepting he wouldn't be coming back to either of them.

As the wine glugged in the glass, she thought about Cassandra's move to a smaller house a few years earlier. Hadn't Alex mentioned he needed to collect all his belongings, as anything that wasn't taken would go in a skip. He had rushed over there that day, saying his mother didn't joke about those kinds of things, and spent two days there sorting it out.

The first sip of wine lined her throat with ice cold silkiness. It hit her stomach within seconds.

'I really must eat,' she said, wondering when she did last.

Grabbing a packet of cheese crackers, she nibbled and sipped, nibbled and sipped, almost in some kind of dream state. Day dreaming but focused, squeezing through her memories of that time.

Alex came home late that night. His hands full with three black bin bags. He dumped them on the floor in front of her, saying,

'Wait until you see some of the gear in this. Pour us a drink, put some music on and be prepared for a trip back in time, baby.'

She remembered jumping up, ignited by his enthusiasm, running out to the kitchen to get the wine. She heard the door close, but instead of returning to the sitting room, Alex took the stairs. Like a wolf, her hackles rose. For in his hands was a box. A long boot box.

That was what she needed to find.

That night when Alex came down, he was in such good spirits she hadn't wanted to ruin the moment. Hadn't wanted to go down the road of thinking the worst about this man who had shown her nothing but love. She chose for once to believe him and now here she was, needing to find that very box as if her life depended on it.

'Up the stairs I go,' she said, carrying the glass of wine with her. By the stairs, she turned back to the kitchen, grabbing the wine bottle from the counter.

'This could take a while,' she said.

Their bedroom gave no enlightenment. The bathroom was a no goer. Never one for clutter, which was surprising for the stereotype of an artist, Melinda liked to keep her colour for her canvases, her walls and rooms she liked to keep blank and clean looking. Under the bed in the spare room, she found some boxes, but none of them turned out to be *the* box. She sat on the bed and sipped.

Maybe she only imagined the box. Or maybe Alex burned the contents. Or maybe he just changed the box.

'If I wanted to hide something, where would I put you?'

She got up and checked Alex's underwear drawer, already knowing it was too small to hold the box she'd seen.

She had asked the wrong question. It wasn't about where she would hide a box. The question was, where would Alex?

If Alex wanted to make sure Melinda never found the contents of the box, where would he put it?

She looked above. 'Dammit, Alex, you know how much I hate spiders.'

Melinda took another sip. 'To the attic I go.'

Chapter 59

Melinda pulled down the attic stairs and, with tentative steps, ascended. Pausing at the top, she stared into the blackness. It was as dark as night. She didn't even know if there was a light switch in there; that was how much she avoided the attic. Turning on the torch on her phone, she moved it from side to side. There, dangling on a beam, was a light bulb with a cord long enough to plug in the socket in the hall below. A spider had made its home around it, spreading it's web out to the wall. That was usually enough to make her quit. Taking a breath, she closed her eyes.

It's just a spiderweb.

Sucking it up, she grabbed the plug, nearly losing her balance after touching that cotton wool feel of the web. She stepped back down and plugged it in. Light poured from the hole in the ceiling. Chest heaving, she took another sip as a reward for her bravery. Then up she went again. Just before the inside of the attic came into view, she took a gulp of breath. She didn't know why or how, but she just knew what she was going to find in there would change her life. Still though, even with this hunch, Melinda Hayes could not be prepared for what she would find. And when she saw it, when it came into sight, she missed a rung of the ladder.

Chapter 60

Holding tightly to the top saved Melinda from falling. She didn't move again until her breath steadied. Didn't look until she was confident she wouldn't faint. There, on the back wall of the attic, were a thousand faces of the same woman at Alex's funeral.

Saoirse Thomas was above her the whole time.

Stepping up, spiders forgotten, she was at least grateful that Alex had taken the time to floor the attic, saying he needed to do it so he could insulate the walls. Impressed with his handiness, now, she saw there had been another reason. She shivered. Both from the shock and the breeze that brushed her skin. A bird chirped from the roof, close to her head, the sound travelling through some gap in the beams. It echoed in the room with no windows.

There was a seat in the corner. Feeling like her legs could go from under her, she sat and stared at the wall. Apart from the huge amount of photos and drawings, there was also a map of Ireland. On it were red crosses nearly on every section. Underneath there was a notepad. Melinda stood and flicked through it.

May 10th

Joe and Christine's wedding in Killarney. Told Mel I was going for a walk while she was getting ready. Drove to Killorglin. Shopkeeper hadn't heard of her.

There were hundreds of entries, all with one or two sentences naming a town and where he had checked.

In the middle of the wall of faces of Saoirse, there was another picture. In it, two children, roughly eight years old, about Lily's age, held hands. The boy was definitely Alex; she recognised him from other photographs. Was the other girl Saoirse? She leaned in closer. There were familiarities to the woman she saw at the crematorium. What made her certain was the way the girl tilted her head to the side, the hair tucked behind her ear. Undeniable.

Alex and Saoirse, both uninterested in the camera, with only eyes for each other. Even at eight years of age.

'It was always her,' Melinda said, slumping to the ground.

Chapter 61

Saoirse sat on the floor, hugging her knees while trying to settle her breath. With Laurie in school, she was free to let the sadness go. It took all her strength to keep it together when she was around. Losing him this time, she didn't know if there was a way back from it. Of all the bad things that had happened throughout her life, Alex dying hadn't been an option. If he could have lived, she would have suffered every instance again, continuously, simultaneously. Her skin was raw from crying. She didn't want to stand up ever again. She didn't want to continue. But she had to, for Laurie because she couldn't just die on the floor of the women's shelter. How would she cope?

Think of a happier time. Think of something that will get you through.

All her happy times had Alex running through them.

Well then think of Alex then.

She closed her eyes, feeling the air dry her wet skin. Settled on an image of Alex, only eighteen years old, looking at her, smiling. All the old feelings came back, how that night she had felt the anger rise in her. The want inside mixed with the fear of getting hurt, the acting brave just to call him out, to confront him on whatever it was between them, naming what it was, trying to label it before they went too far and couldn't retreat.

'Alex, I don't do one nights. I do forever. And if you can't handle that, if you can't go into this wondering the same then get out of my way because

you're only wasting my time.'

An inch from her face. His breath tickled her nose. 'Forever, Saoirse. I'm in.'

And he had meant it, she knew this now. Even though a lifetime had been lived without him, with more time apart than with each other, the forever part had not been doubted. When they saw each other again, the years had melted like crayons on a pavement on a hot day, leaving a mess but colouring the street at the same time.

She remembered what he had said to her one time in the hospital. *When someone wants to control you, they take away your joy. They make you miserable. Because when you are chronically miserable, you get tired and when you get tired you have no energy to fight back. Lethargy allows the controller to thrive. Exhaustion allows the controller to get exactly what they want.*

She had to find the energy to survive this. For Laurie's sake.

And even though every pore, every cell in her body urged her to lie down, wanted her to crack open and cry and grieve for the man that she lost, not once but over and over, there was a little hope present too. Because the way forward was wide. It was open. Not closed off like it had been for years. Not limited or controlled. She was rudderless. But she was also free.

Alex's death hadn't freed her. Leaving Fintan hadn't either. Because there had still been the threat, there had still been the psychological hold her husband coiled tightly around her. Knowing he might have gone into the water didn't abate that. It was the conversation with Vicky that lightened the tight pressure in his chest.

Speaking about the abuse began with Alex in the hospital and had deepened over the weeks in between. When she stepped into the shelter, she had opened her mouth with shock at how much all the women there shared in common, how similar the patterns of abuse were. That started the healing. But it was speaking with Vicky about what that man had done, about what he did in Alex's house, even though she never uttered the actual words, the dispelling of it out into the air, the not denying, the silence in itself an admittance about what that man, what Alex's father did to her dislodged something inside. Since that night, her greatest fear had been Alex finding out. Bigger even, had been the thought of having to relive it by speaking of it.

Yet stepping beyond that fear had set her free.

For the first time in fifteen years, she saw her life clearly. As if a cloud of blackness, a hazy confusion that clouded her days had lifted. All those years she had wondered why she put up with Fintan's abuse, believing there must have been some fault in her that sought his treatment out, she understood now although the patterns had been laid throughout her childhood, the acceptance of what she would allow him to do, all led back to that night.

That night she hadn't done anything wrong.

Yet she chose to carry the shame of it for the rest of her days. She chose to pack up her bags and walk away from the biggest, truest love of her life. Seeing Alex, being around Alex had healed the woman who took all of Fintan's anger. Admitting to Vicky, acknowledging that night had changed her whole perspective, healed that young adult she had still carried inside. She shouldn't have let that man break them. She should have given Alex more credit. Because he loved her, and they could have got through anything.

And now he was gone. And there was no other chance. And somehow, she would have to find a way to live on.

Chapter 62

Melinda rubbed her hand across her legs. The stubble had grown longer than she had ever allowed, she recoiled in horror at the prickly sensation. All her adult life, since probably thirteen years old, she had never allowed it to exist. This was what his death had done to her; she had let herself go. And then, she thought, so what? Is it the worst thing to happen? Who was she doing it for, anyway? Alex wasn't shallow. He would have loved her whether she shaved or the hair grew long enough to plait. It was her. It was her hangups that dominated her life.

No more. Let it grow.

It wasn't that she wasn't good enough. She just picked the wrong men. The ones who hurt people, the ones who needed to hurt people to feel good about themselves, the ones who twisted stories and her mind, the ones that could see her fears of not being good enough and took advantage, and then when she thought she had finally got it right, she went and picked someone who loved someone else.

Alex was never hers; she understood that now.

He had loved her, that she was certain of. What she hadn't known was his love was only on loan.

The right man never leaves, she thought. It was only the ones that were wrong for you that did. She spent her life believing all men leave, but a man can't leave if he isn't yours. He wasn't hers. Alex could never have been hers when he already belonged to Saoirse.

She scraped out some modelling paste, worked it until pliable. Separated it into different sections. Then added different shades. Indigo first, next robin-egg blue, added white to another, then meadow-green. Without thinking about it first, she dabbed at the page. Adding random colours that to an untrained eye would seem random, but Melinda's hands worked viscerally. She didn't stop until Alex's face formed on the canvas. A multicoloured work of skin and hair but still, somehow, she captured who he was. The blue for hair, the yellow for skin, they all made up the essence of her husband. They were Alex. She sat on the floor with her back to the wall and cried.

After her weeping settled, she walked towards the installation propped up against the wall. The abandoned canvas stared with its one eye. Each time she tried to work on it since Alex died, each piece of fabric felt wrong. No material could do the piece justice. Yet she wanted to touch it, wanted to add something.

Melinda walked over to the new acrylics and watercolours. Then, instead of using fabric, she painted the other eye, the other leg, the rest of the body. The paint bled into the canvas and she liked that, liked how it looked because it was a good depiction of grief. It nailed the coiled-up tension on one side, the letting go on the other.

When she finally stepped back, Melinda recognised she had created a mirror image of what was happening inside her.

It was the best piece she had ever made.

Chapter 63

When in doubt, sound it out. Any time she was stuck, Vicky would read from her notes, then stick anything significant up on the wall. What she'd found in the past was it loosened the bind, and an idea got through.

Start at the start, she thought.

She ran through the times. Looked at the pictures she took of the scene inside the derelict building. There were no prints. Nothing to tie Fintan there. She flipped through her notes, settling on Mara's instruction: *Check ambulance.*

Opening the door, she shouted, 'Barratt!'

'What?' he shouted back from the kitchen.

'Dammit,' she said under her breath, then walked towards the canteen. Barratt was chomping on a doorstop sandwich that was threatening to give him lockjaw.

'The ambulance. Did they say why it took so long?'

'There was a crash on the link. Seven car pile-up, if I remember right. Even an ambulance couldn't get through. Ernest Morley started his shift early when they called it out on the radio looking for someone local.'

'What do you mean? Ernest Morley volunteered, as a stand-in paramedic?'

Barratt screwed up his face. 'Ernest Morley *is* a paramedic.'

'No, he's not. He's a dog groomer. Ever see the van with the big fluffy dog on the side?'

'Everyone's seen that van. Must be a side job, Vic, 'cos he's definitely a paramedic.'

She ran out of the kitchen and back to the board. Picked up her notebook and rifled through it until Ernest Morley's name appeared on a page. Not once in their interview did he mention he was the paramedic on the scene.

'Why would he not say anything?'

'What is it?' Barratt appeared at the door, panting with a dollop of mayonnaise on his lip.

'He never once mentioned to me that he was with Alex, his best friend when he died. Don't you think that's suspect?'

Barratt shrugged. 'Maybe he thought you knew. Like I did.'

Vicky pinched one of her eyebrows. 'But how could I know when you never mentioned it, did you? When I asked you to walk me through every piece, every occurrence, when we went through the facts of the day, you kept mentioning, the paramedic arrived, the paramedic performed, you never said, the paramedic was Alex's best friend!'

Barratt wagged his head. 'I was trying to sound professional. There's a standard with you, Vic, you can be intimidating.'

'Really?' She walked closer to him. 'There's not much I ask for except every bit of information you have. This is why I didn't want to work with you, you miss details, vital details like searching for a car that none of ye found either by the way, and now we are weeks into the case and I'm only discovering this now. What else have you missed, Barratt? What else have you fucked up?'

'I didn't ask for this case, Fitzgerald. Remember that?'

'Nobody wants a murder case, Barratt. But when it comes, you make sure you record every detail. You certainly don't omit important facts.'

'All you had to do was ask.'

Check ambulance.

He was right. She should have asked. As much as he should have told her, Vicky just assumed. Oh, Mara was going to eat this up.

'Did you at least interview him? Did you take notes?' She held her hand out looking for his notebook.

Barratt clenched his teeth. 'I didn't, Vic. He was a mess. Babbling about his friend being gone and he had to save him, even though the man was dead. I told him we could go through the details another day. When you called him in, I thought you were asking him about what happened. I didn't realise.'

'Leave me,' she said.

Barratt saluted her and she knew before his footsteps stopped he was going straight back to devour his sandwich, with no regret at all.

She sat with a thud. Barratt might be correct that Ernest presumed she knew he was on the scene but not mentioning anything about it in the interview didn't sit right.

She flicked through her notes. According to Saoirse, Ernest met Fintan in the hospital. If this was the case, why hadn't he recognised the man when she showed him the picture?

She dialled Ernest's number. It went straight to voicemail.

'Ernest, I need to speak to you.'

Chapter 64

Sitting opposite Vicky, Ernest didn't look one bit nervous. Thinner and tired but not one trace of fear. Vicky took a few deep breaths to settle herself. She didn't want him to see how much she was seething.

'You didn't think to make me aware that you were the paramedic on the scene?'

'I made the Garda present aware of the connection, made the hospital staff know too, and the morgue. In fact, anyone who asked me I told, couldn't shut up about it, I was blabbing from the shock. Garda Barratt should recall. I didn't think you were unaware. If I did, I would have told you.'

'Surely you must have realised when you came on the scene and found your friend dying that it was a conflict of interest?'

'Vic, I mean Sergeant Fitzgerald, how long have you worked in Knockfarraig? Five years at least, right?'

'More or less.'

'Well then, I'm sure you have come across most of the residents of the town. If you stopped someone at a red light, could you excuse yourself for a conflict of interest?'

'Speeding isn't the same as a murder inquiry.'

'No, it isn't. But when I responded to the call and found Alex, it wasn't a murder inquiry either. And I did everything in my power to stop it from turning into one. Instinct kicked in, not protocol. Knowing how long it takes to get an ambulance from Knockfarraig to CUH and then the journey back, I wasn't going to make him wait for another ambulance. You've been there, Vicky, where your heart is beating, the adrenaline pumping as you wait for an ambulance to arrive. You know all too well how much every second counts. And even if it gets there fast, even if you can get through the tunnel and all the traffic at lightning speed, it's still a twenty-minute drive at minimum. When you work in life and death situations, you know the difference five minutes can make. No one would want to save my friend more than me, I can assure you of that.'

'Why didn't you say anything when I interviewed you?'

'I just answered the questions you asked me, Vic.'

Dammit, she thought. This was why she couldn't trust anybody to help her with an investigation. It wasn't Barratt's fault. He had done his job to the exact requirements, but he didn't know the ins and outs of the town. He didn't know the people or didn't think to cross reference anything. She had messed up and would spend the rest of the night reading through every piece of information to find out if she missed anything else.

'In the report, it stated that you actually accompanied Alex from the ambulance to the morgue. Is this normal?'

'No. It wouldn't be normal procedure. But finding your friend in violent circumstances and him dying in the back of your ambulance isn't either.'

'Did you see anything unusual when you got there?'

'At first I didn't recognise him; his face was so messed up. Once I did though, I think I blanked out, even now I don't even remember much of it. It was like my whole body went into shock. If it wasn't for my training kicking in, I would have frozen on the spot.'

'Why stay with him in the morgue?'

'The pathologist was going to take a few hours to get there. So I asked them to do me a favour and let me just sit with my friend until she arrived. I've worked in the hospital since I was twenty-two. I didn't want him to be alone, Vic. They understood.'

'Who let you?'

'I'd rather not say. It's a fireable offense.'

'I wouldn't tell the hospital.'

'Oh, they'd find out.'

'I don't have to take any notes, just from you to me.'

Ernest clenched his jaw. Vicky waited.

'Paul, the manager of the morgue, is a close friend.'

'I just can't understand why you didn't mention any of this before.'

'It's not that deep, Vic. I assumed you knew. My head is gone, I don't know my left from right, after I found my friend lying on a floor and then watched him die, then spoke at his funeral. How am I supposed to remember to tell you my name, let alone that I was there?'

'Seems a pretty big thing to omit.'

'See that notebook you carry everywhere? Or that backpack? I thought you already had all that information at your disposal. You never miss a trick; it was a fair assumption that you and that other guard would tell each other everything. When you interviewed me, I thought you had dismissed the information or didn't feel the need to bring it up. And I was glad you didn't because I didn't want to talk about him dying. At all.'

'Did you see Fintan that day?'

'By the time I arrived in the ambulance, his car was gone. There were people outside, don't get me wrong, but I didn't notice anyone that matched his description.'

'Anyone help?'

'A woman made the call as far as I know but I don't think any of them approached.'

'When you realised it was Alex, what happened?'

'As soon as I walked in, before I recognised it was Alex, I knew the person was in big trouble.'

'How?'

'The fact that he wasn't responding. Low pulse, the stab wound was just by the heart, I knew it was urgent.'

Ernest lifted his head, looked her straight in the eye. 'I couldn't stop him from dying. Believe me, I didn't want Alex to die.'

'You never told me you knew Fintan.'

'Because I didn't know there was a link.'

'When I showed you the image of him, you didn't say a word.'

'Because I didn't recognise the man. At all. The image you showed me was blurry. When they released the clearer picture I rang the station and gave them his name.'

'You rang the station about Fintan Clancy?'

'Yes. I told them I knew it was him. Told Garda Ryan I think he was called, that he hurt his wife Saoirse enough to put her in the hospital.'

Derek hadn't realised the link. She pinched the bridge of her nose.

'Is there anything else you're hiding from me?'

'I haven't hid anything. It's all there in front of you, Vic.'

'What do you think happened, Ernest?'

'Fintan attacked Alex, no doubt about it. It's right there on the tape, Vic.'

Chapter 65

They had sat in silence on the drive up to the city. Vicky was in a pig of a mood and the last thing she needed was to make small talk with Barratt. Sitting across from Mara now in his office, she knew it wasn't looking good.

'Let's sum this up, will we? CCTV shows the altercation between a man and Alex Hayes, who ran into the derelict building. His wife, Saoirse, has confirmed the man is Fintan Clancy. No one else goes in, no one else watches the interaction. Next bit of footage is of Fintan getting back in the car and driving off. Records confirm the car is registered to the suspect. Car was located, eventually ...' Mara threw a dirty look at Barratt. 'Found hidden under shrubbery. The murder weapon was inside. DNA came back that the fingerprints on the knife match the fingerprints on Fintan's wallet, which was found along with his phone and passport in the car. Fintan's wife confirmed clothes, car keys and shoes discovered on the beach were his. No activity on the bank account whatsoever since the day before the murder. Coupled with the video evidence of his abuse of Saoirse, and the link between her and Alex – with him helping her locate a woman's refuge – is enough to label it motive. Although a body hasn't turned up yet, we assume it is a case of murder, then suicide.'

'Mara.'

Mara held up a finger. His face was almost purple. 'Don't give me your conspiracy theories, Fitzgerald. You had us running around in circles chasing angles of hitmen and domestic abuse and jealous wives.'

'I had to pursue every angle, Superintendent, you're the one always saying I shouldn't assume anything.'

'And I also tell you when to give it up, Fitzgerald.'

'So, that's it?'

'The papers have lost interest, trial by news has decided Fintan Clancy killed his wife's ex-boyfriend and then killed himself. Since they have it all summed up, they've gone on to another story and my blood pressure thanks them for it. There are no other leads.'

He held his finger up again in warning to Vicky's open, ready-to-speak mouth.

'No matter what you want to argue, there are no other avenues to pursue. Officially, we are still classing him as a suspect, but for now, unless Fintan Clancy shows up on the system, the case is closed.'

'Can I just tie up a few areas first?'

'Fitzgerald, you and Barratt will write up paperwork on this for months. Tie it up and kill the case. It's done. There's a whole town that needs you to carry on.'

'Something's not right.'

'Like what?'

'I don't know.'

Mara crossed his arms, sat back and regarded her. 'Do you know how many times I've heard that sentence from you?'

Vicky pinched the bridge of her nose, a headache brewing. 'A few, I'm sure.'

'At least five times, Fitzgerald. This job, as the years go by, it makes us cynical. There's always a case that can get under the skin, but with you, it's every case. All we can do in this line of work is our best. We unpick the lies from facts and hope the truth will reveal itself. Don't let the job take over your life. Let this one go.'

Chapter 66

Melinda held out flowers as the door opened. Cassandra took the offering and smiled.

'My favourite.'

'Can I come in?'

'Course you can, Mel. Come on and I'll put these in water. Tea or coffee?'

Melinda dangled the bottle of wine in her other hand. 'I think this conversation calls for something stronger.'

Cassandra laughed. 'I'll get some glasses.'

Out in the garden, the women sat across from each other, the half-full glasses resting on coasters on a white, metal table, still untouched.

'I'm just going to get straight to it. Why didn't you ever mention Saoirse?'

Cassandra rocked back.

'Why exactly would I divulge information about my son's ex-girlfriend to his wife? Some would accuse that of being cruel. Especially someone recovering from jealous episodes.'

Melinda's jaw slackened. She took a sip of wine to counteract her shock.

Cassandra narrowed her eyes. 'What? You think Alex wouldn't have told me? There's very little Alex didn't confide in me. With you though he didn't have to, I saw your worst moments for myself.'

'Do you think I killed him?'

Cassandra tilted her head. 'At first I wondered. You had the possibility. Anger is a very bumpy emotion. Rationality goes out the window. I feared something had set you off.'

'Like?'

'Like nothing. It was just an assumption based on past altercations. I wondered if something made you jealous, if something had set you over the edge. Made you hire someone or put someone up to it.'

Melinda's eyes welled. Cassandra placed a hand on her arm.

'I don't think you killed him, Melinda. When Sergeant Fitzgerald interviewed me in the hospital I suspected you, but those first few days, after the heart attack, I was trying to make sense of it and you were the first in the firing line. I know you loved him deeply. And he loved you, no matter how much you doubt it.'

Melinda wiped at dry eyes, eager to stop them before they even thought about spilling. 'Thank you for saying that.'

'Well, I figure, if we both love Alex even a little, we should honour his memory by trying to get on.'

'I'd like that.'

The two women took a sip of their wine simultaneously, their arms resting closer to each other.

Melinda dared to put into words what she came to ask. 'Do you think Alex met with Saoirse recently?'

Cassandra pursed her lips. 'Ah, that. I was hoping we could skip over her.'

'Why?'

'Because knowing what I do about you, I don't think it will be good for your mental health.'

'Do you think they were having an affair?'

'No.'

'Then what? Alex had a past before me, I knew that. What happened between them?'

'Saoirse ran away. Alex needed an explanation.'

'They ended abruptly?'

'You could say that. They had what he called a stupid argument and the next day when he went to apologise, her house was empty, Saoirse and her mother had just upped and left. He never saw her again.'

'Poor Alex.'

'After she left, my Alex turned into a shell, became bitter. Drank. Got angry. His father died around the same time, so we couldn't talk about it like I would have liked. There was too much going on with arranging a funeral, but I could see he gave up. After we buried his father, he clammed up, wouldn't talk to me at all, wouldn't even allow me to mention Saoirse's name. What followed was a few lost months and then he got with Bernice and before I could say get away from that woman, she was pregnant.'

'Saoirse broke his heart?'

'His heart, his mind, his body. Nothing was the same after Saoirse left. That was why I understood your jealousy sometimes. You were perceptive. Just picking up on the fact he would never truly, completely, let you in. Does anyone after being hurt by their first love? How can you ever give fully after losing the love of your life?'

'You think she was the love of his life?'

Cassandra's hand went to her mouth. 'I'm sorry. That must sound malicious. It wasn't meant that way. Their love was innocent. All consuming. The "give everything you have" type of love. When Alex met you, you both had your scars. Please don't doubt he loved you because he did; he definitely did. It's just Saoirse was the groundwork, the tapestry, the one he searched for and could never find.'

'The one that got away.'

'Yes, the one that got away.'

'But then the one that got away came back.'

'Yes,' Cassandra agreed.

'And Alex died because of it. Because of her.'

Cassandra's hand rested on Melinda's. 'From the sounds of it, that girl lost as much as us.'

'Have you spoken to her?'

'No.'

'Do you know where she is?'

'Mel, I haven't seen or spoken to that girl for over fifteen years. Alex taught me that life might throw its worst at you, but it is only how you love that matters. You both loved my son. Don't turn that love into hate. Alex deserves better than that.'

'Have you seen the kids lately?'

'You didn't hear?'

'Hear what?'

'The kids are staying with me. Remember that envelope at the will reading?'

'Vaguely, I was pretty out of it.'

'You might want a sip of wine for this,' Cassandra suggested.

Melinda followed instructions and took a sip.

'I would have thought you would have read about this in the papers.'

'I haven't looked at a paper or watched the news since it happened. I can't.'

'The envelope contained footage of Bernice hurting Alex. Months and months of footage, Mel.'

Melinda held her chest in shock. 'Was she arrested?'

'Sure was. At the moment she's out in bail but because of the video of her being rough with Lily, her visitation rights have been waived.'

'She hurt Lily? That poor girl.'

She bit her lip. 'Do you think they might want to see me at all?'

Cassandra took a sip of wine. 'I was going to ring you actually. This weekend, if you are willing, I'd like to release Alex's ashes over the cliffs of Knockfarraig with Lily and Kenny. You're welcome to join us.'

'You're getting rid of his ashes? Already?'

'Not getting rid of. Releasing. That's not Alex in the urn, Mel. It's just soot. I can't have it in my house, sitting above a fireplace. Alex wouldn't want that. I need to let him go. I think it would help the kids process it some more. It might help you too.'

'That's why I couldn't hold on to the urn. The thought of him in some box is horrible. You're right, he should be free. I'll come,' Melinda said.

Chapter 67

Vicky replayed the CCTV footage again. Before he got out, before he bumped into the car, Alex looked to the left, as if scanning the sky.

She paused the footage. 'What is he looking for?' she said.

Playing the footage, Alex looked down and just before he bumped into the car in front, she paused the tape. She moved closer to the monitor. The pause made the video pixelate. She rewound. Played it again. Rewound, then pressed play again. There was no doubt. Alex smiled just before he hit the car.

According to Saoirse, Alex never met Fintan and had no idea what he looked like, or what car he drove. So, why did he smile before he hit the car in front? Was he angry and wanted to get into a fight with anyone? According to Cassandra, Melinda and Saoirse, Alex never hurt a person in his life, so why start that day?

Maybe that was all it was. After a life of giving in to everyone, after placing his ex-lover in a refuge for abused women, did Alex Hayes wake up that morning and decide enough was enough?

She rewound the footage again. Before Alex smiled, he was looking for something. What was on the left of the road? What was he looking for? She selected maps on the computer then chose street view. Typed in the street and scrolled along the road as if a pedestrian. She could see the fishmongers directly on the right, so she scrolled and continued along, staying on the same side. There was the chemist, the off license and then nothing, just the derelict building he would a few minutes later be fatally stabbed in. Did he smile because he spotted someone? She replayed the video of him driving, checked his eyeline. Alex was looking up. She scanned the opposite side of the street checking what was above. Mostly one-storey buildings; there was nothing in the sky but electricity poles. She scanned each millimetre, only stopping exactly where the car had stopped. Nothing else stood out. She sat back and thought. Thought about who Alex was, about the things he knew, about the things that excited him, about the choices he made in life and the reasons he made them. And then she understood.

Chapter 68

Alex Hayes was not a liar as far as she could tell and Vicky would bet on the authenticity of the tapes sent to her by Brooks and Belmont. There was no doubt in her mind that the man who sat on the couch in that footage was Alex Hayes, and that the abuse inflicted on him by Bernice was nothing short of terrifying. A long history evident for anyone to see. No doubt whatsoever about any of that.

But.

There was one difference between Alex and any of the abused women she encountered. Most victims were too afraid to tell anyone about the abuse, let alone have the strength to hide cameras in their house. Usually, by the time the abuse became consistent, the victim was too scared to do anything that might anger their abuser. That was where Alex differed. It was never about strength with Alex for he knew from the first time Bernice hit him he could overpower his wife. For Alex, it was about proving he wasn't the one hurting the other person in the marriage. Vicky didn't doubt he felt fear. There were times on the tape that it certainly looked convincing that Bernice could kill him.

So, why did he stay? There could only be one answer. Alex stayed to compile enough evidence to convict Bernice without ever having to give a testimony. From his documentation, Bernice would serve time, would certainly lose custody of the kids. He had chosen the perfect place to position the cameras. This told Vicky one fact, for sure. Alex knew a thing or two about cameras.

Driving on the same street as the attack, when she scanned the sky, the only thing she found was the only working CCTV camera on the street. Alex was looking for the camera and when he had spotted it, he smiled.

Alex bumped the car on purpose at the exact spot of the cameras. Alex Hayes wanted to start a fight. And he wanted it recorded.

Chapter 69

Cassandra let Vicky in without a hello.

'Thanks for letting me visit again. I wanted to tell you myself that my superiors decided to close the case.'

Cassandra rubbed her hands together. Self-soothing, Vicky guessed. 'What does that mean?'

'It means I'm not allowed to pursue your son's murderer anymore.'

Vicky pointed to the fireplace. 'No urn?'

Cassandra gave a smile that didn't meet her eyes. 'No. We released his ashes earlier today. I thought it would help but it didn't. Too soon maybe.'

Cassandra gestured for her to sit but didn't offer a drink. 'Do you think he's still out there?'

Vicky sat. Cassandra sat on the single armchair facing.

'A few clothes folded aren't enough. Until I find a body, I can't be sure.'

'You won't let it go, will you?'

'Mara's warned me off, so officially I'll be quiet as a mouse, but under the surface, I'll keep scratching. I just wanted to reassure you I won't forget Alex.'

Cassandra smiled. 'You were always an inquisitive child.'

'Nosy, you mean?'

'In your job, I'm sure that's important.'

'You'd think so. Sometimes my boss would call it troublesome.'

'It's a quest for justice.'

Vicky tilted her head. 'It leans more towards the nosy part; I just can't rest until I know the truth.'

'Ah.'

'Which is why I'm here. I wanted to ask you about that night.'

'Which night?'

'The night your husband died. Your husband, am I right in saying you found him?'

'That's right, Vicky, I mean Sergeant Fitzgerald. Sorry, I forget we're supposed to act differently with each other.'

'Vicky is fine, Cassandra. You were saying?'

'It was me that found my husband's body. He was at the bottom of the stairs.'

'The ruling was he fell?'

Cassandra didn't look up. 'That's right.'

'Was he an easy man to live with?'

'Who, John?'

'Yes.'

'Out of all the words I would call my husband, easy was never one.'

'What would you call him?'

'Abusive. Arrogant. Manipulative. Unkind. Will I go on?'

'If you want to, add more.'

'That's descriptive enough, I'd say.'

'He was alone when he died?'

'Yes. I was at an annual charity function in Crookstown. Alex was at a dance, his Grads.'

'Two very public events. If I check them out, there will be people who will corroborate your story?'

'Plenty. Back then I didn't drink alcohol, so I gave two women a lift home afterwards. There were teachers and pupils at Alex's Grads, so there would be dozens of witnesses, I'm sure.'

'And you arrived home before Alex?'

Cassandra made eye contact. 'Over an hour before.'

'What was your first reaction when you saw your husband at the bottom of the stairs?'

'Honest answer? Contempt. It wasn't the first time I found my husband passed out from a drinking session. When he didn't move at all after a few minutes, I got down on my hands and knees and checked to see if his body moved up and down.'

'You didn't touch him?'

'No way. Touching him didn't go down well if he was drunk; I learnt that the hard way. After a few seconds, I realised he wasn't sleeping it off this time. My first reaction was contempt, but God forgive me, when I realised he was dead my second thought was relief. That man hurt us every opportunity he got.'

'There were some photos in the old file of the scene and something struck me as strange. The way the shoes were on the landing, wait, I can show you.'

Vicky removed some photographs from her pocket. She gestured to the seat next to Cassandra, asking for permission to sit beside her. Cassandra nodded and sighed. Vicky pointed to the picture. 'See, here at the top of the landing there's a shoe, but it bothers me.'

'Why so?'

'Because the way he fell means he hit the right-hand side of the stairway and then bounced off it sending him backwards the rest of the way, which is accurate with the type of injuries he had. But see the shoe?'

'I see the shoe,' Cassandra said, almost bored.

'It's facing the wrong way. Years ago I was at a trial and they had a fall expert and he went into a long, drawn-out detail on how that couldn't happen and it stayed with me, about the angles. Do you understand what I mean, Cassandra?'

Cassandra stayed looking at the photo, her expression unchanging.

'Do I need to get a lawyer, Sergeant Fitzgerald?'

'Nope. This is all off record. That case is completely closed. Whatever else happened to that man is none of my business. I was not a Garda then and I remember well what type of man John Hayes was. Sorry, but he often scared the living daylights out of me and my friend when we used to walk home from each other's houses.'

'Try living with him.'

'The last thing I want is to bring up old trauma, Mrs Hayes. What I want to understand is why Saoirse left Alex.'

'You found Saoirse, though, yes?'

'She found us. She voluntarily came to the station and has been talking to us.'

'So, ask her.'

'She will not discuss why she left.'

'What does it matter, Vicky? It was fifteen years ago. They were just past their eighteenth birthday. Children practically. They broke up. You want to see them as some Romeo and Juliet but they were barely adults. This is a concern. On the news it says the Gardaí are doing everything in their power to find my son's murderer, yet here you are asking me about something Alex had nothing to do with.'

'Cassandra, you've known me for many years, yes?'

'All your life I'd say, Vicky.'

'Exactly, well just in case you haven't picked up on it, there is one thing I excel in and that's sensing a lie. Something happened that night and I believe it holds the key to a million little things, namely why Saoirse and Alex broke up, why she moved away and never came back to Knockfarraig.'

Cassandra chewed on her lip. 'You won't give up will you?'

Vicky smiled apologetically. 'I won't give up.'

'Off record?'

'Off record,' Vicky repeated.

'After I realised John was dead, I ran to Alex's room, afraid that something had happened. I was too late. I came home to a deed already done. To a bed with crumpled sheets when they had been smooth before he left. A scrap of glittery material on the floor, a scrap identical to Saoirse's dress. Blood on the sheet. There was no sign of Alex. Straight away I knew, John hurt Saoirse to watch Alex's reaction when he told him. That was the only reason. He wanted to ruin Alex; he wanted to ruin the pure love between the two of them because that man was never capable of loving anyone but himself.

'I knew my son. Knew exactly how he would react once he knew what that man had done. Knew exactly what way John would react to Alex's confrontation, to what his father definitely would have said. I could see it all. How my son's heart would have broken right there by the door to his bedroom. Could hear my husband's vicious laugh as he told him. There were no bruises on my husband, but I could tell he was dead and for the first time in nineteen years my body relaxed. I knew exactly what I needed to do. He was still warm enough, his fingers still pliable. I placed the bottle of whiskey in his hand, unscrewed the bottle top, let it lie. There wasn't much left anyway, and I knew if they bothered running tests toxicology would prove the rest of the bottle lay in his gut. I took off his shoes and lay one underneath his calf. Sat another by the foot of the stairs. The guards never even questioned it. Everyone knew it was the night of the Grads, that Alex was away. Everyone knew how much my husband drank. I had an alibi for the night. Within minutes of coming home, I rang the emergency services. It looked like he just fell back on his discarded shoes, broke his neck on the step of the stairs. The guard on duty, Wallace something I recall, nearly tripped over the shoes another time he'd visited, when he needed to calm him down. It was a cut and dry case in his eyes; he wasn't as thorough as you. Once they heard from the coroner that there was only the one injury. No other bruising. No evidence of a fight. They closed the book.

'As I waited for the guards, I thought, *I will not lose my son.* So, I made Alex's bed. Hid the piece of Saoirse's dress. Made sure it looked like a typical young man's room.

'The autopsy ruled it accidental death. The amount of alcohol in his system made them treat it as if he tripped up. That day I discovered autopsies got it wrong. That man was a tyrant who never gave the rest of us a moment's peace, Vicky. I thought I was protecting my son. But when the Gardaí arrived, Alex followed a few minutes after and I could tell he knew nothing. He was as shocked about finding his father dead as I was. Maybe he just fell. Or maybe Saoirse pushed him, to be honest, I didn't care. If I admitted I had tampered with evidence, I would have been in the frame, and for what?

'If I had to choose who died between my husband and son, I'd pick the same every time. Do you know how many nights I worried it would go the other way? The man was finally gone. I only wish it was me who had done it.'

'Do you think that's why Saoirse ran away?'

Cassandra shrugged. 'Who else could it be?'

'Well then I need to talk to Saoirse again.'

'What good will it do her or him, Vicky? Can you not just let the girl be?'

'I need to know. Did you try to contact Saoirse that night, to see if she was hurt?'

'The guards kept us up most of the night. The next day I heard she was gone, and at the time I was glad. Safer I thought, because my priority was to keep Alex from knowing. Alex told me later, he got drunk the night of the Grads, he fell over, slept it off in the grass for a while. When he woke up, sober, and realised Saoirse had left, he ran to her house. Her mother turned him away. Said to come back in the morning when things had died down. When he returned the next day they were gone. Packed up. Every sign of them disappeared. She didn't leave a note. After that Alex went to pieces. Everyone thought it was because of his dad dying. At the funeral he was a mess. It helped our case. It worked. Except it didn't.'

'In what way?' Vicky asked.

'Alex tried to kill himself after Saoirse left. I found him one night with an empty pill box. After they pumped his stomach, and I knew he would survive, I sat him down and told him he had to move on, that she mustn't have cared for him, if she could leave without a goodbye. Even though I knew how much she loved him, even though I knew they would never love another the same way again. As much as he was hurting, I couldn't let him find her. Not when she killed his father. Not after what his father must have done. I didn't think Alex would recover after that. He would have forgiven Saoirse for killing his father, he would have forgiven Saoirse anything. But he would never have recovered from the guilt of what his father had done to the girl he loved just to destroy him.

'When she ran, Alex knew something must have happened but he couldn't figure out what. We both wronged him, we both should have given him more credit. It made him love her more. Made him blame himself. When he didn't improve, I started to doubt whether separating them was for the best. Wasn't his father winning that way? So I started looking too. We searched for her everywhere. But she just disappeared. No sign of her or her mother anywhere. Now you can find anyone pretty quickly. Social media makes stalking easy. Back then all we found were dead ends. Alex did something he never did after that, drank until falling. He wasn't an unkind drunk like his father, not to anyone else anyway. There were many nights I stood outside listening through the door afraid he was going to harm himself. And then he started hanging out with Bernice. Instead of lashing out, or self-harming, Alex found someone else to inflict the hurt on him. I didn't know at all, if you're wondering. I didn't know what she was doing to him at home. He protected her, even when I questioned him, even when I knew he was becoming withdrawn. You don't have any children, do you, Vicky?'

'No.'

'From the day a child is born, a mother's life is never the same. After, I could never be reckless with a decision, it was never again just about me. There is always someone else to consider. It is unnatural. We are born selfish, born with only us to consider. Empathy, putting someone else first, is learned behaviour. Women are taught this early, from childhood. Sometimes it is forced. Screamed at us until we conform. Until we learn to put our needs behind the rest of the family. We are second-class citizens on the hierarchy of the heirloom. Secondary characters in our own story. From the day he was born and they told me I birthed a boy; I was determined Alex would grow into a different kind of man and I succeeded. What I didn't realise was in teaching him to be empathetic towards women and not expect the usual expectations from them, I was also teaching him to hand over his control to the one he loved. It was never about gender, as much as I thought it was. It wasn't about me being small and my husband being bigger. With Alex, I learned the lesson is about being made to *feel* smaller. That can happen whatever size you are. It is about getting into someone's head. Once you figure out how to unlock that, you can unravel anyone, the biggest giant you can find. Will you charge me?'

'For what?'

'I don't know? Perverting the course of justice or something?'

'Sometimes the past needs to stay in the past. In a small town, sometimes being the only guard on duty means I have to pick my battles. Sounds to me justice was done.'

'Thank you,' Cassandra placed a hand on her heart.

Vicky pointed to her chest. 'How are you recovering?'

'Since the heart attack, I've been watching what I eat. I go to their rehab and get hooked up with loads of little stickers on my chest, and they watch as I do specific exercises. No joke, I'm fitter now than I have been for the last twenty years. My son is gone, yet I have never felt more alive. It is a very strange situation. When I was told, I was sure I would die on the spot and I very nearly did.'

'And now?' Vicky asked.

'And now I'm still here,' Cassandra said, shrugging. 'Having to take over custody of Kenny and Lily helps. With those two live wires, I barely have time to think. This has been a good thing. It has got me through. In the evenings, when they are in bed and the house goes silent, my chest tightens enough to worry about another heart attack. It is a different type of pain to the attack. This is pure loss.'

'Are you able to cope, Cassandra? I could put you in contact with a social worker or a bereavement counsellor?'

'No need. We are in contact with both. Like I said, those kids are the reason I'm coping at all. Although, I worry about the years to come. If something happens to me, what will happen to them? Hence why I'm doing the bloody rehab. The guys there say I'm doing brilliant and I feel it. It has to work; I plan to stay around for a lot longer. They need me. Can I ask you something?'

'Fire away.'

'The children's summer holidays are coming up and after everything, I was thinking of taking them away. Do you think that would be a problem?'

'You are free to holiday, Cassandra.'

'That's not what I mean. All this with Bernice, the fact she isn't allowed visitation, means they don't have to be here. Every time I drive towards the city I have to pass where the murder took place.' Cassandra's voice broke. 'There's nothing in Knockfarraig for me or the children anymore. If we are going to go, now's the time. I'm thinking of heading somewhere warm, somewhere different from Ireland. A fresh start. If they like it, we'll stay, and if they don't, we'll come back. Course, I'll return if they allow Bernice visitation. Or if there's a trial. If you ever catch my son's murderer, that is.'

'That's looking unlikely these days, Cassandra.'

'Do you believe that man killed himself?'

Vicky pulled at her lip, thinking. 'Bullies like Fintan have no issue dishing out pain to other people but chicken out when inflicting any on themselves. Unless they panic or are so tight in a corner, that there is no other way out. I think he certainly was in a corner. Whether he deemed it enough to harm himself has yet to be determined. Until I find a body, I'm open to all ideas. In regard to whether you can leave, as long as you are not in breach of your custody requirements and leave contact details, and enrol them in a school, then as far as the law is concerned, you are good to go. On a personal note, Knockfarraig will miss you, Cassandra, you helped this community a great deal.'

Cassandra squeezed the sergeant's shoulder. 'Thank you, I will miss you too.'

Chapter 70

The art piece was a butterfly made from dyed rags and microscopic bits of paper. Some were scrunched into a ball. Some suspended as if they fluttered free.

A man stopped beside Melinda. He stood for a long time. She tried to ignore him as he moved from side to side.

He said, more to himself than to her. 'How can cloth and paper make the butterfly come to life?'

She looked at him then and realised he *was* speaking to her. She shrugged. There was no point in giving him an answer.

'If you move to the left, it changes the piece completely.' He walked closer to the piece. 'Are they tiny wings?'

She nodded at him, then laughed at his confusion. He moved back nearer to her.

'Then if I move to the right to see it from that angle, it changes into different shapes and textures, all little butterflies. Move to the middle and it's one gigantic butterfly. How does someone do that? To have the insight and the creativity.'

'You think?'

He tilted his head. 'You don't think?'

'I've stood here for the last,' Melinda checked her watch, 'fifteen minutes, trying to figure out what's missing.'

He stood shoulder to shoulder with her. 'What's missing? You're kidding me, right? You add one more piece of cloth, or take away an inch of paper, and you'll ruin the whole equilibrium of the piece. It's perfect.'

Melinda scoffed. 'Please. It's pieces of paper layered on top of each other.'

'No,' the man said. 'There's way more to it than that. I'd pay to learn how to do that type of art.'

'Oh yeah?' she smiled.

'Yeah. Believe me, if I tried to stick bits of paper to a canvas, it wouldn't come out like that.'

'How would it come out, then?' She recoiled. *Was she flirting?*

'Like it was fit to be burned.'

She laughed, then stopped herself. It was the first time she laughed out loud since Alex died, the first time she had wanted to. 'Well, I'll make sure to tell the artist then.'

His face dropped. 'The artist is you?'

'The very same.'

The man covered his face with his hands. 'Well, that's embarrassing.'

'Don't be embarrassed. You just made my day.'

He smiled, wide, showing a small gap in his teeth. Melinda liked it. An imperfect smile had more character than a Hollywood one. His entire face was interesting; she had to admit. Different from Alex, who was all light, this man was brown-haired with grey streaking through, and dark eyebrows that framed soft sloping eyes. About her age, she guessed.

'At least I was complimentary. Imagine if I didn't like it?'

'Honestly, when you stood there for that long, I thought you were going to rip into it.'

The man looked right at her. 'What you do is astonishing.'

She stared back at him, wondering if what he was saying was just fodder, just some throwaway compliment. Just a way to get her attention. He looked around.

'Have you more work here?'

'No, just the one piece. I wanted to break myself back in. Are you an artist?'

'Not professionally. My parents didn't believe in art as a career, made me pursue business. So, when I made enough money, I bought an art gallery. I come here to get inspired. When I heard about the exhibition this week showcasing pieces by different local artists, I ran. And now I'm glad I did.'

When he smiled at her, it didn't cause butterflies to flutter in her stomach, or make her heart beat faster, or make her squirm. It just made her want to smile back.

'Do you have more pieces?'

Melinda laughed. 'A few.' She didn't add that she had worked night and day since Alex sent her the art materials.

'Would you have an interest in holding an exhibition in my gallery?'

Melinda stared at the butterfly on the wall. She had worked on it as a representation of her own metamorphosis. The man had been right; when you looked at it from the sides, multiple tiny butterflies stacked together to form the whole. What the man didn't see, was behind the initial butterflies, at the very core of the installation, sat small hearts, broken ones, that eventually morphed larger and better formed until they mended, each one growing in size and becoming more open, until they turned into butterflies.

'Did you mean it when you said you would pay to be taught how to do it?'

He smiled. 'If I say something, I mean it.'

'That's good to know. I like that; I need that in my life.'

'Daniel is my name.'

'Melinda,' she said back.

'So, will you let me exhibit your work?'

'If you buy me a coffee, I might.'

Chapter 71

Four weeks later

The exhibition was called *Pieces Of Him*. Voile and netting formed one artwork. Beige and browns and blues for Alex. Pinks and reds, whites and purples for Saoirse. In the piece, they were eight years old again. Melinda's version of the photograph that made everything clearer in the attic. The picture that set her free.

There was another on the main wall. It was the only one featuring a self-portrait. She was facing away from Alex. Looking up into the far corner of the frame; smiling. Alex's hands grasped the corners, as if he was climbing out of the picture. When Daniel had mentioned he had a last minute opening in the gallery, instead of hiding away like she usually did, she had seized the moment and told him she would be ready. She couldn't believe she had accomplished all that work in four weeks. Her hands had worked at record speed, never letting up. She had painted, glued, sewed and embellished in almost a dream state, barely sleeping, not frantic but alive, knowing all too well how time could be taken away, how time could rob you of a precious moment if you let it. Instead of feeling tired, she felt invigorated. Melinda would never again let the creativity inside of her quieten.

Daniel leant close, then whispered in her ear. 'Enjoy tonight, Mel. You deserve every bit of attention.'

She turned to him and couldn't help from smiling at the face that had become so familiar to her, so comforting. 'I'm scared.'

He wrapped an arm around her. 'There's no need to be afraid. Are you proud of them?'

She met his eyes. He waited for her to answer. 'They are the best pieces I've ever done.'

'Good. They deserve to be seen.' He trailed his hand along her jaw. It surprised her when she didn't flinch. 'Allow all of you to be seen.'

Whatever happened later, Melinda knew she was ready to love someone again. In grief it has seemed impossible, but how could she live, what, hopefully, another forty or fifty years closed off from something beautiful? Whether Daniel remained just a friend or their relationship developed into something more, she was open now; she was ready. Sure, some might gossip that she moved on from her husband's death too soon, but she knew the truth. Alex left her long before he died.

Daniel turned to the canvas. 'They are as if you have reached into your soul and poured out the emotion. They are remarkable. You are remarkable.'

Melinda blushed. 'Thank you. It was the only way I could say goodbye.'

'You don't need to say goodbye to Alex for me, you know that, right?'

She nodded. 'I know. It's me who needs to say it. If I don't, I won't let anything good into my life. This is my way of letting Alex go.'

She bumped his shoulder. 'I actually said goodbye to Alex last night. I closed my eyes and imagined he came to see me, to apologise. Words I believed going into that attic that I needed to hear. Even if he was alive today, even if he told me about Saoirse in person, those words are, do I want to say, useless? No. What I want to say is unneeded. If he was alive, I would stop him and say I don't want to hear it. Because his love shaped my whole life. The choices I made stemmed from all the actions he would apologise for. It is all so clear.

'It would never have worked. And I don't think we were meant to. Alex taught me what love could be like. My love for him embroidered into everything. True love, enduring, nurturing, reciprocal love was not the course our relationship took. There are many forms of love.'

Daniel laced his fingers through hers.

'When I married Alex, I thought all I wanted was to love him. But my version of love meant Alex had to fix me. No one can hold that responsibility. I hadn't learnt yet that love takes on the form and flaws of the person who receives it. You can mask it, taint it, twist and restrain.'

She wiped at her eye. 'I don't want to do that anymore.'

'Me neither,' Daniel said. 'With each failed relationship we stack our hurt, like carrying heavy rocks. Eventually, we have to let go.'

Melinda squeezed his hand. 'That's why first love is unforgettable. We have no idea of the pain in store, until it goes. Any love after is less pure, but deeper, because we understand what we might lose, we know the wound love leaves, we felt its cut, know how long it takes to heal, know it can get infected, or damage. Yet we are still brave enough to try.

'Daniel, I want to be brave. I want to trust. I want to create art until I die.'

Falling. That's what being around Daniel felt like. The ground under her ready to give way. Letting down her guard was more than scary – it wasn't anything she had done before. Even with Alex, as much as she had loved her husband, some bricks had been removed but most of her walls had stayed up. How had that helped her? If anything, it had pushed Alex away. Melinda saw it now. Alex was loyalty to a tee; he would not have been unfaithful.

Except to the past, for Saoirse came before. When you stood the two women in a line, Alex's loyalty had to be to his first, had to go to

Saoirse.

Chapter 72

If you wanted access to a woman's refuge, being a member of the Gardaí helped. Normally, no amount of door knocking would get them to open it. With no public phone number, it was usually impossible to talk to anyone there. Essential for the safety of the women, Vicky knew the only way to make an appointment was by emailing ahead. It was pointless to question the manager Lynn over the phone or by email, as she wouldn't acknowledge anyone staying in the building in any form except by conversation in person. Even after being told by Saoirse that was where she was staying, the refuge wouldn't confirm or deny. There was nothing for it but to call in.

Used to these places, Vicky didn't greet any of the women. A Garda triggered many of them. The uniform was a reminder of when they needed help, of the pain they endured. There was no need to bring anxiety; these women had already suffered enough. With her head down, she followed Lynn to her office.

'You wanted to speak to me?'

'You, no, I'm here to speak to a woman staying here. Saoirse Thomas.'

Lynn gave Vicky a look. 'You know I can't share information about the residents.'

'It's not sharing if she told me.'

Lynn folded her arms and said nothing.

'It's a high-profile murder case, Lynn. Saoirse came to me and offered her statement. There are just one or two questions that have been bugging me. If I could have a few minutes, I'll be gone. I promise I haven't compromised her whereabouts. In fact, I have been searching for her husband night and day, so she will feel safe. No one knows she is here.'

'Sorry, you're wasting your time.'

'Come on, Lynn, off the record. No one has to get their knickers in a twist about GDPR. You know how we need to help each other; it needs to be give and take for this to work. You keep the girls safe while I go chase the bad guys who hurt them. We're on the same side.'

'I can't help you.'

'This is ridiculous. Is it too much to ask for us to work together?'

'Vicky, will you let me get a word in for once?'

'What?'

'I would love to help you.'

'Oh, good.'

'But I can't. Against my advice, Saoirse booked a holiday with her daughter. They left a couple of days ago.'

'How?'

'What do you mean, how?'

'How could she afford a holiday?'

'Her friend sent her a present of the flights and hotel.'

Vicky straightened. 'What friend?'

Lynn jerked her head, narrowed her eyes. 'Let me check.' She walked to her desk, pulled out a file, gave Vicky a warning look to step back, and only opened the file once she did. She flipped a few pages. Vicky's stomach lurched at how big the file was. This wasn't Saoirse's first time needing help.

'Ernest, that's his name. Ernest Morley. Saoirse told me they were very close growing up. He wrote her a letter saying she deserved a break. She honoured his wishes.'

'When is she back?'

'Hold on.' Lynn flipped to the last page of notes. 'Exactly three weeks from today.'

Vicky closed her eyes.

'Where?'

'Hawaii.'

'I have to go.'

On the drive to the airport, Vicky wondered where she went wrong. Why would most of the women in Alex's life be running away? Were Cassandra and Saoirse in on it together? And what the hell could they be in on, anyway? Her head was bursting with questions. It didn't make sense that the murderer could be anyone but Fintan, and there was no way Saoirse or Cassandra were meeting with him. Yet, she was still adamant there were no coincidences. How could they both be going on holiday within days of each other? Unless Ernest also gifted Cassandra. But why would he do that?

She sped up. Cassandra had given Vicky her travel details, in case she needed to ask her anything before she left. Their flight was leaving in three hours, which meant check in was in the next hour. She needed to talk to Cassandra before she stepped on that flight. Her hunches were up. Something was going on and she needed to find out.

She ran through what she knew.

Was Fintan involved in Alex's murder? Yes.

'How do I know this?' she spoke aloud.

'CCTV showing the confrontation on the street. Eye witnesses confirming the sighting from his ID. Saoirse confirming from the footage. Fintan's car. Fingerprints matching the wallet, passport and steering wheel matched the knife. Saoirse also confirmed the knife was Fintan's. The knife was covered in blood. Blood that matched the murder victim. Saoirse and Alex's past was enough reason for motive.

Fintan's history of jealousy and violence was enough motive for road rage if they couldn't prove he knew Alex. Most of these were past facts, though. What did she know for definite?'

She tapped on the steering wheel.

'The murder weapon was Fintan's. His fingerprints were all over it. Fintan's car was found abandoned. He left behind his keys, wallet, his licence, his passport, his car. Most likely dead. Yet no body. Why?'

She pressed down on the accelerator. There were still too many unanswered questions.

When she pulled up at the front of the airport, she rushed in and the first person she saw was the last person she expected.

Melinda Hayes turned around and smiled.

Chapter 73

He lifted Melinda's hand by the fingers, barely holding the tips until he raised her arm, he didn't stop until he pulled her nearer, until her body caved to him, breast against chest, breath on breath. She could kiss him if she wished, the way he was looking at her, she didn't think he would refuse. It was what she wanted, that she knew. Instead of kissing her, he swung her around, making her dance. Slipping his arm behind her back, their bodies meshed and from there they rocked from side to side. He bent his head towards hers and she knew there was no going back.

When Daniel kissed her, it felt different from Alex. Alex taught her what love should feel like, but Daniel gave her what she craved. To be adored. To be loved loudly. What she had needed all along was someone to make her their first. Melinda had always been second with everyone, including Alex.

No more doubts. No more checking if she was good enough. Alex spent years trying to help her understand she had always been good enough, but the doubt hadn't left her, and finding out about Saoirse, she understood why. Her doubt, her jealousy had been her instinct. With the right person, there was no need to be jealous. This time, with Daniel, Melinda *believed* she was good enough.

Daniel could leave her in the future. Or she could walk away from him. There were no guarantees in this life; she learned that all too well.

Either way, she would survive.

'Are you ready to do this?' he whispered into her ear.

'Head first,' she whispered back.

'Good. 'Cos I was hoping you'd still be here if I run to the bathroom.'

'Ah, see, you'll just have to trust me.'

'You want anything in the shop? I'm going to pick out a read for the plane.'

'No. I'm going to lovingly stare at you all flight. Or take out the novel I already have in my bag.'

He walked away laughing, and after she watched him retreat, she let out a contented sigh. Arriving early, her gate hadn't opened yet, but she was happy to wait. Heading towards some seats near the departures notice board, she wheeled her suitcase behind her. All her favourite things fit into one rectangle. The rest was in storage or given away. She had arranged with the storage company that when the time came, she would pay them to fill a container and ship it. When she decided where to stick, that was. For the first time in her whole life she didn't have a plan, and it felt wonderful.

Five lines over, she spotted a familiar hairstyle. Cassandra, not alone, heralding Lily and Kenny to the ticket desk. The sign was for Stansted. It crossed her mind to call out to them, say hello after they had checked in, but she thought better of it. Too awkward. What could they say to each other? The words were too big, too embarrassing; the children would not like it, she was sure. Instead, she held back, took her time and wished them bon voyage. In silence, she said, *I love you. Thank you for letting me share your dad with you for a while.*

It was time to move on. A new life awaited her. No more Alex. No more being a stepmother. As much as she would miss them, as much as it hurt her chest to close that door, Melinda had to admit there was some relief there, too. No more waking at the crack of dawn to a foot in the face in bed. No more having to run around on weekends, being a taxi driver for parties and matches and outings. Or feeling like she would never get the hang of being a substitute mother. Making silent lists like that helped her get through each day.

And then a hand slipped into hers and all her excuses disappeared.

'Lily, my lovely,' she said. And her eyes welled because she knew, all those things she listed she would have freely done in a heartbeat if allowed.

'Are you coming with us?' Lily asked.

Melinda crouched down so she was at the same height level. 'I wish I was, honey. Come here and give me a big hug.'

The girl squeezed her tight and Melinda knew this was the goodbye she needed.

'I love you, you know that, right?'

Lily nodded. 'From my head to my toes.'

The tears flowed freely now. 'And you know it doesn't matter where we are in the world, what's in our hearts never leaves, yeah?'

Lily nodded enthusiastically. Then her smile fell.

'Are you leaving me?'

And that's when Melinda realised it didn't need to be a last goodbye.

'Lily, whenever you want to see me, you can. Your grandmother has my number, so whenever you want to speak to me, I'll be there. I'm going to live in a part of the world where my house has fields you can run in and places you can paint. Any time you need me, I'll always be there, you understand?'

'I'm sorry you couldn't be my mother,' Lily said, her own eyes full now.

'You already have one of them. What you got with me was an extra person to love you. That will never change, even if I'm no longer with your dad.'

And then Kenny and Cassandra were beside her. Whether it was taking their cue from Lily, or just because there was no more need for awkwardness, the two women embraced.

'When did you know?' Melinda whispered as they hugged.

'After the will reading,' Cassandra whispered back.

'I'm glad. I'm so glad,' Melinda said. Kissing the woman on the side of the face.

They pulled apart. She grabbed Kenny for a hug, whispered into his ear, 'I love you.' Speaking over his hair, she said. 'You look after them, Cassandra. And if you ever need some help, I will come running.'

Cassandra checked her watch. 'We have over two hours on the other side of security before our flight leaves. You fancy a coffee?'

Melinda beamed through the dam of tears. 'I'll just check in and follow you up. I'm not alone though, is that okay? If you don't mind, I'd like to introduce you to Daniel. I think you'll like him.'

'I'm sure,' Cassandra said.

'He's not a replacement for Alex; I want you to know that. Daniel's not leaving with me, we're just having a break together, then we might do the long distance thing or maybe, one day, he might move. Everything is up in the air.'

'Mel, it's okay. I'm happy for you. Alex would want you to find happiness.'

'You think?'

'I know.'

Chapter 74

It was rare to receive post these days. Other than bills; she could not recall receiving a letter in years, especially in a place where no one was allowed to know where you were. The manager had just handed it to her, with no words about who it was from. The handwriting on the cream envelope was a scrawl she didn't recognise, which instead of alarming, put her mind at ease for it wasn't Fintan's writing. Hurried and scratchy, as if the writer was running out of time. Inside was a piece of paper folded over a thicker piece. A letter wrapped around two tickets. Saoirse read the handwritten note first.

My dearest friend,

Sorry I contacted you here when I'm not meant to. Myself and Lynn the manager go way back, so when Alex called her, she pulled a few strings to get you in. I'm sorry for everything you've had to go through. And I don't just mean over the last few weeks. After all you've suffered, you and Laurie deserve a holiday. I know your heart is broken and all you probably want to do is mourn and lie in bed. Please, I beg you, don't. Go on this trip, no matter what doubt creeps in. You and Laurie need to smile again, and where I've booked is the perfect place to heal. Don't worry about anything. The flights are booked; there will be a driver waiting for you on the other side who will bring you to your hotel. All expenses paid. Don't even think of not going.

I'm sorry I took so long to help you,

Ernest.

Saoirse held the letter to her chest and smiled. Trust Ernest to manage to get a letter in. That was her friend. He could always persuade the most diehard of rule keepers to bend for him.

Even though time and her bad choices had kept them apart, Ernest was always there. Here he was now, knowing exactly what she needed. A holiday wouldn't take away the pain, but a fresh setting from the women's refuge would take the pressure off and give her some space to figure out what her next step should be. Although Ernest was usually pretty spot on with the truth, he was wrong when he wrote he had taken too long. It was her that had hesitated, staying in a marriage years longer than she should. It was her that cut off contact with the people who proved they loved her. Soon, she would have to leave the refuge and find somewhere to live. A scary thought starting again, especially starting with nothing. But nothing was something. Nothing meant anything better was an improvement. She hoped she was strong enough. Even taking a trip, was a bigger feat than she thought possible. She didn't know if she was brave enough. If she could be brave enough.

But she wanted to find out.

Six weeks after Alex's death, Saoirse Thomas boarded a plane to Gatwick and then from there another flight with Laurie. The flights were uneventful, with thankfully no turbulence which for nights had kept her tossing and turning, because good things did not happen to her. The image of the plane plummeting to the ground kept repeating, invading her sleep. She contemplated drinking a brandy or taking some kind of pill to calm her nerves but the counsellor she had worked with at the shelter was big into allowing in all the feelings, good and bad, and she was starting to, trying to, at least.

On the other side, just like Ernest described, a man holding a sign with her and Laurie's name greeted her. Thick warm air hugged her grieving flesh as soon as she stepped outside the air-conditioned airport. The smell of sunshine, of flowers and cut grass, of baked pavements and ocean, of hope and new beginnings tickled her nostrils.

The hotel made Laurie gasp and brought grateful tears to Saoirse for her friend. Ernest hadn't exaggerated when he said he'd splashed out with no expenses spared. She whispered a thank you to her friend for thinking of her. For knowing her. The complex was small but definitely full of five-star luxuries. All palm trees and subtle features that smelt of money. She had never stayed in a place like that before. It was a place you could hide away from prying eyes or from the rest of the world, somewhere you could rest, a place you could heal. Check in was easy, the staff made it as smooth as possible. Still though, as easy as it all was, whether from not being used to flying, Saoirse felt exhausted. The girl at reception told her there was a welcome drink in the bar, but she cried off, not wanting to mingle with the other guests. Because in the middle of all this beauty, the perfect place for honeymooners and couples, it only reminded Saoirse how much she missed Alex, and no amount of sun, or pina colada's or nice receptionists or easy flights could make up for it. All she wanted was to lie in the bed and try to get through the day. It was ridiculous to believe a holiday could distract her grief.

As hinted at, the room was magnificent. All muted colours, beige and browns with gold handles. The balcony gave a view of ocean that was bigger than the sky and in a betrayal of her lethargy, she gasped at the sight.

Life would go on and she would learn to adapt. She had survived losing him once, then twice. She could do it again.

Laurie jumped on the bed. 'This is the best holiday ever. The hotel receptionist said I could get a free ice cream. Can I get it now?'

'Why didn't you get it when we were down there?'

'Because I wanted to see what the room was like.'

'Laurie, can we wait? I'm wrecked from the flight.'

'But I'll miss it then. I can go down by myself; I remember the way.'

'No, I can't let you go down on your own.'

'Why not? I'm nearly nine, Mum. The lift is right there and I know the way. Please.'

'No going anywhere but to get the ice cream?'

'Promise. I'll try and get you one too.'

'I'm okay. I'm going to make myself a strong coffee, that'll perk me up.'

As soon as Laurie clicked the door, she sat on the bed. *She would learn to adapt.*

But the truth was she didn't want to.

There was a knock on the door.

'That you, Laurie?' she called.

'No.'

A chill ran up her. What if Ernest hadn't set up the holiday? What if it was Fintan, luring her there so he could finally get to her, finally finish her off?

'You forgot a bag, miss,' a voice called. A voice with a definite local accent. Checking over the pile of luggage, Laurie's bag *was* missing. With a hand on her heart, she tried to still the rapid beating. Then, reaching for her wallet, she pulled out a note to give as a tip. When she opened the door, her legs buckled. The man wasn't lying. Indeed, there was a porter, holding out Laurie's bag. What caused her legs to buckle was the man standing behind.

Chapter 75

'Are you going with them?' Vicky asked, rushing over.

Melinda laughed. 'Sorry?' With her hair loose and wearing a summer dress, the woman looked about twenty years younger.

'Where are you going?'

Mel stepped out of the queue so she wouldn't delay the person behind. The gesture didn't stop the stares. It looked highly suspicious to have a uniformed Garda approach. It didn't help that Vicky looked furious.

'Sergeant Fitzgerald, for the first time in a very long time, I was excited about something. You keep reminding me of everything that caused me pain. Please don't ruin this for me.'

'I didn't even know you were going to be here. Are you meeting with Cassandra?'

Melinda cocked her head. 'Why are you looking for Cassandra?'

Vicky pinched her nose. 'Please stop asking questions without answering mine.'

'France. I'm moving to France. Or Spain. Well, that's the idea. I've a holiday booked where I'm going to visit a few places which I could turn into an art retreat. After that I'm not sure yet what I'm doing. If I don't like any of them, I might move on to Spain or somewhere else, or I could end up back here in a few weeks with my tail between my legs. For the first time I haven't planned out my future. For the first time, I'm going to follow my dreams.'

'Why now?'

Melinda shrugged. 'Why not now? There's nothing in Ireland for me anymore. I'm renting the house out for a while until I know if my ventures abroad will be permanent. If they are, I'll sell up. The insurance money has given me the freedom to go.'

'France?' Vicky repeated. 'Okay then. Do me a favour and email the station, will you? In case I need to get in touch at any stage. Look, I'd better go,' she said as she scanned the crowd.

'If you're looking for Cassandra, they already went through security.'

'You saw them?'

Melinda nodded. 'Fitting really. Wouldn't have felt right to leave without a last hug.'

'You knew they were leaving?'

A flicker of expression told Vicky she hadn't.

'It shows on the record that you were the one that identified the body ... sorry, I mean identified Alex. Can you confirm this for me?'

She crossed her arms. 'Why?'

'Melinda, in this type of interview, it is usually the Garda who asks the questions.'

'I'm not under caution, am I?'

'No, but I'd prefer for you to answer honestly without the details influencing your answer.'

'It was him.'

'You are sure?'

Melinda's jaw slackened.

'Sergeant Fitzgerald, not even an idiot like me could mistake their husband when he is lying dead in the morgue.'

Vicky let the silence be enough.

'Fine. You want details. He has, he had, a scar. On his ear. Shaped like a V, right on the lobe, at first look you would think it was an earring hole.'

'From that time Bernice cut him,' Vicky muttered. 'And you saw this at the morgue?'

'I did.'

'Any other notable scars?'

Mel thought for a second. 'A freckle on his wrist shaped like a peanut.'

'Okay then. Best of luck, Melinda.'

About to turn away, she stopped. 'One last question?'

'Go on.'

'Do you think someone other than Fintan could have been involved in the death of your husband? Like, one of the women?'

Melinda thought of the women who loved Alex. Her, Cassandra, Saoirse. She thought of Lily. Then of Bernice. She thought of what her husband's death taught her; of all she learnt by loving him.

'I think my husband needs to be allowed to rest now. Nothing can bring him back. Sergeant Fitzgerald, the case is closed now, right?'

Vicky stepped closer. 'Officially, yes. There are still some things I can't put to rest.'

'Will it help anyone involved if you keep going?'

Vicky stopped. Would it help anyone involved? If she followed her hunch, she could crack open the case. There were ways to get a person back to a country. A government could be convinced to revoke a passport – force them to have to leave. But for what? Some hunch that she couldn't prove? And how many lives might she ruin by insisting on that? For the sake of justice, did she want to send some children home to an abusive mother? Or send an abused woman back to a shelter? Saoirse was safe now her husband was presumed dead. He certainly couldn't get to her while she was abroad without his passport. At best, pulling Cassandra away from the airport would ruin her and the children's much-needed holiday. At worst, if she found Cassandra was involved, what would happen to Lily and Kenneth?

As a female Garda, Vicky learnt long ago to choose her battles. To let go of what didn't need to be stated. Yet, she *knew* there was more to the case. Maybe that was enough. There was nothing to gain by pursuing it. The bad guys lost. The good guys left should be allowed a good life. Vicky hoped that was the case. That was what she lived by. Hadn't they hurt enough?

Vicky knew all about pain. Knew all about secrets, too. She understood some pain needed to stay hidden; knew it was safer for a person sometimes to keep the truth to themselves. On paper, there wasn't anything she needed to do. Fintan would have killed Saoirse at some stage, of that Vicky had no doubt. The truth was, if he did go into the water she was glad it was him that died instead of Saoirse. It wasn't her choice who died. But what she could decide was whether to tell or not. Keeping another secret was easy.

'It's like having an itch. Once I scratch it, I'll be happy.'

'The problem with scratching an itch, Vicky, is once you've satisfied it, another piece of skin itches.'

Melinda's eyes lit up and she waved at a man, his hands full with shopping bags.

'You know, I used to watch Alex, when he wasn't looking. It always amazed me how he could continue doing something, so unaware of the love I was tunnelling his way. Sometimes it frustrated me. How could I have such intense emotions while he was oblivious? I said it to him once and he just laughed. Stroked my thigh and said, "I wondered how long it would take you to ask."

'That was Alex. He'd known the whole time. Said it was so hard to pretend to concentrate on what he was doing, but he didn't want to break my gaze by starting a conversation. He didn't want to break the emotion. "I felt it every time," he said. And even now I believe that. Alex loved me. But he could not give me the type of love I demanded, the all in love I found since. He couldn't, because he had already felt it, already nearly broke from it.'

The queue for her check in was dwindling. Melinda pointed to let Vicky know she needed to go. Vicky nodded, giving her blessing to leave. Melinda shifted her luggage, but she didn't take a step.

'You know, Vicky, I found photographs of Alex and Saoirse a few weeks ago. It hurt, felt like a betrayal because he never gave up looking for her, even after he married me. There was a book he had hidden. Inside were hundreds of notes of places and towns he searched. Years and years of searching for Saoirse. And you may not believe me, but I cried at the last date, I lay down on the floor and cried. Not from jealousy. I cried because the last date he wrote was two months before he died. I cried because seeing that made me happy.'

'Because he gave up looking for her?'

'Come on, Sergeant, we both know you are better than that.'

Melinda stared at her, her face open and waiting.

'He stopped looking because he found her,' Vicky whispered.

'Let us all be, Vicky. Each one of us has hurt enough. We all deserve some happiness, don't you think?'

With one last look at the security gates upstairs, Vicky walked towards the exit.

Case closed.

Nearly.

Chapter 76

In the station, Vicky stood at the wall looking at the information she'd tacked up and refused to take down.

'It's gonna be a long night,' she muttered. Taking a box from her desk, she laid out every piece of paperwork single file on the floor, then sat down and started reading the first piece of paper next to her. Most were redundant. A waste of hours she could never reclaim but scouring through the information settled Vicky's panicked heart because until she had gone through every piece, she couldn't quieten the niggle that something in there held the key to the case.

Taking out her note book, she flicked through it, hoping something would stand out. She stopped at her conversation with Lily. About the message he sent.

He said he would find me.

What was Alex rushing to Lily for? She stuck the question on the board.

She took a deep breath as she stared at the papers. This was what she had needed, time to think, without Barratt or the other's making noise and distracting her. Silence was good, it helped her stay focused. She glanced over what she had, stopping at the note left on the coffin. Recognition flashed over her. She had seen that writing before.

Where?

Anyone she spoke to, she had made a point of checking their

handwriting immediately after the interview ended. It wasn't Saoirse, Cassandra, Ernest, Melinda or Bernice.

Who then?

She picked up the autopsy report. All the details Barratt went through in his summary were there, which was exactly the same as the pathologist told her over the phone. Vicky scanned down to the end. Stopped on identification marks.

'That's strange,' she said.

There was no mention of a scar on his ear.

She put the report down. How could that be? Shannon, the pathologist was experienced. And extremely thorough. No way would she not report an old injury.

So, what could it mean? Was Melinda lying about a scar? Did she concoct an elaborate story to appear the dutiful wife?

She read on.

Tattoo on the right arm. A heart emblem with the word Saoirse across it.

Vicky frowned. Why would Melinda look shocked when Vicky told her Saoirse's name if she had seen it before on Alex's arm?

It didn't make any sense.

No mention of a large freckle on his wrist.

Could Alex hide a tattoo from his wife?

Vicky picked up her phone, scrolled until she found the right picture. Approaching the board, Vicky held the picture against it, lining up with the note from the coffin. The note Alex wrote to Saoirse the night before he died was the perfect match to the note at the crematorium.

How could that be possible?

She scanned the rest of the wall. Stopped at the picture of Alex and Saoirse from the night before the murder. Right in the very corner was a sign. She pulled out a magnifying glass she kept in her drawer. Half obscured, Knockfarraig was the only word visible. Vicky thought about her own phone, about how years ago she had linked her phone gallery to the cloud so she would never lose another picture again if anything happened to her phone. Could Saoirse have done the same? Wouldn't a control freak have linked their devices together so any photograph would show up on his phone too?

And, had Alex known this before he took the picture?

Had Alex set a trap for Fintan?

Chapter 77

Vicky strummed her fingers against the cheap counter, hoping it might irritate the woman into conforming.

'Do you have a way of contacting him or at least have his work rota to hand?'

'I cannot give that information out.'

'You can if the man is involved in a murder inquiry. GDPR goes out the window in that case.'

Vicky leant in, looking around first to make sure no one else could hear. 'Look, I know where he lives but he hasn't been there. I'm not asking you to write anything down or put your neck on the line. Just point me in the right direction about where he'll be at a particular time, like say, where or when he starts his shift and I'll just turn up at the same time.'

The woman typed into her computer.

'Sorry, there's no record of any upcoming shifts.'

'Try next week?'

'Nothing. We don't go further than two weeks on our system.'

The hairs prickled on Vicky's neck. 'Has he gone on holidays?'

'Can't be. If he was, it would still be on our payroll system. He isn't here at all.'

'What does that mean? Did he quit? Or was it forced leave, like a suspension without pay or something like that?'

The nurse baulked, then checked behind her before speaking. 'No. It says here in the notes, it's for personal reasons.'

'What does that mean? Mental health grounds, like grief?'

The receptionist looked over her shoulder again and when she saw no one was watching, typed on the computer.

'You'll find him in room 4, ward 2b. That's all I can say.'

'That's more than enough. Thanks.'

With long strides, Vicky rushed to the lift.

At first, she didn't notice him, for she was looking at the room from a different angle, looking around the bed instead of in it. Ernest was not visiting or transporting or treating a patient.

He was the patient in the bed.

'Ernest, what did you do?'

He opened one eye and smiled, not at all surprised to see her.

Chapter 78

'I don't know yet what you did, but I know you played a part in this.'

Ernest held up his hands. 'You got me, Vic.'

The man in the bed was not the same person carrying Alex's coffin. He must have lost the best part of twenty pounds since she last interviewed him. In what? Five weeks. Not only that, Ernest's jaundiced skin was noticeable from the far side of the room. The whites of his eyes were yellowed, too. There was at least three week's worth of stubble on his chin, which was understandable for a sick patient but not from someone known for being immaculately dressed. He lay on the pillow at an awkward angle, as if he'd slipped down and didn't have the energy to correct it.

'You are hardly comfortable lying like that. Do you want me to prop you up?'

He smiled, held his arms out. Vicky, careful not to hurt, looped her arms through and shifted him higher on the bed.

'My hero,' he said.

'What happened?'

He gestured for her to sit. Then looked straight at her. 'Nothing I shouldn't have done years ago.'

'But Alex was your friend.'

'The very best.'

'There was another reason you didn't tell me you were at the scene, wasn't there?'

He shifted, then winced, holding his lower stomach. 'I knew you'd figure it out. Never hid it, so there's nothing wrong with that. I tried everything to help him. Wouldn't change being there for anyone. Wouldn't change any part of what I did.'

'Which is what exactly?'

'My friend was in pain.' He stopped to take a breath. It seemed to hurt. 'I helped her.'

'Her?'

'Him,' he said, fanning his face.

Her.

And then she knew.

Chapter 79

'You were quite the threesome growing up.'

He closed his eyes as if trying to make sense of what she said, but it was too late to pretend or rewind because Vicky was on to it.

'You, Alex and Saoirse.'

He flinched at her name, confirming the connection.

'That bloody notepad.' He rolled his eyes, but he smiled while he said it. 'I want it noted that before this, I was always an honest person.'

'I remember. You used to pick up fallen coins around the shop and hand them over for the charity box.'

He chuckled.

'You were always smart, Vic. Always one step ahead, I know how much you hate loose ends so I'm hoping if I can give you the answers you are still searching for, then you will leave everyone else alone. I always had time for you, even though you like to keep people at bay these days. I never actually said it to you in person, but what happened to you was terrible; I hope you have found some peace over the years.'

Vicky bit down on her lip. 'What's happening to you?'

'Pancreatic cancer.'

'Any chance?'

'Not a hope unless you know someone performing miracles. I'll have two more weeks if I'm lucky.'

'How long have you known?'

'About eight.'

Two weeks before Alex died.

'You had nothing to lose.'

Ernest nodded. 'I had nothing to lose.'

'Why would you hurt him?'

'Because Saoirse would never have got away.'

'And why would she need to get away?'

'He hurt her, he always hurt her. You don't know Saoirse. She's loyal, even if it means she will live in misery.' He closed his eyes. 'I'm in pain, Vic.'

'Don't leave me with questions, Ernest.'

He nodded. His eyelids looked heavier than when she entered the room. She wouldn't have long.

'The plan was only for Fintan to hurt Alex enough that he would go to jail. Alex rang me to say he had spotted Fintan. My job was to intervene and make sure Fintan didn't hurt him too much.'

'Saoirse said Alex never knew what he looked like.'

'He checked the cameras that time he turned up in the hospital.'

'Alex and cameras,' Vicky muttered. 'Did he know Fintan would see the photograph on Saoirse's drive?'

Ernest nodded.

'Fintan drove straight to Knockfarraig looking for Saoirse. Alex was parked up on the lookout, when he spotted him he rang and told me what direction he was driving, so we figured Fintan was heading for Coburg Street. I was near, only on Main Street so when I arrived, Alex was already running towards the building. Like you, Vicky, I know every inch of Knockfarraig; I knew the back of the building had fallen away, knew it led to an alleyway, so I turned the car and drove around.'

He closed his eyes. She had to keep him awake.

'He was there when you arrived? There is footage of him leaving before you got there.'

Ernest opened one eye, enough to warn her to stop butting in.

'He purposely started a fight. He purposely ran to that building. It was only meant to be the two of us threatening him, to force him to leave Knockfarraig. These guys usually only start a fight with the women who stay alone. When they know they have back up they run. Fintan didn't run. He got madder. He went for Alex and tried to kill him. He had a knife. They both went to the ground. That's where I found them.

'He said, "is he dead?" but I couldn't even answer. In shock, I wasn't thinking straight. Then I saw the knife, the body on the ground. Saw Alex's battered face. And then I knew what I needed to do. When I'd gotten out of the car, I'd put on gloves, figuring I might need to rough him up. So I undressed him, made them swap their clothes. Fintan's keys were in his pocket.'

Vicky tried to make sense of it. 'You made Alex change?'

Ernest nodded. 'I told Alex to get out of there. That I would go around the back and wait for the call. Would make sure I was the one that would bring him in to buy him some time. Alex was panicking, shaking like a leaf and I could see he had lost it, couldn't think straight. But I was always like you, Vic, my best talent was seeing a few steps ahead of everyone else. I took the cap from Fintan's head and put it on Alex. Made him put on gloves then closed his palm over Fintan's car keys. I told him to get into Fintan's car and drive to the woods and wait for my call. He did it without question. He did it without even looking back. Like me, I'm sure you have come across disassociation in PTSD victims. Well, he was classic case, no joke. He looked terrified. Shaking. Alex thought he was changing clothes so he could run. So he could get word to Saoirse and warn her.'

Ernest smacked his lips together, the skin on them dry and cracked. Vicky reached over to the bedside locker and lifted a cup of water with a straw, placing it on his lips. Ernest drank greedily, then smiled at her with gratitude.

'Before I got there, Fintan caught Alex by the throat. He tried to kill him, tried to choke him. What Fintan didn't factor on, was Alex having plenty of practice playing dead. He dropped him to the floor and Alex lay there and didn't move. Fintan didn't even check to see if he was alive. Alex was never a fighter, but for the first time, as Fintan was about to leave, Alex fought back. When I arrived, Fintan was unconscious on the floor. Both their faces were battered. Fintan's pulse was slow but he was alive. I thought of what Saoirse had suffered because of that man. He left her for dead that time at the train station.'

He shook his head. 'Alex was a mess so I took over. When he left Fintan was alive. His original plan was to get Fintan arrested, get him jailed for attacking him but Alex had fought back, so it wasn't clean cut anymore. Alex panicked that he'd made it worse because now Fintan could claim self-defence and he would know where Saoirse was. I knew there wasn't any time. Fintan wouldn't have left her alone, would never stop looking for her. He would have always been in her life, always sniffing around Laurie, always getting into Saoirse's head. It wasn't planned. The decision was made when he woke up.'

'What did you do?' Vicky held back the tears, because she already knew the answer.

He stopped for a second, as if about to fall asleep.

'Go on,' Vicky said.

He opened his eyes, and Vicky wondered if he forgot she was there. He tapped his chest.

'Like you said, I had nothing to lose. I knew I would die within months, so I set them free, Vic. I'm a paramedic, right?'

'That's still a sore subject.'

He nodded.

'I know. But I had to hide it from you, it would have been easy to work it out otherwise. I thought about all the times Alex suffered. His dad was an absolute bastard. Then Bernice made him suffer, what she did to him nearly ended him, but I'm sure you've seen the videos of what she did to him by now.'

'You knew about them?'

'Alex told me in case anything happened to the tapes. I thought about Saoirse. About what she had suffered too. She had years with this guy who wanted nothing but to cause her misery. I know what you must think but I promise my intention was to leave. But then he stirred on the floor and groaned. And then I knew what I had to do.

'It wasn't the groan of a man contemplating his actions. It was a growl. A getting ready to gather his strength and strike. I knew it wouldn't end. People like Fintan don't let nice guys win. They don't let the woman they stalked and blamed for all their problems leave with their child and set up home with another guy. He was toxic. Do you know how many women we have to treat in the ambulance whose men hurt them? Do you know how many die before we get there? Fintan was sour. He was vinegar. He was the squidgy dog shit that gets into the grooves of your shoe. Everything around that man turned stale and disgusting. They would never have a life with him, not a life together, not a good life like they deserved. By that stage, I knew my fate, knew I wouldn't be around to help them, wouldn't be the one Alex could call anymore if he needed me. And if that man lived, Alex or Saoirse would need me. After that my mind was made up. I punched him once to knock him out again. With my gloved hands, I picked up the knife.

'Touching Fintan's chest, I located the precise spot of where it beat, then moved lower and drove the knife in, leaving it in on purpose so the blood wouldn't gush out all at once. Then I slipped out the back of the alley without looking back. I live two streets away, so I changed into my paramedic gear and headed to the unit that keeps an ambulance on standby, knowing the call would come. And six minutes later, it did.'

'Why did you want to be the paramedic on duty?'

'Because I had left the knife in. I didn't want him dead until we reached the hospital. If he died by that building, it would have been a murder scene and the gardaí would be called and ye would take over. That wouldn't have worked. The knife went close enough to his heart to ensure he died but further down to buy some time. Around the corner from the hospital, I removed the knife, wrapping it in a surgical glove, I hid it in my bag, knowing he would only have minutes once the wound was exposed.'

'How did you get away with it being a different man at the hospital?'

'How does any doctor or surgeon know who they are treating? They go with the information they have. I was first on scene; I identified the patient as Alex Hayes. There was no other identification on him because believe me, I checked. There was no question about whether he would die, I made sure of that. Fintan barely made it to the entrance of the hospital before he went into cardiac arrest. After the doctor declared him dead, I asked them if I could bring him down to the morgue. They all knew me, worked with me for years. Never had a cross word with anyone there, so of course they were going to let me wheel my buddy down. Grief does funny things to people, and us paramedics and hospital staff have seen it more than anyone. They let me be without question.'

Vicky pinched her nose. 'There's a lot to take in here. Reverse a minute. Melinda identifying Alex. Was she in on it?'

'Hell, no.'

'Then how did you manage it? How could she identify a man who wasn't her husband?'

'Because it was her husband. She identified Alex.'

Chapter 80

Ernest closed his eyes. She waited, then when he didn't speak, she resorted to begging. 'Please. How could she not tell?'

'You'd be surprised at how many over-the-counter medications that could do it. If you ingest the right type of eye drops even in a small amount, it will make your heart rate decrease. We were careful with the dosage. Just enough for her not to notice his breathing. Also, like I said, Alex had learnt how to play dead. Melinda was in shock and couldn't take it in. Being a murder inquiry meant she couldn't touch him.'

'Did it not bother you, tricking a woman, breaking so many people's hearts?'

'We did what we had to do. Fintan would have killed Saoirse and Laurie, no doubt about it.'

'Did Saoirse know?'

'That I killed Fintan? No, she had no clue.'

Vicky pinched her nose. 'But how did you get Alex into the morgue? How did you switch the bodies?'

'It was Fintan that lay in the ambulance. It was Fintan that died. By the time Alex found any of this out it was too late to change it. I admitted to him about the cancer, told him how I fixed it. How I was going to set them free. Alex was almost catatonic in shock; he just followed my instructions.'

'How did you get past the morgue?'

'The hospital staff and the pathologist saw Fintan. Barratt accompanied Melinda to the viewing. The morgue attendant set Fintan up in the privacy room, nice and early, so Barratt and her could identify him. What he didn't account for was me knowing exactly when his lunch break was, and his passcode for exiting and entering the building.'

'Go slow now, Ernest. How would you know this information?'

'Paul is the head of the mortuary. He's also my partner for the last two years. He wasn't in on it, didn't know a thing, and won't find out unless you tell him. If you ask, he will identify Fintan as the person in the mortuary. But he will call him Alex Hayes.'

'How did your partner not recognise Alex?'

'Alex battered Fintan's face, remember? Also, like I told you, me and Alex fell out, we didn't start speaking again until after the day Saoirse ended up in the hospital. I knew Alex wanted to help Saoirse leave, so I kept us making up a secret. Also, I had started to fell unwell so I was a little distracted by that, so I never gave them a proper introduction. Paul knew of Alex, but did he see him in anything other than a photograph? No. Alex and Fintan's hair were of a similar style, same colour; also in Paul's defence, his dying boyfriend was bawling his eyes out, saying someone murdered his friend. There was no reason for Paul to doubt it was Alex. I asked him could I stick around and wait until Melinda came to identify him. He did me the favour of letting me be the one who waited, who walked Barratt and Melinda in. What he didn't know was that I had parked my car by the fire exit and when he went to the bathroom, I had opened the door and hid Alex in the room, behind the door of the privacy room. If Paul had walked in, he would have discovered Alex straight away, but poor Paul was too busy consoling me in front of the door instead. When Paul went on lunch, thinking I was gone to the little church in the hospital to light a candle, I moved Fintan back to the body-holding area, which is basically like lots of large fridges. This was the only stumbling block because it had a pin code on each door, but I had stood over Paul when he got him out and took note. Once he was there, I didn't move him again. Paul got mad at me for that, for moving the body after the identification before he came back; he said I took liberties and went too far, but how could he stay mad at a grieving man? I told him I didn't want Alex rotting on the table any longer. He checked on him and saw Fintan in the right spot. What he had no clue about was as soon as Melinda and Garda Barratt left, Alex jumped up from the table, and following my instructions, used the passcode to leave the morgue. He walked right out of the fire exit and lay down in my car until I could leave.'

Vicky held her face. 'Of all the things I imagined you might say, I didn't expect it to be that. When did you collect Alex from the woods?'

'Before Melinda got there, I went home to change. When Alex saw me put the knife on the dash, he lost it. But there was no turning back by then. He followed my instructions.'

'Did you look at him, Ernest? Fintan, when you were moving him?'

Ernest squinted. 'What? You wondering if I felt guilty? Vic, I'll tell you right now, there is not one bit of remorse running through these decaying veins. For those two, I'd do it again in the morning.'

'What am I meant to do now?'

'Do what is right, Vic. By the time this goes to trial, I'll be long dead. Think first though, if you report this, what happens to Alex? Will he face charges?'

'Well, he helped to fake his own death.'

'I kind of forced him into it. By the time he knew there was no choice.'

'The knife?'

'I placed it in the car when I collected Alex. Brought him a change of clothes and we left them on the beach. He didn't want to run. He didn't want to leave his kids or Saoirse. I promised him I'd sort it. But the first thing we needed to do was get him away from Knockfarraig.'

'That's why he left the message for Lily,' she muttered. 'The note. In the crematorium, did Alex write it?'

'He asked me to leave it for Fintan. He was distraught. It was the least I could do.'

Ernest reached for the red button next to the bed. Then pressed it twice.

'Sorry, I've held out as long as I can. Meant to only press it once to administer a dose but once never hits the spot. Might go drowsy after this. Probably get a few minutes of me making sense. Fire away the questions until I talk about rainbows or something.'

'Must be strong medication.'

'Needs to be for this pain. I'm sorry.'

Vicky blew out a breath. 'You've screwed me over.'

'You've a decision on your hands, Vic. Do you do the right thing?' he mumbled something. Then pursed his lips together a few times. 'Or, maybe the question you should ask is, *what* is the right thing?'

He tried to shift position but thought better of it, the effort too much. When he opened his eyes they had a hardness to them.

'If you ask for a statement, I'll refuse. I'm on pretty serious medication; I'll swear I didn't know what I was talking about. I've put you in a position, I know that, but I thought it only right you know the truth. No doubt over time you'll find out how to prove it. Just think first, Vic, about what's the right thing to do.'

'My job isn't about judging what the right thing to do is. It's about justice.'

He nodded. 'Justice. Look, I don't care about keeping my good name. Just consider them, consider what it will do to them. What would you have done if it was Christian?'

'Don't mention his name in this conversation!' she said, raising her voice.

Ernest smacked his lips together again. This time, she didn't offer any water.

'You loved him, you would have done anything for him, I know that, you know that. That's what Alex meant to me. That's what Saoirse meant to me.'

He sighed, long and drawn out. 'While I'm confessing, I might as well tell all.'

Vicky narrowed her eyes, confused.

'It was you,' she whispered.

Chapter 81

Ernest's head rocked. The morphine was kicking in.

'After they had the fight, I drove to Alex's house, found Saoirse stumbling along the road half dazed. She wouldn't tell me what Alex's father did, only that he was there. She didn't have to tell me, Vic. The bruises on her knees, her torn dress, the blood on her lip, her swollen eye told me all I needed to know. I dropped her home and left her with the promise I would get help. I crept into the house. There he was, just standing outside the bedroom, with his back to me, just waiting for the moment he could tell Alex. I didn't even say a word, just caught him by the shoulders. He was so drunk he didn't even fight back; his body just went with me. Near the edge of the stairs, I shoved him with everything I had.'

'Did Saoirse know?'

'Saoirse left in the night, not even knowing Alex's father died. She left because she didn't want to destroy Alex, because she said once he knew, he would never look at her the same.'

Vicky pinched her nose.

'Did it not bother you, tricking a woman, breaking so many people's hearts?'

'I regret not returning to Saoirse that night and stopping her from leaving Knockfarraig. If I did that, she would never have met Fintan. I regret the years I wasted for them, because I was afraid I would lose them both if they knew what I did. As much as they hated that man, the two of them would never think murder was the answer. With John and Fintan, I don't regret it at all. I am a murderer. Twice now. When I die, when all this comes out, that's what people will know me as. They won't remember the man who spent every day of his adult life trying to save the people that entered the ambulance. They won't see the small boy I watched hide behind the field at the back of his house when his father came home, that man with his voice thick with drink, looking to start a fight with a child. Looking to start a fight with a kid who would never fight back, never provoke, never do anything to hurt another soul. I love him, Vic, always have. Alex accepted me when I was afraid to admit to myself I was attracted to men. He was my first love. Never sexually. Never like that. Growing up with Alex, I understood how beautiful he was. How I wanted someone like him. And then Saoirse came into our lives and I knew from the very first day I met her they were meant to be together. And I loved her. When Saoirse returned, she found out I was seeing a guy in secret at school and instead of acting horrified, she accepted me, encouraged me to go for it with him. She loved me without question. Saoirse was my second love.'

He exhaled deeply, shook his head. 'People will see me as a monster for killing those two men but as I lie here knowing I will soon go to the same place I sent them, still, I don't regret it. What I regret most of all is the secrets I kept. I thought I was doing right. I thought I was respecting Saoirse's wishes not to tell Alex she contacted. How could anyone who has been abused and neglected all their life know love has the ability to heal? I wish I'd convinced her. I wish I'd just told Alex. You may have questioned how someone who claimed to love Alex could stop talking to him for so long, well, it was because I couldn't face him, I couldn't look him in the eye. Because deep down I knew what he really wanted was to find Saoirse. I hope they can forgive me. I hope they see how I've tried to make amends.'

He pressed the button again.

Ernest closed his eyes, and she knew there would be no more conversing. Still, she sat. As time went on, Ernest's breath deepened and his body relaxed, slipping into sleep.

'Do you think he's still out there?' That's what Cassandra asked her. At the time, Vicky thought she was asking about Fintan, now the question made her wonder who Cassandra was talking about.

At the end of it all, Vicky knew only too well about secrets. Or why the past was better left to rot. She was proud of her work as a Garda. Experienced enough to not feel she always needed to prove she was right. Or to always reveal the truth. In a small town, she had learned you had to pick your battles. If she could answer one question after a case closed, that was enough for her. *Was justice done?*

Alex Hayes was alive.

Fintan, who beat his wife on a regular basis and threatened to kill his child, and was prepared to kill Alex, died in his place.

Died and framed as a murderer, in fact.

And they had cremated him which meant she couldn't exhume the body to prove it. Cassandra had already thrown his ashes out to sea.

How convenient.

Ernest, a man who loved both Saoirse and Alex, was in fact a murderer of two people. But within a week or two he would be dead, too. It would be his maker's decision on whether to punish him.

Except for faking his own death and causing the women and the children who loved him unnecessary pain, Alex didn't do anything wrong.

There were no loose ends. No unanswered questions. No bad guy out there ready to strike again.

Yes, Vicky thought, nodding at Paul as he entered the room.

Justice was done.

Chapter 82

Before she could stop it, Saoirse felt the floor nearing. She had finally lost it, finally broke and all her brain could do was turn off, reset, faint and forget. Before her face hit the ground, he must have scooped her up and carried her to the bed. He must have picked up the dropped tip and taken the bag from the porter because when she opened her eyes they were alone. The room came back into focus and all she could stare at were the two cocktails on the desk in the corner. She was afraid to look. Afraid to face the man she saw outside in the corridor.

Until Alex took her hand.

'Did I die too?'

He shook his head. Alex's blond hair moved with him, like it always did.

'Are you really alive?'

He nodded. Touched her lips with one finger. 'I'm sorry for scaring you.'

'Scaring me? You broke my heart.'

She sat up. 'Laurie.'

'Don't worry, she's eating her ice cream out on the balcony. She didn't even act surprised when she saw me, like she expected me here. I told her you just needed some rest.'

Outside, she could see Laurie stretched out on a sun lounger, licking the ice cream methodically. Relieved, she turned to him.

'We cremated you, Alex.'

'Not me, Saoirse.'

The colour drained from her face. 'He's dead?'

'Yes. He can never hurt you again.'

Her voice sounded in broken spurts. 'He hurt me all the time.'

She reeled back. 'Was it you, did you kill him?'

Alex kissed her forehead, and Saoirse didn't stop him.

'No.'

There would be years to listen to what he had to say. Years to hear out what happened. There was plenty of time to figure out where they would live, or how to blend their new family together, or how they would heal. None of it mattered that very second. All that mattered was knowing they had years.

Knowing they had a second chance.

Not a second chance, for that came when they were eighteen. Not a third chance, for that came when she was bruised and broken in the hospital.

This was a fourth chance. A final chance, and this time she would not let it slip away.

It wasn't new, his touch. It didn't feel new to her at all. As he stroked a strand of her hair away from her face, it felt like she was coming back to a place she always felt she most belonged.

Because in the end, it didn't matter how small she reduced her thoughts, how compliant she became, how submissive she forced herself to be, how loyal, or how good she became at keeping secrets. It didn't matter how much she pushed it down, or how much she erased from her memory, she could not hide from what she knew. She couldn't fight the truth. Even if she ran from everyone or every place she had ever known, she couldn't stop how Alex made her feel. Being around Alex felt like finding a safe place when she no longer had a home to call her own. Home was Alex.

Alex was hope and safety and a return all at once. Not a return to him. For it was Saoirse returning to her best self when she was with him, It was returning to life, to finally allowing her desires, her dreams, her wants in. It was a return to love. And she welcomed it with open arms.

Forever.

The End.

If you would like to know more about Vicky

The story of Alex, Saoirse, Melinda, and Cassandra has concluded, but Sergeant Vicky Fitzgerald's life has only just been peeked into. If you'd like to delve deeper into her past and discover what is in store for her future, you do not have to wait long, for on October 13th, all will be revealed.

Here's the prologue:

A flash of light. A crack of thunder. Cold water hitting bones. Ringing in ears and a sharp throbbing in her forehead where she was hit. Worse still, worse than anything else ever, he is gone. And she knows, she knows, before she sees, before his absence is determined by facts that confirm, her life has forever changed.

He is lost to her.

And with him gone, any reason to want to go on leaves too. She will not recover from this. From now on, she will view life as a cruel master of fate. A fate she has no control over. From now on she will only exist. Only survive. In an instant, the light inside her extinguishes.

Check out the next page for cover reveal and blurb!

Also by Natasha Karis

The Three Stories For Vicky Fitzgerald
A treacherous storm. A mysterious stranger.
Three stories that will save a life.

When Sergeant Vicky Fitzgerald finds a naked and disoriented man in the middle of the street, right before the Samhain festival, she already has enough to deal with.

As the town prepares for the celebration, the weather turns ominous, and so does the man's warning. He insists he has a story she needs to hear, one tied to her own buried past.

The man won't say who he is, yet he knows her name.

Vicky is certain she has never seen him before.

But time is running out, and Vicky must choose: ignore the stranger's tale or trust him, even as the world around her begins to unravel.

With lives at risk, long-lost truths resurfacing, and personal ghosts demanding to be faced, Vicky will have to rely on others in ways she never has before. Because by the end of Samhain, her life will never be the same.

Perfect for fans of heartfelt, emotionally layered fiction, this is a deeply moving novel about what ties us to the past and learning to trust again, even when the storm has left you shattered.

Check it out

https://mybook.to/thethreestories

What The Heart Needs
A mother desperate for revenge. A young man haunted by his past. One decision that will change both their lives.

Hidden in the dark, Lorna Thomas watches a man with only one planned outcome.

Revenge.

Driven by a desperate need to avenge the pain her daughter Sara endured, Lorna won't rest until she hurts all the people involved.

But a discovery will trigger a chain of events that will force Lorna on an unexpected, emotional mission. Through heartache and healing, Lorna will learn revenge is not the answer.

But will it be too late?

A revenge story with an emotional twist.

Check it out at
https://mybook.to/whattheheartneeds

The Sisters You Choose
A daughter desperate to discover what happened to her parents. A stranger claiming she has the answer. A secret book that holds the truth.

It is near dark and pouring rain when Abbie Ellis visits her mother's grave for the first time.

Not to mourn or cry.

For the last thing she wants is to forgive.

That night is the tenth anniversary of when her mother, the famous writer Gabrielle Ellis, took the lives of both Abbie's father and herself.

Finally ready to confront her past, Abbie hopes visiting the grave will unleash the anger she has held on to for too long.

But she is not alone.

A woman appears out of the shadows.

The stranger claims she knows Abbie and has a message from her mother.

Gabrielle wrote a secret book, only for her.

If she reads it, will Abbie get the answers she's hoped for all her life?

Will she finally learn what happened that fateful day?

A sweeping, emotional tale of wrong choices, of the power of friendship and enduring love that outlasts even death.

https://mybook.to/thesistersyouchoose

The Breaking Of Dawn

Taken for granted by her boss and friends, Dawn Moloney can never find the right way to stand up to them.

Forced to move back to her childhood home after an attack leaves her bruised and broken, Dawn struggles to adjust.

When her mother suggests she try classes at a local centre for the unemployed, she reluctantly agrees. There, she meets Alayne Adams, who prefers to focus more on Dawn rather than what classes she is taking. Talking about herself is Dawn's worst nightmare, but if she wants to get better, she will have to learn.

Can Dawn finally find the right words?

https://mybook.to/thebreakingofdawn

The Truth Between Us
A make or break holiday. A love that should last a lifetime. A truth that threatens to rip them apart.

When Adaline decides to book a trip away to contemplate her failing marriage, her husband Andrew suggests he join her. As they embark on a last chance holiday to Cyprus, Adaline reflects on her life, hoping to fix what went wrong. But the past contains much pain, and a secret threatens to ruin everything.

Can they still salvage the relationship?

https://viewbook.at/thetruthbetweenus

Send Me Home For Christmas
Four strangers stuck in an airport at Christmas. One snowstorm. Only two tickets home.

Desperate to get home to her daughter for Christmas, a huge snowstorm threatens to keep them apart. In the airport, her path crosses with three strangers just as eager to get home. All longing to get on the last flight, each stake their claim for one of only two tickets left to Cork.

Each one wishing for a Christmas miracle and hoping that maybe, this Christmas, they may get one.

An emotional, heartfelt novella about finding your way home.

https://mybook.to/sendmehomeforchristmas

www.ingramcontent.com/pod-product-compliance
Lightning Source LLC
Chambersburg PA
CBHW030531190726
48283CB00006B/1858